BURNING CARDS

by M. E. Patterson

ISBN 978-0-9838448-2-2
Published by Digimonkey Studios
Printed in the United States of America
First Paperback Edition

ACKNOWLEDGMENTS

Thanks, as always, to Sheilagh, early-reader extraordinaire; to Kurt, my #1 fan; to Chris, expert cover artist; to Robert, razor-sharp editor; and to Katrina, for everything.

And thanks to all of the new fans and friends, local and international, on Twitter and Facebook and everywhere in-between, who have joined this journey since the release of Devil's Hand.

Your support keeps these stories coming.

For Mom and Dad.

Then with a cheerful look he placed his hand
On mine to soothe my soul and mind—and then
He led me in among the secret things.

Inferno, Canto III
Dante Alighieri

A veil exists between the world above and the realms that are below;
and shadow came into being beneath the veil; and that shadow became
matter; and that shadow was projected apart.

"The Hypostasis of the Archons"
The Nag Hammadi Library, codex II, tractate 4

Nowhere

With a wary eye, she surveys the nothing-world around her. Formless dark shapes flit in and out and between massive obsidian spikes that jut angrily at the ash-grey sky, like cruel, barbed spears aimed at God. She suspects there is truth in this. The Prince of Shades rules over this place and it is held together by his seething fury for all that lies beyond his realm. It is Abaddon, and it is the Prince of Shades and he is it and everything it contains. And it is the end of all things, a world pulled from the shadow of the real. A piece of an unholy black trinity. An echo of a dark heaven.

But as she moves through the ash that drifts across the tops of her feet, she knows that she is different from this place. She casts a shadow here, unlike any of the other creatures she has witnessed. A shadow cast upon shadow.

She also knows her own name. And that, she believes, is what gives her power in this nameless world. No matter how the Prince might try, no matter how this place tugs at her memories, it cannot rob her of that.

She exists, in a world of nonexistence. She slips through the bloodstream of Abaddon like a virus, an incongruous something in a sea of naught, and she knows that she cannot stop moving, or she will be found and her name will be lost, her soul ground into the very same dust that stains her naked toes.

And so she runs.

1

THE SHORT, PUDGY MAN WORE a bright blue vinyl jacket that looked altogether too hip for him as he moved through the crowd of the wealthy and famous and powerful. He sidled up to every celebrity at the party, passed within earshot of high-roller conversations, and would have been a nuisance had any of the guests bothered to notice him. But to them, he did not exist, a creature that made little sense in their world-view and therefore not worthy of their recognition.

Trent grinned as he watched the guy pick his way through the crowd. He felt a certain kinship. The pudgy man didn't seem to care one bit about the lack of acknowledgement. He was a man apart from the world he was invading. Trent understood.

He lifted the highball glass of Jack Daniels off the bar, stared deep into its contents, and then shook it lazily, swirling the ice cubes around until they clinked. He absently listened for the sound of Susan's voice, somewhere in that jangling ice. It had become a force of habit, a compulsion. He'd heard her voice in the dying screeches of that shadow-monster atop the Luxor nearly six months back.

After the Blizzard-borne snow had faded back into the earth, and the sharp, stinging wounds to the city of Las Vegas had become dull, dismissible aches, Trent's life had not gone back to normal. He'd sold his services to a cabal of demons, led by the somber Vladimir. The agreement: Trent used his supernatural luck-ruining ability to chase creatures from the Realms of Shadow back to their black world. In return, the demons kept him and Celia out of the news and away from the cops.

It had seemed ideal at first, playing the role of interdimensional bouncer. And with each shadow-thing dispatched, he listened for Susan's voice, hidden between layers of otherworldly moans and screams. He never heard it again after the night of the Blizzard. He worried that his obsession was overtaking what remained of his life. It had soured his desire to play the role he'd agreed to. And that's why he had, only yesterday, told Vladimir that he was quitting. The demon's angry glare had made it clear that Trent's troubles were just beginning.

He lifted the glass of Jack to his lips and sipped, wishing that he had a cigarette. After the Blizzard, he had quit smoking, mostly at Celia's request. The craving came back strong at random moments, worse when he had a drink in the other hand.

He glanced around at the party. It was all one big diversion, a cloud of smoke to obscure the real event: the game. The man who owned the estate, a 'Mr. Gadreel', ran an annual poker tournament, a huge-money affair that attracted the best poker pros in the world, who were then promptly beaten by quiet players they'd never met and never heard of; players that did not need to be in the spotlight; players that did not want to be known and for whom the astronomical pot was irrelevant. For them, the real game was not the poker, but the battle against the other players: a battle of luck and fate.

A famous actress passed Trent and winked, shaking him from imagining what his life might have been like had he won a tournament like this years ago, when he was still gambling professionally. Even worse, he decided. Back then, more money would have meant more drugs, more women, and an even more distraught wife. He managed a sad smile and tipped his grey cowboy hat at... Jennifer? Jessica? He couldn't remember. Something with a 'J'. She was in the tabloids a lot.

He lifted his glass, realized it was empty, and set it down on the bar. He gestured and the silent bartender walked over, grabbed the bottle of Jack, and then scooped ice from a bin beneath the bar.

Trent shook his head. "No ice this time."

The bartender nodded and poured a neat finger of whiskey. Trent gulped it down and put the empty glass back on the counter.

He looked out at the horizon beyond the party, beyond the bikini-clad celebrities and too-toned action stars and Armani-wearing businessmen, beyond the mansion and its multitude of lights and art objects and the odd, giant stone cross that stood just on the edge of the property line, flanked by cacti and scrub. The sky was made up of purple and gold bands, just like the evening that he fell. To the east, the neon lights of Las Vegas glowed dark, obscured by desert dust.

Further up the mountain, through the trees and scrub, Trent could see the dim outline of a massive church complex. He wondered if it had something to do with the owner of this mansion—

"Hey!" came a voice way too loud for a face-to-face conversation. "I know you. You're that guy, that umm... you know... the *guy*...."

Trent turned slowly and arched his eyebrow at the round little man, who was double-fisting a tiny snack tray sandwich and a glass of something bright pink. He had a nose like a vulture's beak and pink, stubby fingers.

"Yeah." He sloshed his drink with excitement. "You're that guy they made all those TV specials about. I remember you. I know you!"

Do you really? Trent wondered. "Yeah," he said, hoping the man would catch the hint and back off. No such luck.

The vulture dropped his pudgy fingers into a bowl of peanuts on the bar. "You were a god, man. For like a week at least. All over the news and shit. All those people died, except *you*. Man, that's what I call luck." Through a mouthful of half-chewed nuts he said, "How ya doin' now?"

Trent saw a refill waiting at the bar, picked up the glass, slugged it back. He grabbed the bottle from the bartender's hand and tossed a few crumpled bills on the counter. He filled his glass and wished the idiot vulture would just leave him alone.

"Thirty-thousand fucking feet?" He made a show of rolling his eyes and guffawing. "No way, man. No way. You gotta gimme something. What was it like? You know, falling? I mean, was it all windy and stuff, or did you black out? I read that somewhere. About blacking out, I mean, when you fall off a building or whatever...."

Trent got up then, deciding that maybe a more definite approach would do the trick. "I gotta go." He took his glass and his whiskey with him.

The smaller man held up his hands as if to stop Trent's advance. "Whoa, you're not goin' off to drink that all alone, are you?"

Trent removed his hat and feigned a smile as he ran his hand through his sweat-streaked hair. "Not in the mood, okay? Go bug one of the other famous people."

The man looked hurt. He let the few remaining peanuts in his hand fall to the floor and then wiped his salt-crusted hands on his white slacks, leaving greasy smears. "Famous people?" He frowned. "You're not famous, man. Not anymore. Hell, I don't even remember your name, just those crummy documentaries. I was only tryin' to be nice."

Trent considered that for a moment. The guy was right. He *wasn't* anybody now, not in these circles anyway. He glanced around at the partygoers—famous, rich, both—all on the short list to a private party that he'd pulled unpleasant strings to get into.

He set the whiskey bottle down on the bar, tossed the remains of his drink back and set the empty glass down too. He took a deep breath and let the burn of the whiskey linger in his throat. His breath caught suddenly. His chest thumped and he reached up, clutching at his heart. His vision went black for a split-second, accompanied by a single punch from a waiting headache. He doubled over with pain. A little too much to drink and his strange influence over luck and fate had a tendency to go off unchecked.

"Hey man, you okay?" The vulture's voice was distant, tinny.

Trent blinked a few times and watched as the barman picked up the discarded glass, fumbled, and then dropped it on the edge of the bar where it shattered, filling the ice bin below with broken glass. The bartender swore. Trent winced, realizing he'd just ruined the guy's next thirty minutes.

After catching his breath, Trent straightened up, coughed and gave the pudgy man a thin smile. "I'm fine," he said, and then apologized to the bartender, who was too preoccupied with cursing and cleaning out the ice bin to hear him. Trent walked away.

The little man fell in next to him and his smile returned. "Did you see that? Glass in the ice bin. That'll ruin your night. I know. Used to bartend back in college. Well, until I dropped out." He elbowed Trent in the side and held out his hand. "Hey, I'm Louis... Louis Bird. Journalist, freelance photographer." He glanced around at the crowd and his gaze fell upon several of the beautiful women. "Wish I could take some pictures here. Damn." He turned back to Trent. "Those fuckers took my camera at the gates, but they can't take my memory right?" He chuckled.

Trent ignored him and kept walking.

"Come on man," Louis pleaded as Trent walked away. "Just one question."

Trent stopped and stared at the sky for a moment. He didn't turn around. "You wanna know about the plane crash right? About the fall?"

Louis hustled back up and moved around so he could see Trent's face.

"Yeah. I bet you get that a lot, huh?"

"Sure."

"Well?"

"It hurt."

"Come on, there's gotta be more to it than that."

"There's not. I fell. I hit the ground. I nearly died."

"Well what about your friends, your family?"

"Adopted. Don't remember my biological parents. Dad sent flowers after the Crash, but I haven't seen him in years. You writin' a biography?"

"Just curious."

"Your name is really Louis Bird?"

Louis shrugged. "Grew up in Boston. Dad was a big basketball fan. Figured my name should start with 'L'."

Trent shook his head. "Look, there's not much to say. I was in a coma for a couple weeks and the world moved on. First thing I saw was my wife...." *Wife*. It brought back memories of Susan, squeezing his fingers in the hospital, begging him to wake up while he waited just on the other side of darkness, trying desperately to find his way out.

"Yeah, sure, but what about after—"

Trent spotted a gentleman in a sharp tuxedo at the far end of the bar. The suit caught his look and nodded. Break time over. Time for the last round, at a new table with the remaining players. Trent had been there all day, playing through the tournament, ignoring the players who gawked at him, who knew him from the old TV specials as the "Luckiest Man Alive". He'd worked his way up the tournament bracket to get to this, the last table, where he'd finally meet Gadreel, a man with information that could lead Trent to Susan. Or, more accurately, a man who might tell him where to find someone called the Medicine Man. Through various sources, Trent had heard that the Medicine Man knew a way into the Realms of Shadow. If he could get there, then Susan could be rescued.

"Gotta go," he said. "Good to meet you."

Louis frowned, glanced at the man in the suit and then back at Trent. "Hey, before you go, can I ask you something?"

"You already did."

Louis chuckled. "Seriously, though. What are you doing now? You know, besides talking to jerks like me at swanky parties?"

Trent thought about it for a moment. How often he'd wished he could tell someone, anyone. He walked daily on the black razor edge of fate, watching the movements of things that would make an ordinary man cover their eyes and blubber like a child. Even Celia, his charge, his arranged "niece" of sorts, herself now an orphan, knew only a fraction of what he'd seen.

He sighed. "You wouldn't believe me if I told you."

He turned and walked off, leaving Louis standing there, brow furrowed in confusion.

Mr. Gadreel's mansion perched like a hulking beast on the edge of a cliffside estate, where it watched over the desert to the east. In the distance, the color-shrouded city of Las Vegas loomed.

The final group of gamblers had congregated in the private poker lounge at the top of the house, an ornate room that jutted out from the side of the mansion and overhung the outdoor pool area. The lounge hummed with quiet tension, amplified by the dark wood paneling and enormous windows that let in breathtaking panoramic views of the night-blackened desert. Below the gamblers' feet, a one-way glass floor let them look down upon the unsuspecting pool-goers below. Supermodels and celebrities strutted across the patio, oblivious to those peering down at them.

Trent didn't need to ogle like some of the old men around the table. He had no interest in what was down there. He had come for a singular purpose. For Susan. He had to know what Mr. Gadreel knew. He had to know how he could get to her, how he could bring her back to this world.

As he took his seat at the game table, he caught a familiar scent and glanced to his left. A woman sat down next to him. He almost didn't recognize her at first. This week she was blonde, with a bob cut. But it was definitely her.

"Trish," he said with a nod. "Nice hair." Her cleavage bulged generously from her simple, V-cut red gown. "Nice dress."

She reached out a red-nailed finger and stroked the tip of Trent's nose. "You're going to thank me for getting you into this, right? Some friends of ours aren't at all happy with you right now." She had a razor-sharp British accent.

"I'm retired. I don't owe them anything. And they're not my friends."

"It's not an office job, darling. You can't just quit."

"Oh yeah?" He began stacking his chips in neat, color-coordinated towers on the green felt. "I've got a kid to take care of now. Got my own problems to deal with. I don't need to play border patrol for you people anymore. Find someone else. And I couldn't give a shit if they have a problem with that."

Tricia pouted. "So full of anger." Her pout turned into a malicious grin. "You know my offer is still open. The War *is* coming, Trent, whether you play your part or not..."

Trent sighed. Tricia had been pushing for him to become some sort of Lord of Hell or something. She claimed she knew a ritual that would give him immense power and dominion over the Realms of Fury, rule over Hell itself. Exactly the sort of thing a demon would offer you. Trent found it almost laughably cliché and didn't really believe it anyway. He'd already turned the offer down a half-dozen times.

"You know my answer." He sent two stacks of chips clacking against each other and shuffled them into a single, color-alternated column. "Sorry you went out in the second round," he said, changing the subject. He had been surprised to hear that. Tricia could beat most of the world's top gamblers while filing her nails. Any of them but him.

"Don't worry," she said, grinning ear to ear. "I just wish you could have been there. Maybe given me some of your luck?"

He chuckled at that. "Luck. Sure."

Half a year ago, he would have believed her. He had assumed then that his good luck was unnatural, that his unending string of wins stemmed from some supernatural source that he couldn't fathom. He'd found out on the night of the Blizzard that he was only half right. His employers called him the Doombringer. He didn't win because *he* was lucky; he won because he broke the other guy's fate, deadened his opponents' chances when their providence rested on a fulcrum. It was a black gift—a curse, really. But he'd learned to make it work for him, most of the time.

"Well," he said, "sorry I missed it. Heard it was a good game."

"That's sweet of you to say." She leaned in close and kissed him on the cheek.

Her breath reeked of sulfur and kerosene and Trent winced at the sudden and overwhelming odor. Trish looked hurt by his expression.

He looked away from her and decided it might be best to change the subject. "Gadreel." He surveyed the old men in the poker lounge. "Which one is he?"

Tricia's answer was short and cold. "He's not here."

Trent rolled his eyes. "Dammit, Trish."

"It's not *my* fault," she said, and shrugged. "He's away on business."

Trent drummed his fingers impatiently on the poker felt. He'd come to talk to Gadreel, not Tricia. Now what?

Out of curiosity, he asked, "What kind of business?"

"Religion."

Trent raised an eyebrow. "What?"

"Religion. He invests in mega-churches, like the ones you see next to the interstate. Texas, Colorado, California. He even owns one here. It's run by Edward Palisade, the gentleman with glasses over there. He's a very popular preacher, I hear."

Trent looked across the table and saw the man she had pointed out. Thin, wiry, in a boring grey suit and blue tie, with short-cut blonde hair and tiny, round glasses perched on the tip of his beakish nose. He looked irritated to be there.

"He represents Gadreel's interests in this game," she continued.

"And those would be?"

"Probably you."

Trent let out a long sigh and gave Tricia a plaintive look. "I thought we'd agreed—"

She interrupted, her voice a whisper. "Don't be a fool, Trent. Everyone here knows who you are. I'm sure it was a big draw to the others when he announced that Trent Hawkins— the Luckiest Man Alive—was willing to attend. I expect most of them are here just to try and beat you."

"I don't *always* win."

"Games you've thrown on purpose don't count. Name the last time you *actually* lost."

Trent frowned. She was right. He hadn't lost. Not one game he could remember in the past two years. "Look, I don't give a shit about some pinhead preacher he throws to the wolves. I need Gadreel. What am I supposed to do with him?" He gestured at Palisade, who was checking his watch, tapping the glass face impatiently.

Tricia shrugged and leaned forward to kiss Trent behind the ear. She nibbled on his lobe for a moment and whispered, "I got you this close, darling. The rest is up to you."

Before Tricia could get up to leave, Trent reached out and laid a hand on her wrist. "Trish," he said, whispering now. "What happened to Zamagiel?"

She furrowed her brow, confused. "What?"

"Zamagiel, the Watcher. You know, the fallen angel I killed on top of the Luxor last year. What happened to him?"

Tricia smirked. "First of all, *you* didn't exactly kill him. Your little girl, Celia, did."

Trent impatiently twirled one of the chips between his fingers. "Yeah, yeah," he said, annoyed. "But I burned the body. He's not still here, right?"

"Why are you bringing this up now?"

He shrugged. "I just want to know. Where did he go after...? You know..."

"To the Realms of Shadow."

"Yeah, I know. But *where*? What does that mean, exactly? Where did he go in the Realms?"

Tricia raised an eyebrow. "We're not talking about Zamagiel anymore, are we? You're asking about your wife."

"Just answer the question." He flipped the poker chip off his index finger and it clacked neatly down atop the stack in front of him.

Tricia shrugged. "It's hard to say, exactly, since 'where' doesn't have the same meaning there as it does here." She looked down through the glass floor at the people walking below. It bothered Trent that she was suddenly refusing to make eye contact. "I have some contacts there, Shades that send me messages. From what I gather, he's the ruler of Dis now. Or... well... he always has been..." She looked up and finally met his gaze again. She gave him a crooked smile. "It's complicated. Time, I mean. In that place."

Trent shook his head. If Susan still walked that place, somehow, then she was in grave danger with Zamagiel in charge. "What is Dis? A kingdom or something?"

"A city. The Iron City. Built by *grigorim* banished from this world. Kind of a thumb in the Prince's eye. The *grigorim* have their own little place. It's a ruin, I hear, but it keeps the wild Shades out. The *grigorim* plot and scheme and...." She shrugged again.

"Thanks."

"Anytime. And don't forget my offer. Dis sits atop the sealed gateway to Hell below. If you want to do some Shadow Realm tourism, it's much easier as the Lord of Hell...."

"I'll find a way there, Trish, but not your way."

"Fine. Have fun playing your little game." She gestured at the croupier, who was approaching the table and motioning to everyone that the poker game was about to begin.

Tricia scooted her chair back, stood abruptly enough to startle a few of the old men around the table, and made a show of adjusting her breasts. She winked at one of the gawking men and sauntered off, butt swaying, needle-sharp heels tap-tapping against the glass floor.

Trent rolled his eyes. His frown remained. He'd come expecting to meet Gadreel. He'd been told that the old man had information, that he could lead Trent to the Medicine Man. And the Medicine Man, in turn, could lead him to Susan, wherever she might be in the Realms of Shadow. Now, if Tricia was right, their old enemy had his own little fiefdom and maybe posed a threat to Susan's survival. Trent couldn't bear the thought. It was all he cared about now. Not celebrities, not poker, not Tricia and her ever-changing hair color and eye-watering scent. Just Susan. He looked at Palisade and his frown deepened.

The croupier stepped up to the table then and began shuffling the cards. No words spoken. None were needed at this table. The crowd that had gathered in the room stood up and moved their chairs back against the walls. Trent, Palisade, and two older gentlemen in fine suits remained seated at the table. Just the four of them for this last game, sat before an astronomical pot.

A flash of the croupier's wrist and two facedown cards slid into place before each player. The blinds went into the new pot with a ceramic clack. Trent glanced at the other players and grinned.

Everyone peered under the edges of their pocket cards. Trent threw in two thousand dollar chips just for fun, and was met by a full round of calls. Palisade wouldn't make eye contact, but instead fidgeted with his tie. The room was dead silent.

"All playing," said the dealer quietly as he dropped one card off the top of the deck, facedown, and then dealt three into the middle of the table, face up—the flop.

In a rare moment of good fortune, Trent had been dealt pocket aces and, combined with the flop cards of an ace, six, and a queen, he already had ace trips. Not too shabby for the first hand of the game. He figured he could win this one fair and square for a change. He threw in a handful of high-value chips that he hadn't counted. Maybe a couple hundred thousand, maybe just over a million. All the money was on loan from Tricia, so he wasn't too concerned. She had a near-inexhaustible supply. He had never asked why. In truth, he didn't want to know the answer. Most of the demons came into wealth by less-than-honest means.

The two older gentlemen quickly folded, but Trent was shocked when Palisade carefully counted up the massive bet, countered it, and re-raised by a million. Trent didn't let his surprise show.

Okay, maybe the guy has triple queens and thinks the best I have is ace-queen for a high double-pair.

He tried again to catch Palisade's gaze, but the wiry fidgeter wouldn't look up from the table and instead spent the tense moment re-stacking his chips in perfect, color-coordinated piles. He poked at his wire-rim glasses, pushing them a bit further up the bridge of his nose. Trent tossed a few more high-dollar chips in to call.

"Call," announced the dealer, and flipped the fourth card onto the end of the line.

Another six and that made Trent nervous. Had Palisade opened with pocket sixes, a devil's hand right from the start? Demons had a ridiculous tendency to land that particular hand.

No way, he thought. *This is just a normal guy, a little anal-retentive but nothing out of the ordinary. Nothing unnatural about him.* Along with his strange ability to influence luck, Trent had been granted a minor gift from Vladimir—he could see the true faces of those around him. When a person was really a demon or angel in disguise, Trent knew, with only a handshake or brief collision. He could even detect the *grigorim*—the bloodline offspring of ancient demons and mortals. He'd made a point of shaking hands or brushing against as many of the gamblers as possible when he entered the room, Palisade among them. Palisade was definitely nothing more than a mortal. *Is he just bluffing?*

Trent laughed. "Nice try," he said. He dumped a few more million-dollar chips on the felt, to several quiet gasps from the edges of the room.

Trent remained stone-faced but stared down the preacher, silently daring him to look up. And suddenly, he did. Edward Palisade's icy stare caught Trent momentarily off-guard. Something about those blue-white faded eyes. He'd seen eyes like that before, but no, not possible. Not another one? He couldn't be—he was too old. The *grigorim* children were just that, children, not adults. Their bloodlines had only begun activating recently. And he looked normal to boot...

But the sudden, unblinking gaze made Trent's breath catch in his throat. He wanted to look away, but didn't want to break his composure. He stared into those ice-blue eyes until his own began to water, but still he held firm.

Palisade spoke then, his voice a quiet, carefully measured monotone, like a man struggling to keep from screaming by enunciating everything with a slow perfection. "I don't have the sixes, Mr. Hawkins. I have three queens. And I'm going to win this hand."

With three queens? Trent had triple aces, already a better hand. He looked down at his chips, desperate now to break eye contact, and that gave him a moment to shut his eyes, to focus on the game and the world and the man sitting across the table, taunting him. Time to win.

In the darkness behind the world he sought handholds to grip, but felt suddenly like a climber whose rocky ledge had turned to windblown ash. And for the first time in five and a half years, he came away empty-handed and for a moment felt as though he was falling backwards, tumbling down into a void that had gone inexplicably silent. He opened his eyes and tried hard to conceal his shock. The dealer laid down the fifth card.

A queen.

Four queens walked all over his triple aces.

Palisade, still staring at Trent, fidgeted with his tie again. A devious smile crept onto his face. Trent felt cold and clammy, and he knew that things were about to go very badly. He wanted to leave. Something wasn't right. Something wasn't right about this quiet, obsessive little preacher. Trent watched him, transfixed by his own confusion.

Palisade seemed to be enjoying it. "Tonight," he said without breaking eye contact, "Trent Hawkins is going to lose."

*　*　*

It was three in the morning and Celia couldn't sleep so, instead, she had parked herself at the foot of her bed and was watching television on a small set that Trent had found for her in Charlie's pawn shop. They had cable, but the signal had been bad all night, all static and buzzing, the image jumping and losing vertical lock from time to time. But it was better than trying to sleep. She never slept well when Trent was gone. She never really slept well at all anymore.

The screen warped and fuzzed for a moment and the volume shot up with a burst of warbling high-pitched noise.

The vertical lock went completely and the remnants of the image danced like a flipbook gone mad. She reached out and smacked the set. It didn't help.

She sighed, got up from the bed and jiggled the cable line where it joined the television. The static twisted, hissed, but wouldn't resolve. She hit it again, harder this time and, without warning, the dancing image resolved instantly to a tiny dot of light that then faded to black. Silence.

"Umm...."

Celia furrowed her brow. Technology never worked right for her. *Probably the stupid magick*, she thought.

She stared at her tiny bedroom closet for a moment before sliding the door open and peering inside. A stack of school textbooks, some stuffed animals, piles of unfolded clothes. Peeking out from beneath one of the piles was a half-opened box. She leaned in and lifted the corner of the lid. Candles, sheaves of paper, unreturned library books, a heavy iron cross. She reached into the box for a candle but pulled back fast.

No, no. I promised. No more magick. She took a deep breath, and slid the closet door shut with a sharp bang. She turned back to see what she could do about the television.

It was on.

But instead of static, the screen was a curious charcoal grey, a mélange of drifting, cloud-like shapes that moved horizontally, as if flowing behind the screen. Every so often, a pattern of white dots buzzed into being with a high-pitched whine and then faded away again. She couldn't quite make out the image. A face? A warbling noise emanated from the speaker that grew louder. She whirled round and discovered that her clock radio had switched on, emitting the same strange warbling, like songs maybe, or voices in some unknown tongue.

"Okay, now I'm freaked out," she said aloud, a slight comfort to hear her own voice above the weird sounds. Definitely people talking, she decided. Some kind of scrambled cable channel or something. She walked over to the clock radio and pulled the power cord, but the warbling only grew louder. The white dots on the television had become clear.

Eyes. Solid, unblinking white eyes.

Her heart felt as thought it might stop from panic. She shoved the television off the dresser, but it still wouldn't turn off. She shrieked, spun around and looked into her dimly lit bedroom. Her hands flew to her mouth in sudden and abject terror. Filling the room were numerous wavering forms; like people, only less substantial, shadows cast against nothing, unfettered by wall, not tethered to any beam of light or errant glow, with circles of unbroken, unblinking white where eyes might have been. They were formless but with humanoid shape of the deepest black, not because they stood where light was blocked, but because where they stood, light died.

They towered above her, elongated shapes that reached to the ceiling, watching with their colorless discs. She screamed and screamed until her throat went hoarse and not a one of the entities moved. They only began a repetitive sibilant chittering, like air escaping from a valve in short staccato bursts, descending in pitch to nothing and then restarting again, over and over and over.

She began to shake and knew that she had wet herself. A sadly humorous notion flitted through her mind about how a fourteen year-old was way too old to be peeing herself. The thought gave her just enough distraction to force her legs to move. She tried to run but realized that her feet were burning with icy cold.

Cold?

She looked down and saw ice gathering around her toes, cracking the hardwood floor with fine striations of crystalline white as though it had burst from below the wood in the shapes of her feet.

Oh no. God no. Please. Not this. Not again.

As the paralyzing panic tried to resurface, she willed herself to action. Her feet slapped loud against the wood as she sprinted across the room and past the creatures. Their eyes didn't so much move as repositioned themselves imperceptibly to watch her passage. The chittering grew louder as she burst through the doorway into the upstairs hallway.

She looked around in horror and then squeezed her eyes shut, clenched her fists, and screamed at the top of her lungs. "*Fuck!*" The curse word tore its way through her throat and she bellowed it over and over.

Dozens of the terrifying creatures lined the hallway, eyes glowing, luminescent orbs white in shadow, unblinking, emotionless and of alien motive. They gathered around her. Their positions shifted constantly as they approached. A claustrophobic panic tightened her gut.

"Leave me alone, leave me alone," she mumbled as she skittered, hunched over, toward the stairwell leading down.

"*Trent!*" she screamed as she reached the top of the stairs. "Oh, God. *Trent, please!*" Her voice cracked, her throat aching from her bloodcurdling yells. "*Trent!*" she screamed again, but there was no answer.

She needed her cellphone. She looked frantically around, trying to mentally edit out the creatures that waited everywhere, chittering louder now, the hissing noise eating its way into her brain like a parasite. Her breath came in burning, hyperventilating gasps.

The creatures were moving, following her, and the scant light from nearby windows and nightlights flickered and died with their movements. As the lights went out, the wall of darkness advanced. She ran back to the stairs, descending two steps at a time. She looked up from her cold, aching footfalls to find more white eyes awaiting her below. Through the bars of the stairwell she could see her cellphone on the coffee table, but the entire living room teemed with the chittering creatures.

She swayed. Her world went awry and she hit the railing hard with her shoulder. It responded with a mighty crack. The post and beam froze for a split-second, groaned, and then burst apart; a blast of steam and splintered wood. A section of railing broke free. Celia went through, falling straight down until her body struck the hardwood floor with a loud crunch. Waves of pain tore through her every muscle, and in her skull, endless ringing, ringing, ringing.

She whimpered. Burning tears sluiced down her cheeks, and as she looked up she saw light glimmering on the silver case of her phone. She reached up and her shoulder popped violently into its socket. She let out a deafening wail of pain.

Her splayed fingers slammed down onto the phone, which toppled from the table and landed on her stomach.

She trembled, barely able to flip the phone open. Even the slightest motion of her arm caused her shoulder to scream in fury. Her breath came ragged. Her back felt broken. Muscles throughout her body tensed and relaxed, tensed and relaxed with throbbing, excruciating cramps. The skin beneath her eyes stung. She tasted blood on her lips. Her belly ached like a knife had been driven through her gut. The hissing and chattering of the ghostly creatures was deafening.

She redialed the number three times before she got it right. Finally, Trent's number.

Jamming the phone against her ear, she curled into a fetal position and mumbled and cried at the unanswered ringing on the line, her voice matching it tone-for-tone with a soft, miserable keening, while the white-eyed alien things moved closer.

* * *

Trent sat frozen, stared at by the other gamblers around the table and the spectators at the back of the room. Everyone knew who Trent Hawkins was—sole survivor of an airplane crash, then professional gambler, winner of every major tournament, winner of impossible hands. They had pinned him with the title "The Luckiest Man Alive" and he had milked it for five years. Then the blacklists and a new sort of crash and he had gone headlong into a downward spiral of drugs and drink and despair. But no one in the poker scene had ever doubted, not even once, his ability to win. He was unbeatable, that's what they all said. He had a gift.

Tonight, Trent Hawkins is going to lose.

Everyone had gone silent at that. Even the dealer had paused, delaying the next hand until the room had regained a measure of its lost energy. No one was smiling but Palisade.

"It shouldn't be such a shock to some of you," he had said with his perfect monotone. "He's just a man."

And then the game went on.

And Trent lost.

For every hand he won, all fair and square, he came up short on two others. He wasn't losing to any unnatural tricks. No magick here that he could see. He was simply outplayed. The other two gentlemen went out quickly, but Palisade remained to grind Trent down. Card after card, stack of chips after stack of chips, the skinny man in the boring suit quietly proved to Trent the difference between a poker professional and a man with a powerful cheat. And with Trent's cheat out of commission somehow, he couldn't stand up to Palisade's expert play.

It had been years since he'd had to face the reality of his failures at the game. He wasn't a great player. In truth, he was an amateur at best, but when he'd pulled a victory on every hand, on every champion, no one had doubted his skill. Now, he looked like a chump.

As the final card of the very last hand was turned over, the room fell silent once more. Palisade, for the first time all evening, stood from his chair and turned his back to the table. He walked over to the huge glass window and looked out over the desert and said nothing.

The card went down and Trent tasted defeat for the first time in five and a half years.

The air burned with tension.

The dealer, in an uncharacteristic moment, loudly cleared his throat to break the silence. "Mr. Hawkins went all-in. A pair of kings wins it for Mr. Palisade. That's our game, gentlemen."

No one moved but Palisade who, still facing the window, tightened his sky blue tie before turning to face the gathered assembly of poker pros and the one unlucky failure. His lips bore a thin smile.

"Mr. Gadreel wanted to thank all of you for joining us this evening. It has certainly been a memorable game." He glanced briefly at Trent, then focused on the others again. "Please feel free to rejoin the party downstairs or at the indoor pool. For those of you still with money to spare—" He paused, as if awaiting a laugh, but none came. "You may find suitable *companionship* mingling amidst the crowd. Please take advantage of the mansion's many beautiful guest rooms if you would like to stay the evening. Good night."

There were murmurs of thanks and a smattering of weak applause, and then the doors were opened. Gamblers and spectators filed out into the hallway. The dealer left through a side door and Palisade moved to follow. Trent leapt from his chair and used an arm to block the wiry man's passage.

"Uh uh."

Palisade stopped, frowned and fidgeted with his glasses. "I'm sorry? I believe you lost."

"I don't buy it. I've never lost like that, not since—"

"The accident. The plane crash?" Palisade turned and walked back over to the table and pulled out one of the chairs. "And what made you think your uniqueness would last forever,

Mr. Hawkins?" He sat down and crossed his legs and placed his folded hands neatly in his lap.

Trent shook his head and carefully shut the side door. "What did you do to my gift?"

"Oh, it's a gift now, not an accident, not a theft from one far more powerful and deserving than you?"

"Who are you? Where's Gadreel?"

"I believe your friend Tricia secured this invitation for you. Mr. Gadreel had no interest in your presence. He would have preferred that you stayed home, with your job and your child. He doesn't even know you're here."

Trent fixed his gaze on Palisade.

Palisade squinted, removed his wire-rim glasses and polished them with the bottom edge of his shirt. "Trent, my understanding is that *you* were seeking *us*. Let's just say that this evening's defeat is a reminder that you cannot *always* call the shots. Walk away. You are on the wrong path. You may be a man with a gift, of sorts, but you are still just a man. You have your role to play." Palisade looked up and smiled. "So play it, and stop agitating."

Trent moved suddenly across the floor, advancing on the seated preacher. He grabbed a handful of Palisade's starched collar and stared into his pale-blue eyes, searching for any sign. When he didn't find what he was looking for, he threw Palisade back against the chair. "Vladimir put you up to this?"

"Please." Palisade rolled his eyes. "That faux-Dracula with his cadre of rejects? He's right now holed up in his bookstore, scared of the dark."

Trent hadn't thought of Vladimir as faux-anything. He'd seemed powerful the last time they'd met. *Scared of the dark?*

"No," he continued. "Tricia was working her contacts to get you an invite. She would never have gotten anywhere had I not approved the invitation. I wanted to meet you in person, find out why you're sniffing around so intently. Something about your dear wife, I understand?"

Trent's eyebrow went up at the mention of Susan. "Where is she?"

"You think that's your role, Mr. Hawkins? Resurrector of the dead?"

"Where's the Medicine Man?"

"Ahh, him. So that's your path then. I should have expected you would go that route." He sighed. "I'm afraid I don't know his whereabouts. Only Mr. Gadreel would have that kind of information. And he would prefer you *not* have it."

"Where is he?" asked Trent through gritted teeth.

"What was it like, Trent? The fall, I mean?"

Trent had no interest in changing subjects. He fished his cellphone out of his pocket and held it between them. "Call him."

After an extensive cleaning, Palisade replaced the glasses on his nose and then met Trent's angry glare. "No."

Trent slammed the phone into Palisade's face, cracking one of the newly cleaned glass lenses and then shoved him backwards against the chair until it toppled over. Palisade spilled out onto the floor. The phone clattered down next to him. Trent pulled the chair off the struggling preacher and hurled it through the plate glass window, sending shards of glass flying into the night. Then he reached down and secured Palisade with one hand by the back of his collar and dragged him over to the window. He slammed him face-first on the sill until he heard the telltale crunch of cartilage. He hoisted the blood-spattered man to the gaping hole. It was at least a three-story drop onto the rocky ground below.

Palisade protested, his breathing more rapid, though he was working hard to maintain his calm demeanor. "You're crazy," he said, blood dribbling from his lips. "Put me down."

"You wanna know about me? You wanna know what it's like to fall?"

Palisade grabbed Trent's wrist with both hands and glanced down twice, his legs kicking and helpless, then he looked back up, his face a mess of blood fronted by twisted, shattered eyeglass frames. He didn't say anything, but Trent could see the panic in his eyes.

"Get your boss on the phone. Now."

Before Palisade could answer, the tense silence shattered. The air filled with an electronic ringing, a silly tone that seemed utterly out of place in the current situation. Trent looked over his shoulder at his cellphone, lying on the poker room floor, lights blinking.

"Let me back inside," croaked Palisade, his voice mangled by Trent's iron grip.

Trent's head snapped back around and he forgot all about the phone for a moment. His self-hatred turned to fury and he growled at the struggling preacher. He gritted his teeth. "Last chance, buddy." He let some of the man's shirt slip through his fingers for emphasis. "You gonna get Gadreel on the line or what?"

The phone kept ringing, the tone somehow growing louder. In between the cheerful musical tones, it sounded like voices oozing through. Shouts, screams, and then it burst to life and the jingly song was replaced by a humming, digitized voice. A girl's voice. Celia's voice? He couldn't understand what she was saying. It barely sounded like speech. And in the background, a strange chittering, a staccato that broke her words with static pulses like a strobe light breaks a dancer's motions.

Trent looked back again. "What the fu—"

The phone exploded, sending plastic casing and electronic circuitry flying across the room and ricocheting off the chairs and poker table. In its wake was a strange, irregular patch of ice that sent spidery veins running through the glass floor and, in places, forming sharp crystalline spines.

Trent dragged Palisade back in through the window and tossed him against the edge of the poker table. The preacher fell to the floor in a heap, shocked and confused by the sudden turn of events.

Trent walked over to the broken glass and touched the ice. It was so cold it burned. *Goddammit*, was all his mind kept repeating, over and over. *Not now, not again. She promised. She promised me, dammit*. He turned to the preacher and jabbed his forefinger at the air.

"Not over," he said. "You tell Gadreel I'm coming back."

Palisade had his eyes closed and gulped for air like a strangled dog. Bloody, frothy snot-bubbles had formed in his nostrils. He could only nod.

Trent swiped a hand across the top of the poker table, showering Palisade with chips, and then grabbed his cowboy hat from his chair, turned and stormed out of the poker lounge.

*   *   *

The preacher watched Trent go through a broken reality, the cracked and red-streaked glass lenses splitting the furious man into a half-dozen crimson doppelgangers. When he was finally gone, Palisade took off the broken glasses and leaned his head back against the poker table, finally able to breathe.

As he gasped in oxygen, he fumbled in his pocket for his phone, dialed and put it to his ear.

"Yes," he said quietly, between ragged breaths. "This is Edward. Mr. Hawkins is leaving the grounds on a black Ducati motorcycle. Please kill him."

The voice on the other end of the line protested.

"No, I don't give a shit what you think or what Gadreel would say. He's not here now. This is my call." He summoned up a rage-filled bark. "Kill him, or *she will*."

Then he hung up, dialed a second number and waited for an answer.

2

TRENT EMERGED FROM THE MANSION elevator and strode quickly out the back entrance and into the crowded pool and bar area. Numerous celebrities gawked at him and he smiled back, trying to pretend that his button-up white dress shirt was not, in fact, streaked with Palisade's blood.

He thought about Celia and the promises she'd made. And this wasn't the first that she'd broken. *She said no more magick*, he thought.

He wasn't any good at being a father. He knew that. And punishment was his weakest subject. He gave in too easy, let her off the hook over and over, but not this time. This time she'd be grounded until....

A familiar voice cut through the murmurs of the gawking crowd and dragged Trent back to the now. "Hey, wait up, buddy." Trent didn't slow as Louis pulled up next to him. Louis eyeballed him, stared at the blood on his shirt and coughed. "Whoa, I heard you lost the game, but Jesus, did you have to kill the winner?"

"Should have," Trent mumbled.

"So where we off to now?"

"We?"

"Come on, I'm a journalist. You're the Luckiest Man Alive, right? This is my big chance for a 'where are they now' interview. Come on...."

"No."

He stopped then and cocked his head slightly. Nothing. The worlds beyond the world wouldn't sing. His mind felt blank, empty, quiet. It had been a long time since he'd heard silence on his mental stage. But he could still sense a change in crowd atmosphere. Murmurings. Startled gasps. "We'd better run."

"Wha-?"

He grabbed Louis by the top of the head and shoved hard, forcing the man to hunch. A gunshot rang out and the crowd screamed. Trent yelled, "Run!" and the two of them ran.

They dashed across the deck, Trent's cowboy boots clattering on the marble tile, Louis close in tow, slipping clumsily through puddles of pool water. "Holy shit!" he yelled, slowing his stride to look back at the oncoming guards.

Trent grabbed his shirt, urging him to move faster. "Run, dammit!"

Another gunshot, then another. A high-pitched twang rang out as one of the bullets ricocheted off the marble near Trent's feet, blasting a polished decorative sphere to bits. He wanted to know the locations of the shooters, to *feel* their connections to fate and luck in the air around him, but something had gone missing in his mind and he could no longer summon that awareness.

He chanced a backwards look and saw a half-dozen of Gadreel's security officers running across the patio, waving large pistols. He had to get to his bike. He refocused his attention forward and saw a large, muscular man without a shirt looming ahead of him.

It was one of Hollywood's famous action heroes, a guy Trent used to love watching at the movies. The muscular actor had squared himself in Trent's immediate path and had his hands outstretched, ready to intercept.

Trent didn't bother to dodge. He dropped his head slightly and barreled forward. The actor's cocky grin melted in the face of real adversity, and Trent bore down on him like a loaded truck with dead brakes. He slammed into the faux hero with a force that sent the actor sprawling backwards, arms and legs akimbo as he hit the ground butt-first, three yards away, the wind knocked clear out of him. He threw his arms up and cowered as Trent leaped over him and continued onward, toward the mansion's exit.

As he and Louis neared the stone archway leading out of the pool area, two parking valets stepped through it to block their escape. On instinct, Trent glanced around for items that might be in play, for things with potential for change, but then he realized with dismay that it didn't matter. Without his strange power over fate, he had to handle this the old-fashioned way.

The valets each raised a handgun. Trent charged. Narrowing the distance would reduce the gunman's options, especially if he could get there before the valet pulled the trigger. At the last minute before the valet fired, Trent dove.

The gun went off and the bullet sailed over him. Trent caught the man like a football linebacker, shoulder to gut. The valet stumbled backwards against the stone arch, caught his elbow on a rock, and dropped the gun. The other valet turned to shoot at Trent on the ground, but with a sharp kick, Trent snapped his shin. It gave him enough time to grab the fallen gun and put a bullet in the hobbling valet's leg, sending him into writhing paroxysms of pain. Then he turned the gun on the remaining attacker, looked over his shoulder at Louis and yelled, "Run! Get out of here!"

Louis, wide-eyed, nodded and stumbled past the fallen guards, through the archway to the parking lot beyond. Trent turned his attention back to the panicked man and growled, "My keys, now!" Then he jammed the barrel of the gun into the man's neck.

Gasping, wheezing, the valet fumbled in his pocket and pulled out a handful of keys. Trent grabbed his, then slammed the butt of the handgun into the man's temple, knocking him out.

Keys jangling, he leapt up and sprinted through the arch as a few more gunshots rang out behind him.

Ahead, he saw Louis stumbling dazedly through the rows of cars. For a split second, Trent felt bad about leaving the little man behind. Palisade's guards had already shot at him once and there'd probably be more on the way. If he left Louis here, he'd probably be shot.

"Come on," he yelled, gesturing at Louis, as he threw a leg over his motorcycle.

Louis looked confused, but a sudden burst of automatic weapon fire snapped him back to attention. He sprinted over and Trent helped him onto the back of the Ducati before squealing off, darting between parked cars for a last bit of cover.

*   *   *

The cellphone ring, loud and obnoxious, dragged Fiamma from her sleep. She sat up, blinked, and ritually swept the bits of ash from her bed sheets onto the ground. The twisting tribal tattoos on her forearms still glowed a faint orange, but had begun to dim. She answered the phone.

"Now?" she said. "It's the middle of the fucking night, pal."

She listened to the voice on the other end, her frown deepening. Smoke lifted from the tops of her fingers as she struggled to grab a protein bar that was lying half-eaten on her nightstand; she needed the protein, always protein. Carbs and sugars burned too fast, and her body lingered on the razor's edge of combustion at any moment. Finally, she got it, ripped off some of the wrapper with her teeth, and bit off a big chunk. The smoke faded to thin wisps and then vanished altogether.

"Fine," she said between bites. "But you owe me, Palisade. You owe me big."

Palisade squawked in her ear.

"No, I don't fucking care who it is. That's not the point. It's three in the fucking morning...."

She held the phone a foot from her ear as Palisade yelled. He didn't yell often, but when he did, it made her worry, just a bit. She never liked being in his presence. She knew what he could do to her if she pushed him too far: he might stop calling.

"Okay, I got it. Heading east. I'll meet him halfway."

She hung up the phone, gulped down the rest of the protein bar, and then got up from the bed. She threw on a pair of jeans that reeked of cigarette smoke, grabbed a too-tight Black Flag t-shirt with holes in the collar, and jammed her bare feet into a pair of black combat boots sitting at the foot of the bed. While she struggled to yank the shirt over her skinny figure, she made her way to her tiny kitchen.

She opened the fridge and pulled out a collection of protein bars with one hand and a gleaming handgun with the other. It was a .357 Colt Python, brand new, with a nickel finish, a gift from Gadreel. She paused a moment, savoring the feel of the cold metal in her hand, and stood in the wash of icy air from the refrigerator. She popped the freezer compartment open too and let the frozen mist pour over her face. She took a final deep breath of the cold, and then slammed both doors shut.

She flipped open the revolver, checking for ammo. Fully loaded. She clacked the cylinder home, jammed the gun in the back of her waistband, and jammed the protein bars in her pocket. *Time to do my part*, she thought. *Just wish I had gotten more sleep.*

She gathered her straight black hair into a short ponytail and secured it with a hair tie as she glanced back wistfully at the bedroom. *Dammit*, she thought. For a moment, her mind filled with images of her last girlfriend, of skin sliding against skin, laughter, and next the smell of smoke and charred flesh and screaming and a look of betrayal and fear that had sent her away from New York forever. She frowned and shook her head to clear the memories. *Long time ago. Not important now.*

Next to the front door was a small side table with her bike keys and a crumpled cigarette pack with one left. She grabbed the keys and the cigarette. With one quick motion she put it between her lips and placed a finger on the tip. Smoke rose. Fiamma grimaced with pain. When she took her finger away, the cigarette tip glowed bright orange.

* * *

"What the hell is going on?" Louis had to shout to be heard from behind as Trent rocketed the black Ducati down the winding mountain path, heading east toward Las Vegas.

Trent glanced in his rearview. Headlights in the distance, gaining fast.

"Just keep down," he said.

He didn't particularly like having the pudgy man pressed against his back on the motorcycle, but he didn't want Louis to end up dead. He guessed that Palisade's guards wouldn't discriminate.

The bike leaned over and slid into a sharp downward turn as Trent guided it to the desert floor and bounced it onto the two lanes of asphalt that formed Route 157, leading east out of Kyle Canyon. Ahead was little more than dust and a scattering of distant houses and old beat-up trailer homes, all bordered to the north and south by looming canyon inclines that blocked out the view to Las Vegas, the only nearby population center.

On an ordinary night, Trent would have enjoyed the peaceful quiet of the night-black ride through the canyon.

Tonight, he needed desperately to get somewhere with other people. The canyon wastes were a burying ground, and no authorities watched what happened here. If Palisade's guards caught up...

Trent heard a screech and saw a black sedan sliding, tires squealing, around the last downward corner. With a thump, it hit the desert floor and gunned the engine into the straightaway. Trent swore.

"Down, Louis, get down!"

Ahead, a small village of ramshackle trailer homes appeared in the darkness. Trent aimed the bike at the roadside and screamed "Hold on!" as he jumped the wheels off the pavement and onto the gravel-scattered desert sand. Dirt and debris kicked up behind the black sport cycle and the sedan followed. Trent could hear its tires protesting as it made the sudden turn.

The Ducati roared into the loose circle of trailers as lights came on and faces appeared in open doors. "What the hell?" someone shouted, their voice dopplering as Trent and Louis whipped past.

Trent didn't slow. Instead, he flipped open a small trigger chamber underneath the bike's accelerator. Back in the gambling days, when he'd had money, he'd spent a lot of it souping up the Ducati. He grinned, ducked into a streamlined posture, and jammed his thumb down on the button. Nitrous canisters burst to life beneath him, jarring a shriek out of Louis and sending the bike screaming forward through the center of the encampment, heading toward the far side, where he had thought he'd glimpsed a hefty pile of debris.

The sedan driver floored the gas to keep up, causing the heavier vehicle to fishtail on the uncertain desert surface. It crashed through a clump of trashcans and tore down a makeshift tarp and two-by-four awning before straightening out, its headlights illuminating Louis's back.

Trent searched the darkness for the trash he'd sworn was there. And then he saw it. A rusted-out old semi cab, glowing faint in the darkness. "Follow this," he said, under his breath.

He aimed the bike at the cab and leaned forward, dipping the nose and straightening out the ride. Behind him, Louis shrieked like a little girl, his voice mixing with the sound of brakes as the sedan driver noticed the looming obstacle. Trent remained focused.

Come on come on come on, he thought as the wreck rushed up to meet him. Sheet metal planks had been leaned against the side at various angles, probably a playhouse for the local kids. He hoped the panel could take the bike's weight, aimed the front tire, dropped his head an inch lower, and held down the accelerator. The bike hit the edge of the panel with a clang, raced up the side and took to the air. Louis' cries melted into a sustained, meaningless yell. Trent gritted his teeth until they hurt and glanced back over his shoulder, just for a second.

Behind him, the sedan driver made one last-ditch effort to avoid the rusting hulk, but it wasn't enough. The car had no traction left on the gravel and sand. It slid at a 45-degree angle and hit the motionless metal emplacement with a powerful crunch. Glass sprayed, metal burst like shrapnel, and the entire conglomerate, car and rusted semi, lifted slightly before creaking back down and going still. Lines of fire raced up from the sedan's hood and into the shattered, bloodied windshield.

Trent turned away, his face impassive. He guided the Ducati through the air until it reached the ground and bounced hard on its shocks. It slid a bit in the sand before he eased it into a slight turn, righted it, and zoomed off into the desert, back toward the two-lane road and the ever-opening mouth of Kyle Canyon, beyond which glowed the sporadic lights of Route 95.

*   *   *

Fiamma loved the feel of the wind blasting her. The air, even in the Nevada summer night, felt cool at high-speed, and she kept the accelerator down as far as it would go. As skinny as she was, she barely had enough weight to keep the Tuono R's nose from shimmying as it weaved in and out of the sparse traffic on the highway, but she didn't care. She liked the power, liked the feel of riding death with an oversized engine. A car honked angrily as she passed. She lifted her non-accelerator hand to shoot the driver the middle finger.

She could see the turn-off waiting in the distance, the feeder sliding off the highway and then the turn that would merge it with 157 heading west. Her mind was laser-focused on her target. Man on a black Ducati, coming down out of the mountains from Palisade's place. She didn't need to know more than that. Her orders were clear, and if they meant more of Palisade's visits, she'd do whatever they asked. Anything for even a moment of relief from her curse. *Besides,* she thought. *It's not the first time I've killed, is it?* It was a cruel and cheap shot at her own psyche. It brought back instant memories of the terrified screaming, the gurgling pain as her mother lay burning in her own bed while Fiamma lay motionless on the other side of the wall, watching the flames lick higher. Listening.

She let out a yell that disappeared into the wind, but it made her feel better, banished the memories. Suddenly there it was, the telltale sound of a high-end bike burning NOS and Trent's black Ducati pouring out of the night in front of her. She sneered and laid on the brakes as she slid the bike off into the dirt median. When she had it stopped and aimed in the opposite direction, she took a deep breath, felt the familiar burning sensation in her throat, and gunned the accelerator again. Dirt sprayed as the Tuono leapt back onto the highway, heading southeast.

In an instant she was upon the jet-black bike. It carried not one, but two riders. She hadn't expected that, but she didn't much care. The extra weight made Trent's bike harder to control and that made her job even easier. So did their lack of helmets. As soon as the Ducati had come up parallel, she used her left hand to reach behind and pulled the revolver from her waistband. Then she aimed it across her own chest and squeezed down the trigger.

Trent glanced over and saw the gun. His eyes widened as he yelled something and hit the brakes. His bike slid back as her gun went off without a target.

Dammit, she thought, and hit her own brakes to fall back to where he had gone. As soon as she reached him again, Trent sent his Ducati sideways and took a glancing swipe at her Tuono. The motorcycles hit with a plastic crunch and

Fiamma dropped lower to keep the nose of her bike steady. Trent floored it again and zoomed ahead.

She'd heard of Trent before: famous gambler, then druggie, then washout that disappeared from the public eye. But she'd never heard of him being a bike pro. Fiamma had been racing since sixteen. The sudden competition irritated her.

Ahead, the neon glowed bright, and she knew that Vegas was a safe haven for Trent. She couldn't risk gunfire inside the city limits or the cops would bear down on her quick. With New York plates and a rap sheet a mile long, she didn't need trouble with the law, even if she *could* take whatever they might throw at her. She had to kill Trent now, before he made it to the city line, leave him bleeding in the desert sand. Time for a different tactic. She gunned the gas and the Tuono leapt forward.

Trent's bike dove to the left of a slow-moving tractor-trailer, so Fiamma pulled hers to the right, barely riding the white line that edged the highway. As she came around the truck's nose, she threw the bike sideways, knowing Trent would be coming out at the same moment. *Fat guy slowing you down? Here, let me help.* She slammed her bike's front tire into the Ducati's rear and then yanked Louis' blue vinyl jacket.

Trent's bike wavered and swerved in the lane as he fought to keep it under control. Louis, screaming, kicked at her and thrashed in his jacket, trying desperately to shake off her grip. Smoke lifted from where her fingers had dug into the jacket and a black halo of ash and melting vinyl began to spread across its surface. Trent glared over at her then, anger in his eyes. She smiled big, baring her teeth.

The Ducati swerved suddenly into her, pinning her left leg against Louis' right. Louis screamed out in pain. Fiamma's smile vanished.

"Motherfucker!" she yelled, still looking at Trent as the weight of his bike forced hers sideways, back into her own lane. She watched his eyes dart forward, then back at her. She glanced forward. Back end of a pickup truck, coming on fast.

She didn't have time to utter another swear. The pickup's tailgate flew up to meet her and she slammed the brakes, swerving to the right. Her bike hit the dusty gravel on the shoulder and slid hard into the desert scrub, coming to a stop in a spray of dust. She crouched in the sand and watched the Ducati disappear. She growled and kicked her boot into the side of a towering saguaro cactus. Smoke lifted off her arms and shoulders, spiraling up from within her thick hair. After a moment of seething fury, she regained her composure, righted the motorcycle, and climbed back on.

*   *   *

Trent needed time to think. After a paranoid, reckless ride through the city, Trent made it to his destination, the closest place he could come up with to take a breather: City Pawn. It was a venerable place on the corner of two sleazy, run-down streets in downtown Vegas, a sort of landmark known only to the desperate folk who lived nearby. Everybody there, for two, sometimes three generations, had sold something to City Pawn. And though most of them didn't know it, they'd all dealt with the very same owner, a man known as Charlie V, a man who changed face every century or so, but who otherwise remained much the same. Right now, he was a diminutive, elderly fellow with a thick, almost comical Russian accent.

Trent knew a lot more than most about Charlie. And he knew that this was a safe place, neutral territory. He hadn't seen the crazy bike girl anymore after she'd slid off the road, but he didn't want to chance leading her back to his apartment, back to Celia who he feared had been dabbling again. Then again, any delay might further whatever situation Celia had gotten herself into. He felt conflicted.

Charlie sat on an old wooden chair in front of the run-down, whitewashed, single story building. He watched quietly as Trent and Louis dismounted.

"What the fuck?" Louis picked at the smoking, melted hole in the side of his jacket. "Who the hell *was* that chick? She didn't come from the mansion, did she? Looked like she was waiting for us. And what the hell is this?" He pointed at the scorched blue vinyl.

Trent ignored him. He was thinking about Celia, guilty about coming here first and not home. But the rational part of him knew that things were different with the teenager. He was her guardian, but not a normal father. The world they lived in was different from the one occupied by everyone else. And the gulf between them widened with every passing day. He loved her, but worried that it wasn't enough. And his diversion to City Pawn gnawed at that worry.

But I couldn't have gone home first, not with that woman chasing me.

He couldn't bear the thought of putting Celia back into danger. He'd already done enough of that on the night of the

Blizzard, and he could tell by her behavior even now, half a year later, that she'd been left irreparably scarred.

"What is happenink, Mr. Trent?" Charlie was a tiny man with an old, wrinkle-lined face and a copse of scraggly white hair that flitted about his head, changing at the touch of even the slightest breeze. He was also, as Trent knew, a bona fide angel, despite neighborhood rumors to the contrary. "Your bicycle is lookink fine."

Charlie had held onto his bike for years, when Trent had first left Vegas. After his return, on the night of the Blizzard, Charlie had loaned it back to him, but Trent knew that the day would come when he'd need to give the bike back, or buy it outright.

"I've got problems, Charlie. Someone's out for my blood, and I think Celia's dabbling again. I can't stay long."

"Ahh," said Charlie. "I see. Let us be goink inside then, for just a moment." He got up from his chair, opened the door to City Pawn, and motioned for Trent and Louis to head in. Charlie followed and locked the door behind them.

Inside, City Pawn was sparsely decorated, but uncommonly clean. There were no crazy neon-colored posters, no illuminated sale signs, nothing that screamed commerce. Just a scattered assemblage of metal wire display racks and wooden shelves, all bearing used goods at basic prices. Trent had always thought the bright fluorescent lighting made the place look more like a tiny grocery store than a pawnshop in a seedy neighborhood.

"What is beink the problem, Mr. Trent?" Charlie raised an eyebrow as he leaned his miniscule frame against the glass checkout counter, which held a locked assortment of guns and boxed ammunition.

Trent jerked a thumb at Louis. "First we gotta call a cab for this guy."

"Whoa, whoa, whoa," said Louis in protest. "What is this about a cab? All that and now you're just gonna ditch me in the middle of the city?"

"You live somewhere, right?" Trent eyed him suspiciously. "You can't find your own way home?"

"That's not the point." Louis' face screwed up in anger. He jabbed a finger at the closed door. "Out there I was shot at, chased by gangsters, then run down by a motorcycle chick, and *then* she frickin' burned me with her bare hands." He grabbed a chunk of his ruined jacket and shook it for effect. "Last thing I want to do now is go back to my apartment by myself and wait for... for whoever they are... to come back and finish me off. No way. I'm sticking here with you until I get some real answers."

Trent sneered. "Do you even have the slightest idea what's going on?"

Louis shook his head, frozen by Trent's sudden fury.

"I saved your ass because I felt sorry for you. But now it's over. You stay with me, you're gonna end up dead. I can promise you that. You're going home, Mr. Bird. Now. And I think we'd both prefer it if you were conscious." Trent balled up a fist. "Be easier to explain to the cabbie that way."

Louis hesitated, his face shock-white. He coughed. "Well how do I know she won't come after me at home?"

"She's not after you," Trent replied. "I'm the target. You were just in the way back there." He watched a range of expressions bounce across the pudgy man's face. "Go home, man," he said.

"Fine," said Louis, but he looked thoughtful. "Hey," he said finally, as Trent ushered him out the front door. He fished a business card out of his pocket and stuck it in Trent's hand. "Call me, okay. I want your story."

Trent nodded, then shoved Louis through the door and shut it behind him. He rolled his eyes as he listened to Louis gripe outside. A part of him wanted to let Louis in on the big secrets, to tell him the whole story. But there were rules. He turned around to see Charlie hanging up the phone.

"Taxi on the way. So what is beink the problem with little Celia?"

Trent frowned. "I got a weird phone call from her. Phone went nuts, exploded, ice everywhere. She's gotta be screwing around again. She promised me, Charlie."

Trent felt anger boiling up and it collided with his wavering sense of fatherhood and made him swear. What had she done this time? Destroyed the apartment? Hurt herself? What? He'd put it off too long already. He knew it was time to confront her. Time to go home.

"You need to go, then. See to her. Discipline is good for young children."

"Sure. And I need info, too. Somebody named Palisade wants me dead I guess; little preacher bastard that works for a guy called Gadreel. And this girl, this... fire-girl... apparently she's on the payroll, too."

Charlie's lips became thin and flat at the mention of Gadreel. He went very quiet, as though searching for the right explanation. Finally, he said, "You were messink in Gadreel's business, yes?"

"Just wanted some info."

"I am givink you great info, Mr. Trent. You do not need to go to one such as him."

"Who is he?"

"Bad."

"How bad?"

"Bad for you, especially."

Trent nodded. "So what is he? Angel, demon, *grigori*, what?"

"I am not so sure, but most likely demon."

"So Vlad's behind this then?"

Charlie shook his head. "Vladimir has no reason to be upsetting your arrangement." He studied Trent's face for a moment. "Or does he?"

"I quit."

"Oh."

The air hung still for a while as Charlie worked to understand.

"You are workink for no one now? Not for the demons? Not for angels? You are neutral?"

"I told Vladimir and the other demons where they can stick it. I'm looking for Susan now. That's all. I'm not on anyone's side. I just need to get these *new* assholes off my back."

Charlie walked over then and patted Trent on the shoulder, an act that required him to reach up. "You go see to Celia now," he said calmly. "I will be here when you get back. We will be talkink about Gadreel and fire-girl and maybe I can have more information for you then, okay? Give me a few hours. I have a few calls to be making. I am thinkink you will be fine until then."

Trent nodded. Then a thought occurred to him.

"Hey, Charlie. Tricia keeps on about me becoming some sort of Lord of Hell. Says I could go into the Shadow Realms that way, to Dis. I guess Zamagiel's running the place now—"

Charlie shook his head. "No," he said, interrupting, "that's not beink the path you want to be takink. It's not for you, Trent. That role."

Trent pursed his lips. "So it's real then? Hell, I mean."

"Oh, yes. It is very real." He cocked his head to one side. "Well, as real as anythink is in that place. It's a place out of time. It has always been, and has never been."

"And this Prince everyone is on about? He runs the show?"

"He was beink an angel once. Great and powerful. Cast out of Heaven."

Charlie walked over to one of the shelves of knick-knacks and retrieved a small porcelain angel, medieval-style with white-feathered wings, a yellow disc behind its head for a halo, and an outstretched arm, hand holding a silver sword aloft. He held the figurine up for Trent to see, and then, unceremoniously, dropped it to the floor. It struck the linoleum tile and shattered, breaking into three pieces and some dust. He bent down and picked up the large chunks.

"Part of him," he said, holding up the first broken piece, the angel's legs and part of its torso, "became the Realms of Shadow. He was refusink to fade into nothing, so he becomes a realm of nothink instead."

He tossed the piece back to the floor and held up the second chunk, the angel's upper torso and head. "Another part of him is becomink the Book that you found, hidink all these years until Miss Celia was discoverink it. It is the part of him that is knowink the ancient secrets and the ways of their usink. It is the angel that was once Raziel."

"Yeah," said Trent. "I've seen what it could do."

Charlie shook his head as he dropped the piece. "You've seen nothink, Mr. Trent." He held up the last bit, the outstretched arm and sword. "But the worst of all is beink the part of the Prince that brought his fallink from Heaven. It is his domination, his drive, his sword."

"Where did that piece go?"

The old Russian shrugged and tossed the sword-arm to the floor, where it broke into a few smaller fragments. "Nobody is knowink. Some say it was comink here, to this world. Reborn. Apart from the Prince somehow. The Prince is sendink his shadows here to be findink and bringink it back. To makink himself whole again."

Ancient angelic history lessons always made Trent's head swim. He still had trouble accepting it all, despite having grappled hand-to-hand with the very creatures Charlie described. He had no reason to doubt.

Charlie continued, "And if he is gettink all three pieces back to the Realms—"

Trent saw where this was going. "Then he invades, with all his ancient power intact."

Charlie nodded, his expression grim.

"But I don't understand... what does he want with Celia?"

Charlie kneeled and scooped up the bits of the shattered statuette. "I think she is beink just a pawn," he said, without looking up. "A piece to be movink across the board. A card to be playink. That is why you must be protectink her, not just from him, but from any who might be workink on his behalf."

"You mean he has allies here."

The old Russian stood and deposited the handful of debris into a nearby trash bin. "Oh, yes," he said, and clapped his hands together to shake off any remaining dust. "Zamagiel was one, and there are others who are seekink to—how do they say?—be ridink on his coat."

"Coattails."

"What?"

Trent shook his head. "What about this Gadreel? Could he be working for the Prince?"

"Perhaps. I would be keepink him far away from little Celia if I were you."

Trent chuckled. "Don't worry. After tonight, if she's been playing with magick again, she's gonna be grounded for months. She won't be going near anybody."

Charlie nodded. "Good. Now you should go. See to the little girl. No more delayink your responsibility as a parent. Be makink sure she is leavink the ancient magicks alone. No good for her."

"I will."

Charlie smiled and headed for a back door that Trent knew led to the old man's tiny, paper-cluttered office. He and Charlie had been friends for a long time. He'd even learned later that Charlie had visited him in the hospital room after the Crash, though Trent remembered none of it. Charlie had never said why he appeared in the hospital that day, and Trent had never asked.

He took in a deep breath and collected his thoughts. He prayed that Celia hadn't done something too dramatic, too visible. The last thing he needed was the police coming around, especially if Vladimir and the demons were no longer upholding their promise to keep Trent and Celia off the law's radar. Their situation was tenuous enough already.

*   *   *

Fiamma watched from the parking lot of a seedy old motel as the yellow cab pulled away from City Pawn across the street. She'd seen the small, round man get in, but no sign of Trent Hawkins.

She stared at the City Pawn sign. She knew the place and it meant that things had grown more dangerous for her. Palisade hadn't mentioned anything about Neutrals being involved. He'd only asked for a hit on a mortal man—a famous man, perhaps, but still just a mortal. Nothing about the supernatural. Nothing about his alliances. She let out an irritated sigh.

She needed to wait on this, figure out a better course of action. She watched the taxi drift off down the street with the fat man inside. *But I can get some more info while I wait*, she thought. She revved the Tuono and pulled out of the hotel parking lot.

Nowhere

SHE KNOWS THAT THIS PLACE does not exist, yet it bears a kind of order, transformed by unending chaos, bolstered by the many things that have become a part of the Realms, things that should not be, standing as bulwarks against the cyclones that sweep across the barren black, wiping away everything and reforming it in an endless loop of timeless reconfiguration. Susan is one of these things. She has a name. She cannot be wiped away, reformed, or reconfigured. She is.

As she moves across the sometimes blistering, sometimes freezing black sands, she toys with the names in her mind. Susan. Trent. Zamagiel. The only names that she can remember from her past life, her life in the world that exists. She needs to find another name, a very important name. She doesn't know why, yet, but she longs to learn it.

What is the true name of the Prince of the Shadow Realms?

When she became a part of this place, a part of the Prince, Susan heard his mind, sensed his motives and desires. He wants more than the black and the cold and the dust over which he now reigns. He wants to lord over something, not nothing. And when the girl, Celia, trapped for but a fleeting moment in the darkened realm, returned to Susan her name, that was when Susan became something, and the Prince wanted to rule over her. And so she ran.

With her own name, she is a rogue element, no longer a pure part of the Realms. She senses that through great effort, she may hide her actions, her thoughts, her location. The Prince cannot find her by ordinary means. He has to send creatures—hunters—after her. He has to name them, so that they might walk where she walks. He does not like naming things, for he knows all too well the danger of rebellion.

And so she runs, and she searches, all the while keeping an eye on the darkest of the dark places, watching for the things that might be seeking her; named, powerful things. Things with white faces and long, metal claws where fingers might have once been. Things with mouths full of razors.

Her white dress billows in the cold desert winds, or it would, if it existed. It is but an artifact of her imagination. She can shape things here. She is not as powerful as the Prince, by far, but she can give names of her own, at least to some things. She has named her Dress, and therefore it is.

She gathers it around her bare ankles as she ascends a small outcropping of stones against a jet-black, leafless tree, twisted and ugly, its branches unmoving even in the harshest of winds. She reaches the apex and enters a cave carved into the trunk of the massive tree. It is a place, a tree, a cave, that should not exist, that should not be. It is, because the occupant of this place also has a name and has made it so.

"The Shadow of Lilith," says Susan, her eyes wide as she beholds the tired, ugly creature sitting upon a rock within the tree-cave. A woman, or some semblance of one, a sickly grey hag, a wretch aged beyond measure and mortality.

The woman looks up at Susan with dead-black eyes and lets out a triumphant, hungry screech. Her voice is thick with raspy mucus that drips from her teeth and sprays as she lets loose a terrifying, high-pitched howl that echoes up the vertical shaft of the hollowed-out tree. And with an impossibly fast motion the woman launches forward, her stringy black hair reaching in parallel with clawed fingers. She reaches for Susan, screaming as she advances.

"I am Susan."

Lilith stops suddenly. Her noise becomes a sustained hiss. Her hair swirls inelegantly about her head, moving of its own accord. Her naked flesh is sallow, blemished and broken by sores, and as she shuffles backwards, away from Susan, her sickly breasts sway; ancient, dry husks.

"What it is you want from the Shadow of Lilith, from Karina, from the Shade-Queen?" she asks quietly. "Why is one with a name entering my house? Such things are forbidden."

Susan, calm, lets her white dress fall to the ground once more. "What is the true name of the Prince?"

Lilith sits down on her rock and snorts. Black mucus dribbles from her nose and she makes no motion to wipe it away. "I cannot answer this," she says. "It is forbidden."

"You know his name, then."

Lilith grins. Her teeth are black, yellow, rotted, and too few. "I give that secret to another, for a boon. Now I know not."

"Who did you tell?"

"The *grigori*, Zamagiel, it knows, but it dares not speak of it." She scratches at the coarse hair between her legs. "It fears reprisal." She snorts and waves a too-thin, rotting hand. "Begone, dead mortal. Karina's house is no place for a dead-child."

Susan had expected the old woman's stubbornness, but she had hoped she might get the answers without doing the one thing she fears. *If it comes to this*, she thinks. *Then so be it.*

"I offer you a boon," she says, finally. "In exchange. Tell me how I can find the *grigori*."

Lilith looks up, her black eyes wide in their sockets. A long tongue slips from between her broken teeth and licks across her rotting lips, which break into a lascivious grin.

"A boon? For old Nyx? For the grey hag? Just to see the rebel lord?"

"A boon. Name what you will."

Lilith reaches one hand to her head and taps a long, crooked, clawed finger against her temple in a mockery of consideration. Her other hand fumbles between her legs.

"A kiss," she answers finally. "You will give us a kiss."

Susan feels a lump in her throat. She had hoped for something less. She takes a long, deep breath.

"A kiss then."

Lilith claps her hands together like a child. More black mucus spills from her nostrils as she snorts happily, twisting and writhing upon her rock-seat. Finally, she settles and begins tracing a circle on the floor of the cave with her finger. She speaks quietly as she draws.

"The *grigori* rebels all fear the Prince. He is their greater. But Lord Zamagiel knows his true name and so the Prince spares them his wrath. They hold a city of their own shaping. They name soldiers of their own, guards to keep the wild Shades out. You will not find yourself in their company easily. You will need a weapon, something special...."

Her voice trails off, and as she finishes the circle, the rock floor inside it becomes something else—a liquid, black as oil and bubbling. Without hesitation, Lilith thrusts her hand into the viscous, churning fluid. Her arm twists and moves as she mutters, "What will I find? What will I find?" And then, suddenly, she draws out of the black pool a dagger, silvery and ornate, with an ivory handle and gleaming blade. It seems to sing in the cave's half-light. The blade of a *cherubim* soldier. Lilith's face betrays her surprise.

"Better even than we expect. A good weapon. Strange to find it there." She stares at the blade for a moment, then shrugs her naked, withered shoulders and tosses it to Susan.

As soon as her fingers close around its handle, Susan feels a strange sensation and hears a whispering in her mind. A whispering of a name. A name she once loved. A name she still loves. She remembers love.

Trent.

She smiles, clutching the angelic weapon, but her smile fades fast as she looks up at Lilith. The hideous creature is already standing, already moving across the cave. Her hair whips and tugs at her scalp, as if attempting to pull the hag more quickly across the room.

"The *grigori* mass in their iron city, the city Dis that rings the black pit," she says, licking her desiccated lips. "Cross the river Acheron and beyond the Styx you will find them. But I doubt you'll survive, even with that trinket." She laughs then, a loud, raucous peal. "They will take your name, dead-child."

Lilith moves within inches of Susan's face. The smell of the grey hag's skin is overpowering, a horrible miasma of rotting flesh, sulfur, and dead vegetation. She can feel tingling sensations as the hag's thick strands of hair weave themselves into her own, encircling her scalp, pulling her closer to the waiting, gangrenous lips. She closes her eyes, trembling with fear and revulsion.

"What does this journey mean to you?" Lilith whispers, her foul breath dancing across Susan's lips. "Why do you seek such things? Why do you offer such a boon willingly?"

Susan does not hesitate. Only a single word comes to her thoughts and to her lips. "Love," she says.

With a hungry, overpowering strength, Lilith draws Susan close.

3

WHAT HAS PALISADE DONE TO me?

Trent blinked and, in the microsecond of black, searched for the sense of fate that always accompanied his dark gift. Still nothing.

He made me normal.

There was something about being normal that elated him, but only for a moment. Without the ability to doom others, to drag another's fate through the temporal mud, he'd never find Susan. He couldn't face Shades with bare hands. He thought about the dagger he carried in his waistband. He could feel the cool blade pressed against the skin of his lower back. *At least I have that*, he thought.

He looked up as his bike glided onto the Strip, the heart of entertainment and gambling in Las Vegas. Everywhere the neon lights burned against the night sky; a dull grey-orange canvas blanketing the stars. Taxis zipped past him. People in outlandish club fashions and expensive suits strolled up and down the flyer-strewn sidewalks. Corporate-salaried casino barkers fought with wild-eyed, longhaired street preachers for attention. And everywhere the ringing, the goddamn ringing that made Trent hate this place with a passion, this raucous nightmare carnival.

He and his wife, Susan, had left once, to escape the noise and the drugs that had been eating Trent alive, only to come back when the economy turned sour and Susan had only one job available to her. And then Celia and the Blizzard and the demons and their world fell to pieces. Susan fell into the black. Everything changed.

He thought about Celia again, teeth gritted. *She promised.*

He didn't know much about being a father, let alone an adoptive father, but he figured preventing your kid from toying with world-ending black magicks was probably a reasonable course of action. He wondered if she had found the Book again. Had she ever thrown it away? Had the foul green-covered tome, with its terrible secrets and strange sentience, convinced her to lie to him? He knew she'd been keeping a secret, something so deep that it terrified her to even think of it—he could see it in her eyes when he probed. What was it? He felt a twinge of fear at his own line of thinking. Was he angrier with Celia for breaking the rules, or was he angry at himself for leaving her alone?

I don't know how to be a dad, he thought. *I'm worthless at this.* He took a deep breath.

Heading northeast, Trent guided the bike beyond the Strip, along Las Vegas Boulevard, past the corner where it met Fremont Street, where casinos and clubs started transforming into run-down motels and adult video stores. He zipped along, weaving in and out of the multi-lane traffic until he reached the highway. He gunned the engine, worry and anger squeezing his accelerator hand just a little tighter as he sped up the ramp and headed for suburbia.

After the Blizzard, Trent and Celia had moved into a small, sparsely furnished two-story townhome in a neighborhood just north of the old industrial airport. The demonic cabal for whom Trent had agreed to work paid the bills. As with any neighborhood near an airport, it wasn't the best part of town, but it wasn't the worst either, and prying eyes were kept to a minimum. No one in this part of Vegas much cared what their neighbors were up to.

He rolled into the short gravel driveway, glancing around as he shut off the engine and dismounted cautiously. The quiet made him nervous. He had half-expected fire engines and police. Nothing. Dead silent. It was the middle of the night, but the lights in their place were off, both floors.

Trent pushed open the rusty iron gate that led to the front path and made his way to the front door. What had happened? A nightmare maybe, transmitted over the phone? He would never have considered such a possibility before the Blizzard, before meeting Celia, but she was a strange child and he'd seen stranger things.

Maybe it was nothing. Just a bad night. She's probably fine, asleep or watching TV.

He turned his key in the front door, heard the deadbolt clank, and gave the door a tentative push. It creaked open, all quiet still.

Trent moved inside and glanced around, looking for signs of damage, fire, ice, something. That's when he saw the broken bannister. He followed the curve and fragments of lingering wood splinters that pointed down, toward the floor in front of him. And that's when he saw Celia, lying on the floor in a puddle of darkness, unmoving.

What the hell?

He flipped on the light and realized with sinking dismay that she wasn't lying in shadow at all, but blood, seeping from a ragged gash in her side that still harbored fractured pieces of wood railing. He rushed to her side and knelt down.

"Celia, kiddo... Oh my God...oh jeez..." He looked around frantically as though searching for some help. "What...? Oh shit, oh fuck, you're bleeding Cee...."

A faint cough escaped her lips as he stroked her cheek. Still warmth there, but not much. Her feet looked blistered, frostbitten and blackened at the tips. *Oh no*, he thought. *Oh God please no.*

He stared at her still countenance and couldn't control the sudden twitching of his own face as he studied the puffy lines on hers. Ice lines, she called them; whenever she cried, her tears froze to her skin, leaving burning welts. Trent hated those lines—they betrayed her bloodline, one that could be traced back thousands of years to the dawn of man and to a lust-fallen angel, the first to be cast from heaven, a *grigori*, angels that consorted with the wives of men.

He brushed back a lock of fine blonde hair from her face and found himself angry that her lips weren't moving, that they sat firm and thin, almost peaceful, when he had grown so used to seeing her ever-present frown. He couldn't shake the feeling this was his fault, that he had lied to himself to justify his failed fatherhood, had blamed her for things she had not done. "Goddammit!" he screamed.

And then her body spasmed, coughing, and her eyes fluttered open, her right eyelid drooping unnaturally as though she'd had a stroke. Bloody tears streamed down her cheeks, freezing. She mumbled something. He moved his ear closer.

"Celia! What...? I don't... I can't...."

She said it again, louder this time, her voice hoarse and raspy, teeth stained red with blood. "I'm sorry."

"Sorry?" Trent didn't know what to think. "I should have gotten here sooner. I'm so sorry, kiddo. Hold on, hold on. I'll get you to the hospital. Just hold on...." He grabbed the bloody cellphone off her chest and began to dial 911.

"I'm sorry," she repeated. "I... brought them here."

He looked down at her, frozen in mid-dial. "What did you say? Who did you bring?" His mind raced with images, things he had seen, things he had fought, things he'd only heard about.

"They're here now." She coughed up a glob of blood that fell onto the corner of her mouth and made a gradual descent down the side of her face. Before her eyes fluttered shut again, she said, "They're looking for the Book...."

*   *   *

The pudgy little man in the ugly jacket—Fiamma had determined from his apartment register that his name was Louis Bird—lived on the third floor of a ratty walk-up in south central Vegas. She'd carefully followed the taxi there, watched the guy slip out and make his way nervously up the stairs. She wanted him to settle in for a few minutes, get good and complacent before she dropped in. She took a long drag on her cigarette, blew it out through her nostrils, and then tore off a hunk of protein bar with her teeth.

"Hey gorgeous, whatcha eatin'?" A young kid, college-aged, waved at her from a nearby porch. She gave him the finger without making eye contact. Then she swallowed her still-smoldering cigarette, popped another in her mouth, and did the finger-lighting trick again. That shut him up quick.

She exhaled smoke and watched the parking lot for signs of Trent. She wasn't ready to take him on again, not quite yet. She needed to know more about him, what it was that Palisade seemed so reluctant to tell her. She couldn't shake the feeling that she had been pulled into a firefight without the right gun.

Should be about time, she thought as she drew the Colt pistol from her waistband and chambered a round with a metallic click. *Let's see what he knows.*

Before the echoes of her second knock on the front door to Louis Bird's apartment had faded, she put a hand on the doorknob, growled under her breath, allowed anger and rage and despair to shoot up through her veins into her palm and fingers. The metal doorknob hissed and smoked before turning bright orange. Fiamma lifted her booted foot and kicked hard. The door burst open and she stood in the smoke-filled frame, holding the glowing knob in her hand. Bits of liquid metal dripped sizzling to the threshold.

Louis looked up at her from the couch and shrieked. She dropped the doorknob and it hit the floor with a clunk. Her boots thudded against the apartment's wood floors as she advanced on him. He climbed frantically over the back of the couch, fell, and hit the ground. He wouldn't stop yelling.

"Shut up, *now*," she said, sticking the gun barrel against his forehead.

He did.

"Now," she said, "we're gonna have a nice little talk."

She looked around his apartment. Sparse, a small television, a desk with a laptop, stacks of books and biblical codices on every flat surface, loose sheets of yellowing parchment, photos covering the walls like wallpaper, most held up by tape and thumbtacks; nearly all of them were photos of Trent Hawkins. She grinned.

"You're going to tell me everything you know, *especially* about the cowboy. And if you behave, you might avoid a trip to the burn ward."

Smoke curls seeped from her nostrils as she withdrew the gun, then plopped herself down in Louis' armchair. The smell of singed fabric filled the air, sweet and acrid.

Louis glanced toward the open front door, but Fiamma caught his glance. "Think you can outrun me, fat man? Wanna try? Get it out of the way up front?" She grinned.

She was a little surprised, and impressed, when he took off toward the door at a fast hustle. "Whoa!" she shouted and leapt from the chair. She reached him just as his first leg crossed the threshold.

"Help—!" he shouted into the night, but was cut off when Fiamma grabbed his collar and yanked him back inside.

She slammed the door shut, then shoved Louis against the nearest table. The sudden impact bent him backwards and Fiamma leapt onto the table, straddling his neck and shoulders, pinning him atop a stack of books that had begun to smolder. She wrapped her fingers around his throat and could smell charred flesh. The sickly sweet odor made her feel good, in command. She smiled wickedly and brought her face down close to his.

"Are we going to talk now?" she whispered. "Or are you going to be another in a long line of unexplained spontaneous combustions?"

He nodded, unable to form sounds with her burning fingers crushing his trachea. She could see the terror that she had invoked in his bulging eyes. She loved it.

She let go and climbed off of him. He stood and hobbled forward, staggering around the bare room until he caught a wall to steady himself. He rubbed his throat where a red ring of blisters had formed.

Fiamma leapt onto the table and perched atop the stack of books like a vulture. She pinned him to the wall with her stare. "Start talking, Bird. First question: who are you? For real... none of this freelance journalist crap." She gestured at the stacks of books and papers. "What's all this shit for?"

Louis lowered his eyes and let out a choking sigh. He didn't make eye contact as he spoke. "Freemason." He was trembling. "You know what that is?"

Freemasons were a supposed secret society, hundreds of years old; they had lodges, ran charities. That's about all she knew. "What do the Masons have to do with Trent?"

"We're watching him. You too, probably."

"Who?"

Louis shrugged. "They don't tell us about each other."

Someone watching me? That complicates things, she thought. *Unless he's lying, the little shit.*

She wrenched a protein bar from her pocket and tore through the wrapper with her teeth. Between chews, she asked, "So why all the pictures? Don't you already know what he looks like?"

Louis clammed up, refused to look at her. In a second she had him against the wall, feet off the ground, the Colt pressed against his temple. She could see he was shocked by her strength.

"So help me God I will *end* you! Only reason I haven't yet is I'm not gettin' paid for it. Figure I can easily wrench a contract out of Gadreel for your murder too. So you better talk before I start making phone calls." It was a bluff. She only ever talked to Palisade, and he never let her decide on new targets.

Louis hesitated a second too long. Fiamma pulled him an inch off the wall, then slammed him back, cracking the sheetrock. She gritted her teeth. "Don't fuck with me, shitbag."

"Alright, alright," he managed to choke out. His face was turning purple as she squeezed his throat tighter and his shirt collar was black and smoking where it had brushed against the side of her hand. "Trent... he's blooded, okay. Like you, I guess, but different—"

She cut him off. "No one's like me!" She pulled him away from the wall and sent him flying. He crashed into an end table and knocked it over, spilling books and loose papers as he slumped to the floor. He crab-scuttled backwards as she crossed the paper-strewn living room toward him. He stopped when his back hit the glass balcony door.

"Please, please!" He held up his hands in defense. "He's... Trent... there's something different about his bloodline. He's not just lucky. He's... he's not lucky at all, actually."

"Then what is he? Why does he always win? Why does Gadreel want him dead?"

"I... I don't know about Gadreel." He kicked his feet uselessly against the papers as she came closer. Smoke billowed from the backs of her hands and the top of her head. "But Trent... he... we think he's the Doombringer. The only one. We've never seen anybody like him."

"A what?" Her eyes narrowed to angry slits.

"The Doombringer. He can twist fate, but only for other people. And he can only make it bad."

"And you people...?"

"The Masons... we have a fragment of an ancient script, a prophecy. Written by an angel. Trent is somehow the key." She took another step closer. He turned his head away, unable to gaze upon her horrifying, angry visage. "God, please! Leave me alone! You can't... you're not a member! They're going to kill me for telling you all this!"

"You worry about *me!*" she shouted. She towered above him, smoke rising from her in thick, undulant coils, like ethereal black snakes reaching for the ceiling. The room reeked of cooking flesh. Small fires were lighting upon the scattered piles of paper at her ankles.

"Please," begged Louis. "Please let this one go... please! It's bigger than both of us! He's too dangerous— You can't just— He'll ruin your fate too!"

She put a combat boot on his chest and pressed down until he couldn't draw enough air to speak. She spoke quietly. "You ever wake up in the middle of the night to find fire climbing the walls of your bedroom?"

Louis shook his head, eyes squeezed shut.

"Do you know what it's like, being a kid, watching your home burn down around you? Being so terrified that you can't move? Hearing your mother screaming, then coughing, then nothing, just groaning wood, roaring fire, as you lay there in bed sheets and ash, wondering why you haven't died?" She jammed her hands down onto a pile of manuscripts that instantly burst into flames. She swept them off the table and onto Louis, who covered his head with his hands.

"Don't tell me what I can't do!" she screamed, her voice cracking, on the verge of sobs. "Fuck Trent Hawkins! No one can ruin my fate! My goddamn fate is already ruined!"

*   *   *

Trent wasn't the least bit surprised when the old Mexican with the scarred face wandered into Celia's hospital room, sometime near dawn. Ramón had a way of just appearing when he wanted to, and he always seemed to know where to find Trent. He didn't say anything as he entered, just glanced around the dim room, leaning hard on his cane for support. His southwestern-style dress shirt, light blue with faint pinstripes, was rolled up at the sleeves to his biceps. The massive black and red ornate cross tattoo that covered the length of his right arm stood out in sharp contrast to the light-colored shirt. He stared at Celia for a few moments, lying in her bed, eyes shut, tubes protruding from her nose and mouth, face freshly scrubbed of blood.

Trent looked at her too, though he almost couldn't bear to. It bugged him that they'd scrubbed off her makeup, the overly thick black eyeliner he always teased her about, calling it her 'raccoon look'. But he'd come to know it, to love it, and seeing her pale and blank hurt.

The doctor had questioned Trent at length about the blood, since they'd found no external wounds on Celia's body. Trent didn't bother explaining that her cuts and scrapes healed quickly with exposure to water, a side effect of her *gibborim* bloodline. He just shrugged and said he had no idea. He could tell that they didn't entirely believe him.

They'd also asked about extended family. Trent told them the truth: she had none. They'd all met unusual accidents in the past few years; the whole family up to the grandparents, wiped clean from the earth, long before Trent ever met her. He didn't tell the hospital that part, but for Trent, it was another source of guilt. He knew Vlad and the other demons had set him up as her caretaker after the Blizzard, after the fallen angel Zamagiel had killed her parents. But what else had the demons set up?

"So what's with her?" Ramón asked, his voice a hoarse mixture of smoke-lung gravel and a southwest twang.

"Unconscious."

"Ordinary or otherwise?"

"Otherwise, I'm guessing, though the doctor says it's just a head injury that sent her out."

"She didn't find the—"

Trent cut him off. "No."

Ramón let out a long sigh, then dragged a metal chair over to the foot of the bed and sat down, cane across his lap, facing Trent. A wheeled plastic cart sat between them, its top strewn with papers.

"You know why I ask—"

"Yeah, I know." Trent frowned.

Celia had taken possession of The Book of the Angel Raziel after she found it in Charlie's pawnshop. And, in turn, the Book had taken possession of her. In the tumultuous events of that ice-filled night, Celia had done horrible things while under the Book's power. Things she wouldn't talk about. Trent had only managed to pry out brief mentions of a horrible fight at the police station. But he had seen the things the green, leather-bound tome could do. He knew it had taught her terrible secrets, truths that lingered behind her eyes in every conversation they had. He'd been relieved to know that she had broken Raziel's dominion over her and tossed the foul thing away before that night's end.

"If Raziel finds her again—"

"I said, *I know*." Trent glared at him. "I haven't seen it. She's been acting normally up until tonight. I mean, as normal as you'd expect. Nightmares, stomach aches, that sort of thing, but nothing supernatural. Anyway, she doesn't have it anymore."

Ramón looked out the small hospital room window and watched early morning birds bouncing along a high-tension wire. "How long's she been out?"

"Since I found her. Doctor says it's not anything obvious. He figures she could wake up anytime."

"And you?"

"I think it's something worse. I don't think she's coming back without help. They took something from her."

"They?

"Don't know." He thought about Celia's last words: *they're looking for the Book*. He suspected that he would have to go looking too. Whatever the connection between 'they' and The Book of the Angel Raziel, somewhere along that mysterious strand lay Celia's salvation. He needed to find out more. He hoped Charlie was coming up with some good leads.

Ramón tapped the end of his cane on the floor a few times, as if each beat marked the passage of a thought through his mind. Finally, he looked back up. "You're losing direction, Trent. I hear you quit the job Vlad gave you. And now, this...."

Trent had first met Ramón on the night of the Blizzard, as the worst of the storm descended. The old Mexican had told of his own history as an angelic prophet, before his fall into the black, cast aside by God. And he'd explained that when he and Trent had collided on the night of the plane crash, there had been a sudden trade—Trent's immortal soul for Ramón's cursed gift. It had saved Trent's life, but at an unthinkable cost. And for the past six months, Ramón had served as an ersatz mentor, though both of them knew that he'd kill Trent if he ever got his powers back. Still, Trent found himself confiding in the old man.

"I just can't do it anymore, Ramón. I'm nothing but dead luck and it's killing me. I want my life back. I want Susan. This—" He pointed at Celia's unconscious form. "This never would have happened if Susan were here. She'd be a good mother. I'm just nothing. Not a dad, not even a person anymore, not really. I can't adopt a teenager. I can barely run my own life, or whatever's left of it."

"That why you started a brawl up on the mountain last night? Because you're a shitty dad?"

Trent met Ramón's stare. "That why you're here? To lecture me?" But Trent knew that if Ramón had heard about the firefight at Gadreel's, he'd probably also heard the bigger news about Trent's loss of his power.

Ramón produced a deck of edge-worn playing cards from his back pocket and slapped them down on the plastic cart between them.

Yep, thought Trent. *He heard.*

The deal between him and Ramón had been a simple one. Ramón wanted his powers back, and Trent wanted his soul back. Neither knew how to do it, but neither could kill the other, for fear of losing that which they hoped to recover. So they'd found themselves at a stalemate. But with Trent's powers stripped away, it cast the situation into a whole new light.

"So you heard," he said.

Ramón didn't answer. He just smiled and began to shuffle.

"See," said the old Mexican as he riffled through the cards, "the question we're at now is one of the most fundamental facing humanity. It's the ultimate dilemma, God's nasty trick on your kind. You aspire to godliness, aspire to heroism and altruism and love and all that bullshit, but to do so, you have to subdue each other. No man can be the hero unless others play the villain."

He finished shuffling and set the deck down and burned the top card off into a discard pile.

"So," he continued, "let's say that you're playing the hero today and I the villain. And so, we each have our strengths. You have your plans, your end-goal." He shot a card across the small table. It tinked against an empty juice glass. Then he placed a card in front of himself. "And I have mine." He dealt them each a second card and then reseated the deck on the plastic surface. "And we fight for our goals, our ideals, our passions." He turned over the top card and laid it face up. The suicide king. "We draw swords."

Trent chuckled. "Nice theatrics, but it's not a fair fight if you're using magick."

"No magick, just coincidence." Ramón smiled. "Any club would have worked just as well."

"Could've been hearts, or diamonds."

Ramón nodded. "We can't fight with either can we? But diamonds usually lead to fighting. So do hearts. Both drive our actions, but in themselves they're not weapons." He laid down two more flop cards: a six of hearts and the queen of hearts. "Hearts are especially dangerous. They lead mortals to war, but if shot through…." He pointed a finger at his own chest and pulled an imaginary trigger. "You're eatin' dirt."

"You trying to tell me something?"

"Poker's a battlefield, Trent. We have diamonds to fight over, hearts to drive us on, and clubs to smash our enemies. And through it all, we're watching the numbers, sizing the casualties."

Trent lifted the corner of his two pocket cards and peered beneath. "You forgot spades," he said.

Ramón raised an eyebrow. "Spades come out at the end. We use them to dig the graves."

A moment of silence, and then Ramón quietly pulled a fourth table card, a six of spades. He smiled and winked, a devilish gleam in his eye. "How many years have you played this game, my boy? How many hands have you won without even trying?"

Trent shrugged.

"You should know how to play well by now, shouldn't you? But it's not that easy, is it? Poker's about more than money and luck."

The expression on Trent's face went sour. "Never claimed to be a great poker player. Just had a great cheat. At least until recently."

"Cheats become crutches. Especially in poker. You get caught, or the cheat stops working, and then you're throwing good money after bad cards. Playing in when you should fold." Ramón turned over the card on top of the deck and placed it beside the others. The ace of spades to complete the board.

"Don't 'bad cards' me, Ramón." Trent sneered. "You, Vlad, the others, you might not like my goals. You want me to do your work, play a good little soldier. But I have my own games to win."

"You quit now and you're playing the wrong game, Trent. Sitting at the wrong table, I suppose, if I can extend the metaphor. And when you're done, you'll have nothing left. You'll chase that all-heart flush draw all the way to the bitter end. You're drawing dead, Trent, and you know it."

"What's your point? You gonna complain to Vlad? How many Shades did I take out last month alone?" He didn't pause long enough for the Mexican to answer. "Eight," he said. "I eliminated eight fucking creatures that everyone else on this damn planet doesn't even know about. And I was doing what was asked of me. And where did it get me? How much closer to Susan, to a normal life?"

"You don't *get* a normal life. You don't even know what you're hunting for or why—"

Trent threw his hands up. "My wife. I'm hunting for Susan, dammit."

"You still don't understand, do you? Where she is, there's nothing you can do now. You can't pull her back from the Realm of Shadows, from Abaddon. You just can't. And if you keep on this path of self-delusion and destruction, if you keep up this suicidal hunt—"

Trent slammed his fist down on the plastic. The juice glass bounced off and shattered on the floor. "Then I'll die trying."

Ramón lowered his head slightly and gazed long into his opponent's eyes. Trent met the stare. The fallen angel's intensity made his skin crawl. "Trent," he said, finally, "how much have I told you about the Prophecy?"

"You? Not much." Trent shrugged. "But Vlad hauls that bogeyman out every time he wants to try and scare me into playing interdimensional bouncer."

"It's not a bogeyman. It's quite real. On the night of the Blizzard, those *cherubim* were trying to stop it by killing you. At least that's what they thought. They misread their hand."

"So everybody knows this Prophecy but me, huh?"

Ramón shook his head. "Nah, we've all got different little pieces of it. Fragments that some angel left behind before he went dark."

Trent raised an eyebrow. "I thought you said *you* wrote it."

Ramón stared at him for a long moment, then smiled. "I said I wrote some of it. The last part, to be exact. Another one of the Fallen wrote the first parts. The angels got some, we got some, even the Prince of Shades knows parts of it. And, don't you doubt it. The Prince has got his allies here, demons, angels, even some mortals, who think they understand him well enough to get their fair share after the invasion rips the world apart."

Trent nodded. "Yeah, Charlie said something similar."

Ramón gave him a "well-there-you-have-it" look, then cleared his throat and intoned: *"When the Doombringer dies and walks and dies again, only then will the darkness come back unto the world like a curtain, rejoining what was projected apart, and the days of man will give way to the eternal night of shadow."*

"Sounds ominous," said Trent. "So I guess you have another reason you haven't killed me yet. You demons like your little status quo. You really think that if I die, the Prince will invade?"

Ramón shrugged. "Prophecies can be wrong. They're more like guesses."

"I get it now." Trent shook his head, chuckled. "That's why you've been making me play bouncer. You guys think it's holding off this big Prophecy, huh? Long as I keep toeing the line, right? You keep me alive, I fight the Shades, everyone wins except the Prince. And the *cherubim*, with their hand already busted, are sittin' on their hands, waiting to see how it plays out?"

"Something like that."

"So you don't want me to quit. But you don't want me to find Susan, either."

Ramón looked away then, out the window at the birds again. He sighed. "Trent, I can't do your job for you. You've been given this task. You can protect the world around you, hold off this Prophecy, if it's true, or just go after your selfish wants. Your choice." He turned back to meet Trent's stare. "But know that what you choose has consequences."

Trent eyed him suspiciously. "Sounds like a threat. But you can't kill me. Not with your powers bound up with my soul."

"Powers you don't have anymore."

Trent huffed. "You wanna kill me? Then get in line. You've got a skinny punk-rock chick and a mysterious church owner ahead of you."

"Look," said Ramón, with a shrug, "I'm just giving you fair warning. One last bit of advice. Don't turn your back on your responsibilities. Not for mortal love. Consider the ramifications."

Trent thought long and hard, but every idea coalesced back into an image of Susan, waiting there, in the black, eyes filled with tears, both Zamagiel and the Prince chasing after her. "Sorry," he said finally, "but I'm getting my wife back, even if it kills me. And I guess if your Prophecy is true, well... then *you'll* have a real problem, huh? Won't matter to me. I'll be dead."

Ramón frowned and gestured at Celia, unmoving in her hospital bed. "What about her?"

A lump rose in Trent's throat, his false bravado conquered. "She... uhh..." Trent stuttered for a moment, and then regained his composure. "I'm not gonna die," he said. "I'm gonna get my wife, protect Celia, and then maybe we'll talk again after that about this *job*."

"What if going into the Realms of Shadow to retrieve Susan *is* your death, Trent? Then the Prophecy will come true."

Trent fixed him with a steely glare, mostly to buffer against his own uncertainty. "That's a risk I'm willing to take."

"Then I got nothing but sorrow for you," replied Ramón. He picked up his two pocket cards. "I regret it's come down to this. I thought by now you'd know when to fold." He dropped his cards face up on the plastic cart: a six and a four, both clubs. He had triple-sixes, a devil's hand.

Trent didn't hesitate to toss his own cards down, a three and five of hearts, a flush that easily beat the old man's triple. "Sometimes you can win with all hearts," he said without even a hint of a smile. "Sometimes you're drawing thin, not dead."

Ramón's eyes narrowed and his nostrils flared.

Trent shrugged. "You can't always predict everything, can you? War's like that. Sometimes you win, even when you're not supposed to. Maybe your little Prophecy is just a bunch of hokum."

The old Mexican huffed and gathered up the cards. He stood shakily, gripping hard the top of his cane as he used his free hand to slide the box of cards into his back pocket. Then he turned his back on Trent and Celia and walked over to the hospital room window.

"So where are you going next? Back to see Gadreel?"

"Maybe."

"You even know who he is?"

"Not yet, but I'll find out."

Ramón nodded. "I'm sure you will."

"What's that supposed to mean?"

Ramón ignored the question. "So that's your answer then? You're giving up the mantle of the hero to save your girl? Running off to be a lover, not a fighter, huh? All the rest of us be damned?"

Trent smiled and pointed at Celia. "For the next couple of hours," he said, "I'm going to help this little girl. And you're gonna stay here with her until I get back. I'll tell the nurses you're the granddad."

Trent could see Ramón's reflection in the windowpane. He saw the old man arch an eyebrow. "You sure about that, Trent? You trust me with her?"

"No, I don't. But you only hate *me*, right, not her? So I figure you're as good as anybody. I can't just sit here doing nothing, watching her fade away."

And he couldn't. He'd quit hunting Shades in part because he'd seen it beginning, the growing distance. It had happened with his own father when he was a boy. He'd been adopted too. He'd started wondering how long before Celia hated him. And that's when he'd decided to do something different, to throw out the job and focus on his new family. To become a father, to try and bring his wife back from wherever she had gone. He loved Susan so much. And he wanted to love Celia too, wanted to be the right kind of father. He would do anything to save them. He wanted a real family, even if he had to force himself to live in an imaginary world; even if he had to try and love a teenager he barely knew. Even if he had to defy a prophecy.

"I'm choosing to trust you, Ramón."

Ramón nodded. His reflection, peering out from within the dark frame of the window, was sad, contemplative.

Trent got up from the chair. "Besides, after the fight I started at Gadreel's, there might be some people lookin' for me. I don't know anybody better than you to tell them I said 'hi.'"

Ramón chuckled.

"Hey, and if that fire chick comes by—and she's blooded, I'm betting—maybe you can con *her* into the shade-hunter job. You know, since I quit and all."

Ramón's reflection in the glass broke a thin smile.

NOWHERE

HER LIPS ACHE AS SHE moves across the dead land. No matter how many times she rubs at them, the faint burning and the discomfort will not end. She knows she has made a terrible choice.

She stops every so often and stares at the gleaming, silver dagger, a strangely brilliant object amidst the unending void of the Realms. She feels as though she has been traveling for ages. The landscape changes constantly, but never in a way that conveys a sense of time or distance. Only the dagger remains constant.

Trent. She senses his connection to the blade, though it is fading, cooling like heated metal, and she fears that the unworld will steal his memory from her when it does.

The next time Susan stops to rest she finds herself in a small glade of rock spires, like apocalyptic trees, twisted and set solid in writhing, impossible shapes. The density of the spires gives the place a forest-like atmosphere and, were it possible to darken the Realms, the shadows cast here would do so.

She clutches the dagger tight and glances around. Something is wrong. She can sense another, more powerful, presence. Not a passing shadow or nameless thing, but something worse, something in the employ of the Prince. Something named. She has been found.

With a sudden, ear-splitting screech, the creature lurches at her, elongating into existence from deep within a long shadow, its body an amorphous mass of smoke and razor sharp teeth.

Susan runs.

Her naked feet pound against the black rock and though she scarcely remembers the sound of her own breath, she hears it now, feels her own lungs aching and pounding like machines and in that moment of flight she remembers a little more of what it means to be alive. She remembers *fear*.

The creature bounds after her, its body alternating between a formless, gaseous mass and a solid, muscled thing that ripples and smokes. She ducks behind a rock spire and the creature barrels through, shattering it into a thousand shards and forcing her back the way she had come. Ahead, she sees a thing that is new, something she has never seen in this place: a river.

Though dark and hardly moving, it is clearly a liquid flow, a winding cut in the black landscape. She heads for it, desperately trying to stay a few steps ahead of the furious thing that pursues her, leaping and slipping through the shadows, teeth gnashing.

She reaches the edge of a rock outcropping above the river and stops, silver dagger drawn. She turns to face the oncoming creature. She watches its footsteps across the rocky ground, its massive, bounding stride and she realizes something. With every footstep, the creature is changing the realm around it. The air shimmers with every impact and the ground itself becomes softer, more tractable for the creature's gleaming claws. Rock spires bend to avoid the rushing thing, or become brittle as it crashes through. As the creature advances, Susan thinks of her dress, and Lilith's reaction to her name, and she knows then what she can do.

"No!" she screams, as the creature bears down on her. "This ground is...." And she remembers something from the other world then. Freezing, cold, clear. Memories of winters in Minnesota with her grandparents flood her mind for just a moment. She remembers the cold substance, the sheets of it that coated the ground and made her slip and fall and break her arm. She screams out the name of that thing.

And with the naming of it, the rocky, black ground at her feet becomes suddenly blue-white, cold, frozen and slick and the bounding monstrosity comes down claws-first, not expecting the sudden change and, like a dog on ceramic tile, its forward motion collapses and its vector shifts. It slips sideways, skittering claws against the new surface. To compensate, it attempts to shift form, to become gaseous and ethereal, instead of solid and out-of-control.

"You are Solid," she whispers.

The creature slumps down on the ice, solid and whole, forward momentum still carrying it, sliding and screeching, toward the cliff-edge and as it slips over the ice-encrusted rock, the thing lets out a terrified howl and then plunges down into the black river.

Susan stands at the edge, dagger gleaming in her grip. The ground becomes black rock once more. As she watches the river and the thrashing monstrosity within, she is horrified to see black, tendrils twisting up from the fluid, encircling the howling creature. Within seconds, the creature is trapped, held fast, and then pulled below, like a fly into a spider's web.

She knows she must cross that same river. Lilith told her so. She scrambles down a nearby rockslide until she finds purchase on the ground below, and then approaches the dismal shore. Tendrils twist up out of the muck, sliding across the rocky ground toward her.

"No," she says, now understanding her place in this realm more fully. "There is a Bridge."

With a loud rumbling, a rocky land bridge rises up out of the river, black fluid dripping down its sides and running in rivulets. With an initial sense of trepidation, Susan takes her first steps onto a part of the world that she has shaped, a change that she has made unto the Realms of Shadow. The tendrils writhe and slap wetly against the rock but cannot reach her. Below, she sees the solid body of her attacker, floating lifeless and desiccated in the sludge.

And as she moves quickly across the new bridge, she hears rumbling and splashing from behind and knows that even as she walks, the Realms are reclaiming her creation, dragging the firmament down beneath the fluid once more. She can shape things here, but only for a short time.

Her creations, like the mutable, ever-changing landscape, cannot last.

4

FIAMMA THREW DOWN THE KICKSTAND and slid off the Tuono, seething. As she moved through the vast church parking lot, a faint haze of smoke accompanied her. She had to stop twice to retrieve the last two protein bars from her pocket and wolf them down. She had begun to feel ill, and the pain in her extremities refused to abate.

The Church of Our Angel of Restoration stood a good clip west of Las Vegas, high up Mount Charleston, overlooking Gadreel's mansion nestled in the steep forest below. Orange and tan desert shimmered in the distance and Fiamma took a moment to watch the dust devils swirl and flit from place to place as if guarding the mountain via their own indeterminable patrols.

She hated the place. She hated all churches, in fact, but this one in particular. To her, it reeked of lies and calculated control. A church owned by a demon, Gadreel, its flock swindled by the smooth tongue of Palisade. As a child, she'd lost her own father to religion when he suddenly left the family to pursue 'a higher calling'. She found it ironic that, at twenty-five, she had ended up working for the Fallen.

She reached the front door to the church, guarded by two men in sharp business suits. She knew they had guns tucked inside their jackets. One of them held out a hand as she approached.

"I'm sorry miss, but—"

Fiamma balled up her right fist and slugged him in the throat. The punch left a mass of rising blisters on his flesh. His spine cracked against the doorframe. The other guard moved to retrieve his gun, but she moved too quickly for him. She jammed her hand inside his jacket, pulled out his pistol, and then kneed him in the groin. He fell over, clutching his nether regions. She stepped past the moaning guards and kicked open the large wooden door to the church.

The atrium was dark. Fiamma stepped inside and let the door swing shut behind her. Without hesitation, she raised the pistol and broke the serenity by firing several shots into the air. "Palisade!" she bellowed.

As the gunshot echoes faded, the sounds of running footsteps grew louder. The door at the far end of the atrium burst open, along with the doors on either side. Through all three poured armed guards in black, wearing Kevlar vests and wielding assault rifles.

I hate this place, she thought.

A chorus of mechanical clicks filled the room as guards dropped to their knees and formed an impromptu firing squad, all barrels aimed at Fiamma.

She scowled and threw the gun to the floor. "Palisade!" she shouted again, sharper and louder this time. "Come out, you little prick!"

The guard at the front of the pack waved his rifle and shouted, "On the ground, now!"

Fiamma gave him the finger. "Fuck off."

"My dear, what is the problem? Can't our appointment wait until morning?" Palisade's voice drifted across the room from a small door off the east wing of the atrium. He stepped through, adjusting his glasses, backlit by the dim glow from the room he had just left. He was wearing sweatpants and a t-shirt and looked thoroughly irritated to have been woken in the middle of the night.

Fiamma knew that Palisade lived in the church, or more accurately, in a small building at the back of the campus. She visited frequently, a task she hated but longed for with every waking moment. Palisade had a strange gift. With a look from his steel-blue eyes, the wiry man could tear away Fiamma's pain. He could deaden her powers, make her normal, extinguish the fire that threatened at every moment to eat her alive. And though it only lasted for a day or so, the temporary reprieve from her curse brought her the only joy she could find. It was like a drug, and she needed it desperately. So she came back over and over, like a beaten dog begging for table scraps.

She glared at him.

"You must learn some self-control. This could have waited." He sighed and waved off the guards, who began retreating back down their respective hallways. He motioned for Fiamma to come to him. "Fine, you've done your job and shall have your pay, even if I am a little tired for this right now. But next time, please—"

"He's not dead."

Palisade, who had turned away, looked back over his shoulder and raised an eyebrow. "I'm sorry?"

"Trent Hawkins is still alive. The deal's changed."

He turned to face her again and furrowed his brow. "I don't think—"

"Who the fuck is this guy, Pal?" She advanced on the sleepy-eyed preacher and jabbed him in the chest with her index finger. "You left out a lot of details. Like why the Freemasons are tracking him. Or the fact that he's a Doombringer."

Palisade frowned. "He's not anymore. This should have been an easy task for you, child."

"Don't 'child' me, you little shit. There're Neutrals involved, too. Did you know that?"

"Neutrals? Who?"

"Trent called him Charlie. Runs a pawn shop downtown."

"Ahh, I see." Palisade took off his glasses and cleaned them with the corner of his t-shirt. "Charles is in danger of breaking his oath. Not entirely unexpected. We can deal with this."

"I don't understand—?"

Palisade raised a hand to silence her. "Neutral angels escaped the Fall by taking an oath of neutrality. And in return, they take no sides in the Great War. Have you learned nothing from working with Gadreel? I'm betting he's never even told you the truth about your father."

Palisade had never talked of her father before, and the sudden mention set her blood boiling. She balled her fists. "What do you know about him?"

He turned his back and replaced the glasses. Without looking at her, he said, "You are correct, the deal must be changed. This... minor irritation, this Neutral... must be removed. Then Mr. Hawkins. And then you will receive your prize, for the normal payment of course." He paused and then said, maliciously, "How I do love our little sessions. The knowledge that I'm the only one who can touch you in that way—"

Fiamma cut him off. Through gritted teeth, she asked, "You want me to kill Charlie? Kill an angel?"

The preacher stepped through the door to his private chambers and then stopped, one hand on the doorframe. A slight glance backward. Eyebrow raised, he said quietly, "You've done it before. And I suspect you will do it again."

* * *

Clouds masked the coming dawn as Trent rode back across the city to Charlie's shop. The breeze had picked up too, and the increasingly overcast skies made him nervous. Las Vegas had plenty of rainy days. But after the Blizzard, after knowing the source of that maelstrom, Trent could never look at a cloudy sky the same way again.

He parked the bike in front of City Pawn, just as the first rays of dull grey light from the dead-flat eastern horizon peeked between the buildings. In the far distance, a faint thunderclap rolled. Trent frowned.

Charlie shuffled out of his office as Trent stepped into the store. The place was rarely locked, either because the old man lived there round the clock or because he didn't need to. Being a Neutral, Charlie had made sure that City Pawn was a place where the ancient rules still held sway. Members of the host, fallen or otherwise, were honor-bound not to enter the shop without Charlie's permission. No magick prevented it, just ancient agreements. Trent thought about the impertinent *cherubim* that had trespassed on the night of the Blizzard. Now he understood why Charlie had been so irate at them. And anyone else, thugs or thieves, drunks or drugged-out hookers, well, Charlie just didn't care that much about them. And Trent suspected that any who tried to steal from Charlie V would never want to do it again.

The old man rubbed his eyes. He still wore the same jeans and t-shirt that Trent had seen him in earlier.

"You been sleeping? I thought you were gonna find me some clues?"

"I never sleep, Mr. Trent. Only dream."

Trent blinked, shook his head. "Okay."

"I am havink some good information for you now. Sit down."

Trent grabbed a nearby metal folding chair, spun it around, and sat down on it backwards. He ran his hands through his hair and took a long, deep breath. Before Charlie could begin, he said, "Things have gotten worse. Celia's in the hospital, unconscious. And she's let something through, summoned them maybe, I dunno. Before she went into the coma, she told me they're looking for the Book."

"Raziel's book?"

"What else would she be talking about?"

Charlie thought for a moment. "This is bad. Things are changink quickly, Mr. Trent. I think the War may be upon us."

Trent frowned and shook his head. "The War, Charlie? You on about this too? Vlad's been using that for six months, and I've seen nothing but the usual. Some Shades try to come through, I beat the hell out of them, they go back. Rinse and repeat. There's no war. I don't care what you or Ramón say."

Charlie nodded. "Oh, but there is. It is no myth."

"Well it's not my problem anymore. I quit, remember? I only care about Celia right now, and I'm going for Susan after that. So what's this new information you've got?"

"I am knowink more now about Mr. Gadreel. It is no good. I still am not knowink *who* he is, exactly. The information is… confusink. But he is hiring someone to kill you."

"No shit. She tried once already. What do you know about her?"

"Her name is Fiamma. From New York City. Her father was a priest. Her mother died in a fire."

Trent thought about the hole in Louis' jacket. "Burned down her own house, huh?"

"With her mother in it."

Something about the story tickled a memory that Trent couldn't quite dredge up. A sense of déjà vu. He opened his mouth to say something, but couldn't think of anything. "Shit," he said finally.

"She's a very angry woman, Mr. Trent. Always burnink, eatink her alive. And Gadreel's assistant gives her something that she cannot refuse."

"What?"

"Solace."

"Fucking Palisade," Trent said, and then it all suddenly came together for him. Palisade. The loss of his own powers. Solace. "He can deaden bloodline powers, can't he? That's what he gives her."

Charlie nodded.

"But wait," said Trent, confused. "How can he affect me? I'm not blooded. I stole my power from Ramón. I'm just an ordinary mortal otherwise."

Charlie shrugged. "I am not able to be answerink that. There is more to you than is understood now."

Trent frowned. If Palisade could suppress others' powers, that made him dangerous. If he could suppress Trent's demon-stolen powers, that made the wiry preacher *very* dangerous.

"What else do you know about Palisade?"

"He's a very sick man, Mr. Trent. Very sick. He has done things, to people, to children. He was spendink many years in prison, until Gadreel was settink him free."

"And now he runs a goddamn church." Trent shook his head and looked out the window at the grey morning hanging dim on the city of Las Vegas. "I hate this place."

Charlie smiled. "Do not be despairink so much. I have good news, too."

"Yeah?"

"I am findink the Medicine Man for you."

Trent's eyes went wide. "You know where he is?"

"Not yet, but soon. For now, you need to be helpink little Celia."

"Yeah." Trent felt confused, shameful. He wanted so badly to find the Medicine Man, to find Susan, but he also felt responsible for Celia's injury. He needed to help her. He loved her, not in the same way as his lost wife, but still.... "I don't know what to do, Charlie. I'm not even sure what's happened. Who did Celia summon?"

"Hard to say. But I am hearink of strange things in the drainage tunnels."

"That's not news." Las Vegas played host to miles of drainage tunnels, built to prevent flooding in the streets during the infrequent, but torrential, rainstorms. Trent had spent hours in those same tunnels during the Blizzard. All manner of destitute, ruined people lived down there, as well as a few, like Mary, who chose to remain in the dark, helping those who could not help themselves.

As if in response to his thoughts, Charlie said, "More strange than usual. Mary called me—"

"Really?" She had helped Trent out on the night of the Blizzard. She'd led him to Zamagiel's hiding place atop the Luxor's giant black pyramid. She'd helped him end the fallen angel.

"Yes. She is sayink that she saw—"

But before he could finish the sentence, the metal door to the shop let out a horrific, tortured shriek. Both Trent and Charlie turned quickly and watched as the door glowed orange, screaming with stress and then slumped inward off its melting hinges.

In the doorway stood an unnaturally thin woman, black hair, black shirt and pants. Smoke drifted from every part of her and small flames flickered along her shoulders and sleeves.

Trent leapt from the chair to face her, putting himself between her and Charlie. "What the hell?"

"Exactly," she said as she advanced on them. She pointed around Trent at the old man. "Him first, then you."

"No," Trent replied. "I'm tired of your shit, girl. This ends now."

She shrugged. "Don't care what you think, cowboy. You're both gonna burn."

His adoptive father had always told him that a real man never, ever hit a girl. But then, his dad had never mentioned girls that could burn a man alive with a touch. Trent grabbed the chair and swung it like a club.

Fiamma raised an arm to block the metal chair, which, as it struck her flesh came apart in a sharp-smelling cloud of smoke and debris. It didn't even stop her stride.

Trent backed away, shooing Charlie to stay behind him. Fiamma yelled and burst forward, hands outstretched like claws. Instinctively, Trent blinked and searched the black world in that nanosecond for variations on the girl's fate, for ways to change her assault, but the space beneath his consciousness was dead. Empty. He was still normal, and he regretted it now.

Her fingers clawed at him as Trent ducked forward, came up under her arms and shoved hard against her sternum. The blow sent her sprawling backwards across the room. She collapsed against a rack of used evening gowns that burst into flame on contact. She struggled to her feet, not even bothering to brush off the melting nylon that clung to her glowing skin. She was a shambling, blazing monstrosity.

"You motherfucker," she said.

"The shotgun," whispered Charlie from behind Trent. "Loaded."

Without thinking, he rammed his fist through the glass and grabbed the double-barreled shotgun from the display case. As he leveled the gun on Fiamma, he could see glass shards sticking up from his skin. Blood ran in rivulets down his arm.

"Hold still."

She didn't listen. From behind her back, she drew out her Colt pistol. Trent pulled the shotgun's trigger.

Time seemed to slow for a moment. Trent watched, fascinated, as the empty casing ejected from the side of the shotgun, as the shell burst from the barrel. And there was a sudden boom, and a zip, and then the shell hit Fiamma in the breastbone, celebrated by a faint spray of red and an explosion of smoldering fabric bits from her thin black t-shirt. She dropped the Colt to the floor as she staggered backwards, clutching at her chest, eyes locked on Trent in a furious, pain-dimmed glare. Her blue eyes twitched, blinked once as her mouth opened and closed like a fish gasping for air. She broke the momentary silence with a sharp, gurgling inhale as she pulled her hand away from her chest and dropped a melted hunk of lead onto the floor. It hit with a bang and stopped dead on the linoleum.

She moved forward then, smoke pouring from her nostrils. "You think you can kill me, cowboy? Better creatures have tried." She reached out and grabbed the shotgun and its frame glowed red, becoming superheated, forcing Trent to let go. It clattered to the floor.

Trent stepped forward, smiling.

Fiamma grinned.

"Whatcha gonna do?" she said, quietly. "There's a contract on you, and I intend to get my pay. Nothing personal."

"This," said Trent, and with a quick motion of his left hand brought the angelic dagger out from behind him and jammed it into Fiamma's right thigh.

The silver blade embedded itself all the way to the hilt. She screamed out, stumbling backwards, and crashed into a drum set. Pure and unbridled fury changed to sudden fear. She clutched at the dagger's hilt, trying desperately to pull it from the wound. She kicked against cymbals and punctured snare drums as she thrashed and wailed, a discordance of violence and agony. Smoke lifted from her hands and steaming tears ran down her cheeks as she struggled to wrench it from her flesh, but the dagger remained whole.

"Run, Charlie!" Trent grabbed at the old man's wrist, trying to pull him toward the door, but Charlie resisted.

"No," he said. "I've made my choice."

Trent stared at him, uncomprehending. "I don't—?"

Charlie cut him off with a smile.

It was done. Charlie had broken his oath. After thousands of years of neutrality, the angel known as Charlie V had taken a side. He felt sick. Of all the foul, twisted, malevolent creatures he'd met in Las Vegas, demon and angel alike, never had he met one as honorable, as oath bound as Charlie V. He turned away, heart aching with regret.

"Don't be worryink, Mr. Trent. You can consider this my retirement."

Trent didn't know what to make of that statement at first. He looked at Charlie, shook his head, and then looked at Fiamma.

Clenching her eyes tight, she tugged at the knife, slicing and serrating the edges of her wound, eliciting ever-growing streams of blood, but still it wouldn't budge. "I'll kill you!" she screamed, her anger punctuated by chokes and coughs. Her teeth shone red with blood. "I'm gonna fucking kill you both!"

Trent glanced at Charlie again and started to say something, but the old man put up a hand to stop him. "Just go," he said. "Talk with Mary. Help Celia. I am takink care of the fire-girl for now.

"But—"

"Go." Charlie's voice commanded suddenly an authority that Trent had never heard before. The tone made his heart seize. He was compelled to obey. He turned to the door and ran, leaving the angel's dagger and the fire-girl and his only real friend behind.

*   *   *

Her leg burned with a fire unlike any other she had known. Not the hot, consuming flames that she had felt inside every moment since childhood. Not the blazing fury of heated metal. This was a cold, perfect burn. A pain that made want to turn her eyes skyward and repent. Her breath came in ragged gasps and her fingers trembled as she pulled helplessly at the dagger.

"It is hurtink, yes?" Charlie stood above her.

She nodded, eyes shut, teeth gritted in determination to free the searing blade from her flesh. With every passing second, she felt the hateful part deep inside her diminishing, as though the blade were forcing it lower. Her soul ached.

"Please," she said, "make it *stop*." She screamed the last word and her eyes opened to see Charlie wincing, his face wrinkled with concern.

"There are things in this world, simple things, that are havink the power to judge," he said quietly. "That knife is one. It is judgink you."

"Goddammit." She yanked on the hilt of the blade, bringing torrents of tears to her eyes. "Take it *out*."

"It is judgink your potential future, not just your past." He shook his head. "Your future must be filled with pain and sufferink."

She screamed, her wall-rattling cry guttural and wordless. Her sobs boiled over, great gouts of anguish poured from her lips. She locked eyes on Charlie, his concern now replaced with a strange sort of fear.

"Repent, child," he said with anxiety in his voice. "Be askink the Lord for mercy. Please."

"No," she said through clenched teeth. "God—" She flopped uncontrollably on the floor, gasping in pain. She struck a hat stand that fell over, spilling the straw cowboy hats down around her. The hats smoldered. "God has done nothing for me." Her fingers clawed at the linoleum. She screamed like an animal at the ceiling. "God has tortured me my whole life."

Charlie shook his head as tears rolled down his cheeks. He looked up at the ceiling. "I cannot abide this." He stooped, grabbed the blade and easily slid it out of Fiamma's flesh. It sang as it came free.

Fiamma's shuddering slowed and her gasps abated. Charlie knelt over her, fluorescent lights casting his shadow, and the shadow of the dagger, long over her trembling body. He held the dagger in his right hand.

"I'm sorry, child," he said. "With you, God has done wrong. I will end your pain for good."

He brought the dagger up, grimacing.

Fiamma screamed as the blade came down, but as the glimmering tip of the silver dagger dipped into the shadow across her chest, a grey-green, shriveled hand oozing with sores and pus, bristled with short black hairs, came shooting out of the black. The fingers clawed for the dagger's hilt and gripped it strong. With a ferocious tug, the hand tore the knife from Charlie's grasp and revoked it into the black, never once touching Fiamma's skin.

The room went quiet, the silence broken only by Fiamma's ragged breathing. Both of them remained still, paralyzed by the sudden turn of events. Charlie looked at his empty hand, then at Fiamma. Her face bore a tear-streaked mask of animal fury, now punctuated by a malicious grin.

"*You've* been judged," she said, with a bloody but triumphant grimace.

Her arms shot forward and she wrapped her fingers around Charlie's neck. They struggled and thrashed together for a moment, until she put a boot heel into his knee, shattering it. She let go of his neck and kicked him to the ground. He fell hard among the pile of burning hats and Fiamma climbed atop him. Wailing in anguish and triumph, she squeezed his throat again, tighter and tighter, drawing billows of black smoke as she bashed the angel's skull over and over against the pawn shop floor.

NOWHERE

THE AIR IS THICK WITH the unexpected smell of salt and something else and Susan remembers garbage. The odor of rotting vegetation lingers in her nostrils. Ahead she sees a marsh of sorts, a swamp, in which other, humanoid figures churn while softly crying out. All of their eyes fall upon the interloper, the woman in white whose feet move dirt as she walks. They call out to her, but she does not answer. She moves closer, fascinated and terrified of the writhing mass of bodies slapping wetly at the muck. And then she notices another figure, a small man sitting near an outcropping of dead, twisted vines. She remembers him somehow, though she cannot place his name.

He is elderly in appearance and, like the others, his form is erratic, though in only the most subtle of ways; a slight repositioning of an eye for a moment and then his white hair is more grey, or less, and then his hand touches his face and then it is not there at all. Still frames in motion. She looks at her own image, peers down her chest at the white dress, the gentle curves of her breasts beneath the fabric, the sliding exposure of flesh as her legs scissor in and out of their linen confines. Unlike his, her form is solid, unchanging. She stares at the man again and he looks back at her now, with sadness in his eyes.

"How have you come here?"

"Who are you?" she asks.

He lowers his gaze and then looks out over the struggling, lamenting bodies in the marsh.

"Who are you?" she asks again, but receives no answer. After a moment's pause she tries, "I made a bridge. I crossed the river."

The small old man turns his tired eyes on her once more. "A bridge? Across the river Acheron? How have you the rule to shape such things?"

She shrugs and then peers at him more intently. Something odd about him, something that tugs at her thoughts. "I know you, don't I?"

The old man merely blinks.

Suddenly, she brings her hand to her mouth. She remembers him. She remembers far more than she might wish and she knows, all at once, that this is the man who attacked her in the hospital, her first day on the job. He had been trying to kidnap a child whose name Susan cannot now remember. But *his* name, she does remember. She gasps.

"You're Salvatore! Oh, God!" She stumbles backward away from him.

For a moment, he seems lost in thought. His eyes slowly widen and his mouth forms a weak smile. "I *am* Salvatore," he says, obviously delighted by the new revelation. "I am! Why have you brought me this gift of a name? Who are you, girl? Speak!"

"S-Susan," she says. "You... you tried to kill me, and my husband, Trent. You wanted that little girl...."

The old man stands up suddenly as though a great weight has lifted from him and he turns and moves in her direction. She stumbles backward again and falls onto her backside in a pool of fetid muck.

"No," he says. "Please, do not fear me. I am Salvatore, yes. But I did not kill you. I never meant to hurt anyone. A demon did that, not I. A demon that had deceived me."

Susan whispers, "Zamagiel."

He stops. Rage burns across his face as he repeats the name under his breath. He balls a fist, clenches hard and then unclenches several times in succession, a motion that to Susan appears like broken film, alien and impossible in its animation. His teeth are gritted and brow furrowed and he snorts at the air. Finally, his countenance softens and sorrow returns to his features.

"I'm sorry," he says. "So very sorry." And he reaches down to offer his hand.

They sit together upon the edge of the marsh and watch the struggle in the filthy black water, naked limbs clawing at the starless sky and mouths and eyes gaping, panicked, oozing rotten fluid.

"How do you have such power, Susan? How are you able to shape this place?"

Susan tells him that she does not know, but that she knows the location of the demon Zamagiel, their common enemy. She does not tell him of the Shadow of Lilith and the granted kiss.

"The city Dis is a stronghold," he says. "We cannot possibly pass within its borders. Even if you could shape an army, the *grigorim* would destroy it. Only a Lord of Hell itself could subdue the horde of Fallen that now occupy that place. They would end us and we would return here, to be like these souls for all eternity—" He gestures at the marsh-dwellers.

"How are you not like them already?" asks Susan.

"These are the souls cast out by angels and demons that take to flesh. The demons throw them out with force, banish them to this swamp and rob them of their lives and mortal skin. The angels—" he pauses and looks off into the distance, lost in thought. "The angels," he says quietly, "they ask permission of the most pious. They ask for this sacrifice...." His voice trails off and then his head turns, slowly, and his gaze meets hers. "For the glory of God, they ask this, and the most pious of men gladly give it.

"Zamagiel and I struck a bargain. I was permitted to remain in the body, to give Zamagiel time to grow his power. At the end, I suppose he could not bear to let me languish in such a fashion as the others." He nods at the moaning souls. "So here I sit, looking over the fate I was spared."

Susan looks out over the marsh and discovers, among the screaming, crying, moaning souls, the rare few who say nothing, whose mouths and eyes are shut as they bob, silently, in the fetid wash. "I see them," she says. "They're so quiet. How long must they stay like that?"

Salvatore eyes her curiously. "It is no matter of time," he explains. "There is no time in this place. Every second is none and all. Every moment is eternity. They, like we, simply remain. Abaddon is beyond time. Abaddon encompasses time."

"But I feel it. I feel time moving."

"Then some part of you still remains in the mortal realm. You still feel the tick of the coil's clock." He is quiet for a moment and then he says, "I do not feel such a thing."

Susan considers this for a moment. "Who are you, Salvatore? I met you once before, but you were him, the fallen angel. Who are you really?"

Salvatore sighs. "I am—I was—a man, a husband, a frightened father. And I suppose I will always be a *gibborim*—a child of Zamagiel, a child of the *grigori*. And I know now that I am a coward. I ran from my life into the arms of one playing at the role of God. I told myself I was serving Him, but it was a deception. I was only serving myself and my fears. I left her fatherless, because I feared her. I feared what she might become someday."

"Who?" asks Susan.

"My child," he replies. "My daughter. You've let me remember her name, and the thought of it still burns my heart." He closes his eyes and then whispers, "I'm... I'm sorry, my dear Fiamma. I'm so sorry."

Silence washes over them like the putrid thick air of the swamp. Even the lamenting souls go quiet. There is a faint whistling on the breeze. Salvatore's head snaps up and he scans the horizon.

"What?" she asks, but before she can finish, he grabs her hand with his own and they leap from their resting place.

"We have to leave," he says. "Something is coming. For only the most powerful creatures do the souls cease their cries, for fear of reprisal. We must flee."

"The Prince," she says. "He's sent things after me."

"Come," Salvatore insists. "You've given me a greater gift than you can ever imagine. I intend to repay it in kind. I know this place far better than you."

A cold wind sweeps through the marsh valley, forcing aside the stagnant waves of rotten fog, and Susan takes this as a cue to action. She grips the withered old hand tightly and lets Salvatore lead her away across the marsh, where a narrow path picks it way between the dripping spires and languid vines.

"Run," he says, his voice quiet but insistent. "We must run."

Susan runs, feeling the sharp stones digging into the soles of her feet. She feels a wet, rubbery mass on her ankle and looks down to see hands clawing at her, black, gleaming arms ending in frail, withered fingers struggling desperately to grasp her ankles and drag her back into the swamp. Moaning, open mouths gape at her below sunken, dead eyes. Ooze drains from every pair of desiccated lips, preceding an unending chorus of awful half-choking cries.

"My God," she says, and makes the mistake of looking back, to see what foul thing could be chasing them.

A hand successfully grapples her leg and she goes down. Her face splashes into a muddy pool and her chest strikes the ground hard and, were she in the mortal realm, she would have expected to feel the breath knocked out of her. She grabs the mud with her fingernails and pulls herself forward, kicking away the hand that has grasped her ankle and she struggles to stand back up, watching as the Prince's minions bear down on her through the swamp.

Salvatore shouts for her to keep moving, but she stands transfixed by the sight of the horrible creatures advancing through the bog: a half dozen tall, too-thin shadows like emaciated giants, with glass-like obsidian skin and hands that are little more than pointed, triangular fingers extending long from the wrists, palm-less and in constant motion. They do not run, or even touch the ground, but instead float along, propelled by the cold wind at their back and the breeze they carry with them pushes away the swamp fog as they come. Dirt and debris swirls and churns the air in their wake. Their motions through the spire-trees are erratic, inconsistent. They cross in and out of the path, deftly avoiding obstacles and their long, pointed arms sway with every sideways motion. The mournful souls in the marsh shy at their passage and sink beneath the fluid surface.

"Please, Susan!" shouts Salvatore, louder now. "You have to run!"

"No," she says quietly. "I can stop them. With a Wall."

And being so named, a wall bursts noisily from the swamp, a blood-red mass of flat, rough-hewn iron that ascends skyward, lifting wailing bodies from the filth, only to tumble haphazardly down the sides of the metal partition, flopping wetly before splashing once more into the muck. The rusted crimson surface peaks at eight feet and slams to a stop, throwing a spray of water into the air. The cold wind at the backs of the oncoming Shades buffets against the barrier suddenly, eliciting a mournful howl that echoes along the wall's length, which stretches away to the horizon in both directions.

All is quiet.

Susan, fighting a sudden fatigue, watches the wall, hands on her knees. Rivulets of swamp water drip silently down its sides. A lone body trapped atop the narrow divider finally succumbs to gravity and slumps over the near side, tumbling end over end, limbs flailing uselessly before it hits the fetid water with a smack and then sinks beneath.

"Come, Susan," says Salvatore. "Please."

She looks at him, sees him gesturing, beckoning her to come, and then she looks at the wall again. The water is running up?

No, she realizes. *The wall is moving down.*

"It is unmaking itself," he says, shouting. "We have little time. You cannot hope to shape this realm permanently. Your will is not as strong as his."

Susan turns then and moves to rejoin Salvatore. When she reaches him, he grasps her hand and they stumble away into the black swamp.

5

ASTRIDE THE ROARING DUCATI, TRENT sliced through downtown Las Vegas, zipped up onto the highway, and merged into moderate traffic heading back toward The Strip. His head hurt, not just from the battle with Fiamma, but also from the rattling guilt, worries, and the multitude of half-considered possibilities grinding against each other like stones amidst his thoughts.

Celia in a coma, watched over by a terrible demon that Trent barely trusted, who had begun throwing out veiled threats, backed by a mysterious Prophecy.

Mr. Gadreel, out to kill him for some reason, using a hate-filled, fire-bearing woman as his proxy.

Charlie, giving up his oath of neutrality after millennia.

Some new type of shade, summoned as a group, searching for the Book, but to what purpose?

And Susan, still out there somewhere, in the black, waiting for him.

Trent banged a blood-stained fist against the handlebars of the bike and then, as if to make a point, swerved in between two cars, gunned the accelerator to pass the one on the right, then threw the Ducati back in front of the guy, swerving wildly in his lane for a moment. The driver of the car laid on his horn and gave Trent the finger.

He needed to find the Medicine Man, to find a way to Susan, but his responsibility to Celia weighed more heavily. Would he risk dooming the world, everything and everyone, for a chance at bringing Susan back? Would he trade Celia's life to regain hers? He shook his head, forcing the question out. He feared his own answer.

First, he had to get Celia some help. If the things she had summoned were lurking in the tunnels, searching for the Book, then maybe their continued existence here was linked to Celia's unconscious state. Maybe if he could banish them, as he had so many Shades over the past few months, she would wake. Then they could hide, get Charlie to tell them where the Medicine Man was, rescue Susan....

It all sounded so implausible.

He veered the bike down an exit ramp and headed for The Strip. He had decided along the way that if Mary knew something about these Shades in the tunnels, the sooner he could talk to her, the better. He wanted to get it over with, and he fought back the little voice that questioned how he was going to do that without either his angelic dagger or his power to bring doom.

Getting to Mary quick meant a riskier entrance to the tunnels. The long way, starting in a drainage ditch on a destitute street south of the neon, had better odds since the

Metro didn't police the street much. But that way involved a couple of cross-tunnels, and the grey clouds looming on the horizon suggested rain. At least one of those cross-tunnels flooded quickly, and Trent had no intention of drowning. Besides, there was a shorter entrance, right on the south edge of The Strip. The Metro had a bigger presence there, but Trent was hoping that his luck would hold.

He parked the Ducati a few blocks away, in a pay lot he had no intention of paying, and walked the rest of the way. He'd learned over the past months to be careful. Hunting Shades sometimes meant a chance notice by a cop. Explaining his actions wasn't an option, so it was usually easier to slip away on foot, down some back alley, and return for the bike later. On one occasion, he'd accidentally gotten the bike impounded after stabbing a lurker shade on a busy Saturday-night street. Snake had cleared that mess up—somehow—but it had been a tense couple of hours wondering if he'd ever get the Ducati back and trying to imagine how Snake would manage to keep his name and face off the Metro bulletins.

In the distance, a quiet roll of thunder sounded. Trent glanced at the sky as he cut down a back alley between two cheap-slots casinos. There'd be a good thunderstorm later. He pressed his grey hat down tighter on his head.

When he finally rounded the back wall of a low-rent convenience store, his heart sank. Just off the edge of the road, by the tunnel entrance, two cops were smoking cigarettes, leaning against a Plexiglas bus stop. They were on their beat: guarding the tunnel entrance.

It was a shit beat, but after the Blizzard, the TV footage of frozen and drowned corpses being dragged out of the tunnels had launched a tidal wave of scorn on the Metro. The department had responded by adding a dozen or so patrols near commonly used tunnel entrances. They shook down itinerants that came too close, made a show of cleaning out the folks that camped just inside the tunnels, and generally harassed anyone trying to use the drainage ditches as a respite from the hot desert sun. The new focus had little effect on those living deeper in the tunnels, but was a constant annoyance and created a need for Trent to memorize beat schedules at the various points of egress.

Trent took a deep breath, steeled his jaw, and loped across the street. He'd come this far and decided to at least give it a shot. Maybe the old trick of just "looking like you belong" would work here.

When he reached the Metro officers, Trent didn't even stop. He gave them a thin smile, waved, and moved to walk past, toward the ditch. But one of the officers threw down his cigarette and stepped into Trent's line holding up his hands.

"Hold on, bud," he said, shaking his head. "No one's allowed in there. City ordinance. Come on, you know that."

Trent did his best not to falter. He smiled wearily, nodded. "City?" he said. "That's who I'm with. Just inspecting this entrance." He pointed at the sky without breaking his gaze from the cop. "Storm's coming. Making sure it's cleaned out."

The officer glanced at his companion, who shrugged and continued to smoke. "You don't even have a city uniform," he said, looking at Trent's burned, stained dress shirt. "You look like you could use a new shirt."

Trent rolled his eyes, trying to stay in character as best he could. "Seriously? I'm not even supposed to be at work today." He took his eyes off the policeman and turned them to the sky. "I mean, come on, you can see the rain coming. I wasn't even on the schedule but now they want me to come down here on my day off and check this shit out before it floods The Strip." He plucked at his own damaged shirt. "Yer damn right I need a new shirt. This was from the tunnel I just cleaned out over on Tropicana. Some asshole Mexican in there with a campfire, gutting chickens. I had to throw him out by force." It didn't seem like a very good lie, but he hoped the overt racism would sell the story. He fished in his pocket for his cellphone, all the while grumbling about "calling his supervisor" and "they're not gonna be happy about this."

"Okay, okay, okay," said the cop. "I'm just supposed to ask. You say you're with the city, fine. I don't really care that much. But you just better come back out in the next hour. We'll still be here, waiting for you."

Trent locked eyes with the cop again. Smiled. "Fine," he said. "That's just fine. I won't be long."

With renewed confidence, he strode past them. Then he stopped and grimaced. The Colt in the back of his waistband. For a split second, he thought that maybe they hadn't seen, but then, "Holy shit, he's got a gun!"

Then the click.

"Hold it! Don't move! Hands in the air!"

A number of possibilities galloped through Trent's brain. He could run for the tunnel entrance, but since he had a visible gun, there was a pretty decent chance they'd just shoot him in the back and claim self-defense. No one would look into it too closely. He could surrender, but then his mission was shot. No seeing Mary, no finding the Shades, no helping Celia, and probably the next twenty-four hours in lockup before he could get hold of Snake and have *him* correct the situation. And that's assuming Snake *could*, and that he *would*. Trent had quit after all.

Reluctantly, he decided on Option C, turned, smiled, and swung a clenched fist straight into the nearest cop's temple. He'd beefed up his punches quite a bit fighting Shades and could drop a man pretty quick.

His aim was off, though.

The Metro officer lurched back, dropped his handgun, but remained standing, dazed for a moment but still conscious. The other officer spit out his cigarette and fumbled for his gun.

Trent had no intention of shooting either of these men, and kept the Colt in his waistband. He just needed to put them to sleep for a while, so he could disappear into the drainage tunnels.

He stepped forward and threw a right cross at the dazed officer. His knuckles collided with flesh and bone and he could both feel and hear the crunch. The muscles in his arms screamed in protest, but the cop went down fast, eyes rolling back in his head. Trent turned to the other cop. Cars on the busy street screeched to a halt. People were yelling. *Gotta move fast*, he thought.

He reached the other cop a second too late. The officer raised his gun. Ignoring the potential consequences, Trent slammed his chest against the pudgier, older cop, pinning the gun between them as it went off. Trent felt a rush of cold pain across his left arm as the bullet sliced through his shirt, ripping the top layer of his flesh, drawing blood. It never would have happened had his powers been active. He growled and tackled the officer to the ground. Arms grappled, fingers clawed at chest and shoulders, face and hair, all the while the loaded gun between them, dancing between hands trying to wrest control. Eventually, Trent won out and knocked the pistol from the cop's hand. It fell into the dirt nearby.

He slugged the officer in the side of the head, even as the man clawed at Trent's back, desperate to push him off. And then the cop gripped the Colt from Trent's waistband and drew it between them. He pinned his arm against the cop's wrist and grabbed at the trigger guard as the cop tried to raise the Colt.

And then it went off.

Trent wasn't certain who had pulled the trigger. Both hands were wrapped around it. He wasn't even sure which direction it was pointed. But the widened eyes and weakening arms of the fat cop beneath him told him everything. Trent staggered to his feet.

The wound in the cop's chest gaped, oozing, and the gun fell loose from his grasp and caressed the bullet hole. He brought sticky, red fingers up to his eyes. Tears ran down his cheeks as Trent stumbled backwards.

People nearby yelled. A woman screamed. A man descended from his pickup truck and ran toward the scene of the shooting.

He hadn't meant to kill the Metro officer. The man was an innocent. Trent wasn't a killer.

"Fuck," he said, sprinting for the drainage tunnel, leaving the Colt with the dying policeman.

As he stepped into the cool, dry tunnel, the pickup truck guy hollered in his wake. "Goddamn coward!" the guy yelled. And, "Come back here, you fucker!"

But Trent plowed ahead into the dark, which grew deeper and cooler as he went. Soon, the chasing footsteps faded. Few folks had the stomach to follow someone deep into the tunnels.

Another twenty minutes of jogging and a couple of ninety-degree tunnel turns led Trent to an area that widened and became what many of the tunnel dwellers now referred to as The Church. It was more than that, really. The Church also encompassed a massive graffiti art gallery, where denizens decorated the drab industrial tunnel walls with multicolored murals—some beautiful, some hellish, and some incomprehensible; the works of the mentally unwell, vomiting out their inner fears and tribulations in acrylic paint.

The Gallery and Church had always been a solemn, quiet place. In a way, it was a place of neutrality under the city. Fights seldom broke out here. Graffiti was used to decorate, not for one-upmanship. But today, Trent found the area *too* silent. No voices, no quiet mutterings, nothing. At least, not until he reached The Church proper.

As he rounded the tunnel into the massive cross-join that made up The Church itself, his jaw dropped in disbelief. The elaborately decorated and furnished area was a ruined mess. Benches had been turned to piles of smashed wood. Unlit candles lay scattered about the floor. The tunnel walls looked as though they had been *peeled*, with curlicues of stone jutting out in places. The crude, but functional altar was now just a collection of cracked planks. Behind it, the wooden Jesus— donated by an aboveground church that had been dismantled and bulldozed to make way for a nondenominational mega- church—had been transformed into little more than a mass of broken body parts. The Savior's thorn-crowned head lay on its side a few feet away, wooden eyes focused on the tunnel ceiling.

And all around, dozens of bodies.

Tunnel dwellers, some that Trent had met previously, lay scattered about the place in various states of decay. Some had skeleton showing through maggot-riddled flesh that only barely held to the bones. Others looked as though they had only recently died.

Trent stood, transfixed by the madness. He couldn't bring himself to move, not until he heard moans coming from a pile of corpses near the altar.

Trent rushed over and unceremoniously shoved the top corpse off the heap. Beneath, lay Mary herself, the spiritual leader of the underground refuge, and a true Angel, of the heavenly sort, who had some thousands of years ago committed herself to the betterment of those lost in this place. Trent knew little else of her strange history, and he had never worked up the courage to ask.

She reached up a withered, but still intact arm. Whatever had done this had struggled to work its foulness on one as powerful as the Angel Mary. "Trent," she said, her voice crackling as she spoke. "Trent Hawkins."

He grasped her outstretched hand. "Shit, Mary. What happened here?" Though he already knew.

"Things," she said. "Shadows, like black curtains. White eyes. Only white." She coughed and sputtered. "David," she said.

"Who?"

Mary repeated the name and Trent finally remembered. David was an orphaned child that Mary had taken in recently—a good kid that the state had failed. Mary had become his adoptive mother, of sorts. Trent glanced around the room at the piles of dead bodies. He saw no children among them.

"He's not here," Trent said. "He's not here, Mary."

"David," she said again, punctuating the name with a bloody cough. "Has the Book."

Trent dropped her hand at the mention. "Wait, *you* had it? You had that damn thing this whole time?"

Mary nodded, almost imperceptibly. "Found it. Hiding it. Knew something would come, eventually."

Trent shook his head, confused. "But— David? A kid? Why would a kid have it now?"

"Running," she muttered. Her eyes rolled back in her head. "Keeping it safe. From them."

Trent reached down again and put both hands on the sides on her face. "No, no, no, come back to me, Mary."

Her eyes returned, but only slightly. "They're after him, Trent." Her eyes went away again as she stared off into one of the cross-join tunnels. Her body went limp. Her head dropped to the concrete. "After him..." And her voice trailed off into nothing.

*   *   *

Sweat ran in torrents off Fiamma's body as she limped through downtown Las Vegas. The midday sun beat down and glowed white-hot upon the sidewalk, the glare of which forced her to squint and shield her eyes. She stumbled awkwardly along, her clothes drenched, shedding steam, sweat vaporizing, smelling of burning plastics, hair and skin. Her body was deteriorating, the cells self-immolating within her flesh and organs as her body ate itself alive. She burned and writhed as she walked, screaming in torment.

Only once had she ever come as close as this. As she staggered along, jostling irritated tourists and jaded casino barkers, her mind flooded with unbidden memories of her mother's demise, of the flames licking at her bedroom curtains and the horrid smells of smoke and cooking flesh.

The pain ripped through her insides, unbearable, and she wanted to scream, tried to even, but the sound wouldn't come. It felt like awakening from a dream, only to find herself paralyzed in the bed. She grabbed a telephone pole for support, slipped and hit her knees on the ground, then slid forward, leaving tiny fires in the scrub she brushed against. A cloud of smoke followed her as she regained her footing and lurched toward a convenience store. Crowds of people parted to let her pass.

She half-burst, half-fell into the shop, clutching at her chest with one hand and hung from the door handle with her other. The doorbell wouldn't stop beeping. The pain that had started at her leg now burned in her abdomen and ate at her lungs. She coughed out thick black gouts of smoke. The few people in the shop looked at her, wide-eyed, and backed away.

"Oh shit!" yelled the man behind the cash register as she released her grip on the entrance and tumbled to the floor. "Someone help her!"

But no one did. She looked up, and through the smoke haze pouring from the corners of her eyes, she saw no Samaritans, none willing to offer aid. *Must... keep... moving....* She searched her core for strength, for energy that could be diverted to whatever muscles hadn't yet succumbed to the inferno. She made it to her feet again, took a few steps forward, then collapsed against a shelf of snack foods. The shelf collapsed, spilling bags of chips and candy bars and small rectangular packets of gum. Everywhere that plastic touched her, it melted, birthing noxious fumes.

The customers had seen enough and made haste to leave. The cashier flipped open his cell phone and was yelling at someone on the other end. A crowd gathered in the street, peering cautiously in through the store's glass front.

Fiamma could smell her own flesh cooking and felt melting plastic sticking to her skin, melting, searing. She flailed in the mess of snacks until her blistering, crackling hands came up with protein bars. She jammed the bars against her lips, the plastic fused to her flesh. Two of her front teeth snapped out with the first bite, but she pressed on and ate and ate and ate, one bar after another, her moans becoming wails and then tortured screams as her lungs regained strength and stability.

"Help! Goddammit help me!"

Even at the rate she was eating, she knew she didn't have long. The fire had taken hold, like a building gone up in flames. Her hair was gone, her skull seared bald and ashen. She knew that nothing short of a miracle could save her and she would burn to death from the inside out as the spineless pieces of shit outside the window watched, gazing with wondrous expressions at the freak show demise.

"You *fuckers*," she screamed, her voice cracking, crying, sobbing with every frantic, trembling bite.

She closed her eyes and, for a moment, entertained the fleeting notion that maybe she deserved all this. *Maybe this is my judgment. Maybe this is Hell, right here inside me.* A feeling of calm passed over her as she took a last bite and listened to the sizzling of her own skin as she waited for the end.

Suddenly water came pouring down. Every molecule of it besieged her superheated skin. A lone woman in a red evening gown had run in from off the street and grabbed a water jug from the store refrigerator and opened it over her. Steam billowed up in great clouds as the water hissed against Fiamma's skin, and some of the pain abated.

As soon as the first gallon had run dry, the woman in the evening gown grabbed another water jug from the fridge and rushed back over. Another wash of liquid purity seemed to tear away, with every splash, the nightmares searing Fiamma's flesh. She closed her eyes again and let her mouth hang open as the water sluiced against her burning body.

*   *   *

His footsteps rang out, cold and loud, as his boots clomped against the concrete tunnel floor. He couldn't stop running.

He wouldn't. *A kid*, he thought. *My God, not another one.* He had watched too many children suffer since returning to Vegas, and his thoughts were full of righteous fury at the things that had come unto this world to do this kind of harm—things, he reminded himself, that Celia had loosed upon the mortal coil.

Shit, Celia. First her, then Mary, now this kid. Everyone's dying around me and it's my fault. His chest ached, and not because of the exhausting run. *Is this what I've done to the people near me?* He ran a hand along the tunnel wall as he splashed through puddles of stagnant rainwater. His fingers bounced across jutting curls of torn concrete and exposed metal rebar. The path of the white-eyed shadows, deconstructing the world around them. The path that led to the boy, and to the Book. He hadn't the foggiest idea how he was going to defeat them.

Everything had gone wrong. He felt as though he'd been so close to the Medicine Man, so close to Susan, but now he'd taken a thousand steps back. A mystery man was after him, had put a supernatural assassin on his trail. Celia in the hospital. A pack of Shades on the loose, looking for what might be the most dangerous artifact in existence. And here he was, slogging through the tunnels after them, with his powers drained by Palisade and his angelic dagger lost to that fire-crazed lunatic woman. He didn't even have a gun—he'd left it lying there with the dead Metro officer—and that thought reminded him that he had just killed a cop.

What the hell am I gonna do?

He'd fought Shades before without the dagger. He'd fought Shades whose fate he couldn't turn. But never had he fought a whole group of them with nothing. He faltered and looked back the way he had come.

God, I wish Susan were here. He thought about her wry smile when he told her something crazy. He pictured her raised eyebrow, that expression she made the moment before she'd tell him how it was going to be, before she'd set him straight. She always put him on the right road, showed him the path through the forest, even when he couldn't see it for the trees.

He pictured Susan on the hospital bed after the miscarriage. He never understood how she could smile as she gripped his hand. "It's okay," she'd said, tears still staining her pale white cheeks. "We're still okay, baby. Just you and me."

And then he pictured Celia in the hospital bed, eyes closed, lips parched, hanging open. Not okay. *He* had let things get this far. He blamed himself, his inattention to the girl, and his obsession with Susan. *She's dead, Trent. She's goddamned dead.*

A noise reverberated suddenly off the tunnel walls. Trent strained to listen. A little boy's cries. Screams.

"No," he said out loud, without thinking, before plunging ahead. "Stop it," he shouted. "Leave him alone!"

And then he rounded the corner and saw them, a mass of humanoid figures made of black nothing, standing in a ghostly fog of dying light from a nearby manhole cover. In an instant, their eyes—white orbs with no pupils—shifted imperceptibly to face him as though they had been staring at him all along. He struggled with the thought that maybe they had. He pulled up short and surveyed the scene.

The child, David, lay motionless in a large puddle of trash-strewn muck, surrounded by red. Trent couldn't even make out the boy's features anymore. His face was torn and peeled away. Flesh clung to his bones, withered and tight like a corpse freshly torn from an ancient grave. His clothes were little more than decayed shreds. In the moments between his scream and Trent's arrival, those *things* had sent the child David careening through time, a boy dead and gone ages ago, only not. He was now a thing destroyed, a grime-stained mass of dead flesh, still clutching a small, green leather-bound journal. The Book.

The shade closest to Trent moved then, advancing in stop-motion, never crossing the space between two points so much as altering its position from moment to moment. The thing poured around him and he felt cold and pain and saw his skin aging, pulling tighter to his bones. He felt as though the creature were drawing him, molecule by molecule, into itself, into some other shadowed realm where time moves differently, as his skin constricted around him like a vice. It felt like a moment and an eternity at once.

Trent stood paralyzed by pain. He thought of Celia and Susan and Charlie, and summoned the strength to issue a guttural shout and throw himself into the creature's ethereal form. The creature's body billowed around him, but followed, as Trent smashed against the concrete wall of the tunnel. The shade's ethereal form struck too and it let out a weird, high-pitched staccato chittering. Trent leapt backwards out of its deadly haze and faced down the group. His skin relaxed.

How the hell can I kill these things? It's like fighting smoke.

And then he noticed that as they moved toward him, the white-eyed Shades avoided a slanting beam of light from a sewer grate in the ceiling. He remembered the Render from all those months ago, atop the Luxor. He remembered how it thrashed beneath his fingers as he jammed it into the brightest light in the state of Nevada. The screams as it burned away. Susan's voice deep within the noise.

Light. I need light.

Trent stepped backwards and fumbled for his lighter. He had promised to quit smoking, but he still carried the lighter and an occasional pack. Force of habit. He found the lighter in his left pocket but it slipped through his soaked fingers and into the grime at his feet. He dropped to his knees and splashed in the fetid water, searching for the lighter as the Shades leapt closer and closer. His skin tightened again—the pulling sensation increasing with every passing moment.

And then he felt metal, pulled up the lighter and thumbed the wheel. It sparked, then died. No luck. The Shades came closer. His vision warped in pinpoints like a bad drug trip. He thumbed the lighter again. A tiny flame came to life at the top.

The shade that had surrounded him backed away in aversion to the flame. "That's right," he yelled. "Get back!" He waved the lighter, summoning the bravery to get back to his feet. He advanced on the Shades. The pack meandered and slid around, encircling him. "Oh, shit," he mumbled.

And then the chittering began in earnest. With every passing second, as Trent frantically waved the lighter, the noise grew louder. Sharp, chirping staccato ate at his brain.

His eyes watered. His head ached. The skin and muscles of his face tightened painfully.

"Get back," he tried, weaker now.

He lurched at the nearest shade with the outstretched lighter, but slipped and fell. The lighter popped loose from his fingers and splashed back into the water.

No, please, he thought. *Please, I can't go out like this. I can't let her down. She needs me, dammit.*

And then, as death seemed imminent, he heard Louis Bird's voice, behind him somewhere, yelling something in another language, rustling papers. The language sounded like Latin to Trent, but *weightier*. The chant ended with a booming yell of some strange word. And then nothing.

"Shit," said Louis.

Trent closed his eyes as his body slumped into the foul-smelling water. The Shades would kill them both. He wondered if he'd see Susan on the other side, or if the Prince would torture him for eternity. He suspected the latter—he'd done enough to piss the Prince off. The darkness circled around him once more and he felt the tightening of skin, the strange sensation of *going away*.

Louis rustled some more and yelled out a few more arcane words. Still nothing. Trent heard the little man cursing and flinging papers.

Then Trent's hearing went altogether, and his vision. Nothingness encroached as the creatures folded their shadowy structures around him. The damp ground went away. He waited for death.

Light came instead.

A searing, burning light cut through the darkness enveloping Trent, and his vision returned in time for him to see brilliance wash over everything, illuminating the water and the grime-covered tunnel walls, pouring through the Shades like white razors, blurred by speed.

Louis yelled something, screamed really.

Then quiet. Trent lay there, stunned. The white orbs, the feeling of pulling away, gone. Only Louis Bird's splashing footsteps and astonished mumblings of victory remained.

"Did you fuckin' see that?" Louis whistled as he reached Trent and extended a hand to help him up. "Man, oh man. I can't believe it. Two of the scripts were duds, but that third one... Shit, I wasn't even halfway through." His words were nearly breathless. "To be honest, I didn't think it would be so easy. Hell, I didn't even think it would work, but—"

Trent held up a hand to cut off the rambling. "Thanks," he said, and grabbed Louis' proffered hand and climbed weakly to his feet. Filthy water had soaked him to the core and dripped off every part of him. "Guess we're even now, huh?"

Louis smiled and slapped Trent on the back. "Just glad I could help."

Trent looked around. No Shades to be seen. He walked slowly to the bloodied corpse of the boy, reached down, and pried the green journal from the child's fingers. Then he passed a palm over the remains of David's face and closed the one intact eye. He stared at the child for a moment as he pocketed the Book. Then, without another thought, he scooped up the boy's limp body and slung it over one shoulder.

"What the hell are you doing, Trent?"

"Boy needs a proper burial."

"Now?"

"You got a better time?"

Louis shrugged.

Trent looked Louis in the eye. "Who are you? Really?"

Louis chuckled nervously. "That's a popular question today."

Trent used his free hand to gesture at the filthy tunnel. "You wanna stay down here? Start talking."

"Okay, okay..." Louis sighed. "You ever heard of the Knights Templar?"

Trent raised an eyebrow. "Secret society, right? Like the Freemasons?"

Louis rolled his eyes. "Not like the Freemasons. Bunch of losers in their stuffy lodges with their idiotic secret handshakes. No, we're nothing like them—"

"So you're one of the Knights Templar, then? What does that mean?"

"We have our hands in everything. But I'm not even supposed to tell you that much."

Trent shrugged and walked away from Louis, back down the sewer corridor with the dead boy slung over his shoulder. "I don't know what you did back there, but thanks," he said without turning around.

Louis followed him. "I don't really know either. I grabbed whatever scripts I could get before the apartment burned down—"

Trent stopped, but didn't turn. "Your apartment—?"

"Burned down, yeah. That damn girl again."

"What did she want?"

"You."

Trent said nothing.

"Guess she didn't find you, huh?"

"She found me. Her hunt's over now. I left her for Charlie to deal with." But he hated the words even as he said them. He knew his false confidence was a lie. He felt like he'd thrown Charlie under the bus and he suspected Fiamma wouldn't go down quite so easily.

"Charlie's dead."

Trent's shoulders slumped and the boy's head rolled gently against his stained shirt collar. He turned. "You saw—"

"Yeah. I got there as the place was burning down. Ran inside to see what I could do. Only found this note in the old man's pocket." He fished in his pants and pulled out a crumpled piece of paper. "He was already dead. She smashed his skull in. Dunno why she didn't search the place. Just burned it down and left, I guess. Must've been in a hurry."

"You weren't there to help," Trent said quietly. "You were there to plunder the remains."

Without asking, he snatched the note from Louis and unfolded it. It read, simply, "Mary called. Shades in tunnels." He crumpled it and threw it down into the muck. His teeth ground together as he thought about Charlie and Mary. Both dead. His fault. He'd just lost his only remaining friends. He turned away. He didn't want Louis to see his tears.

Nowhere

"Over here," calls Salvatore. "We can hide."

He and Susan manage to stay one step ahead of the Prince's hunters, but only barely. Now they stand waist-deep in the murky waters of the Great Swamp, near its edge. In the distance they can see the unchanging silhouette of Dis, the *grigorim* city, and it looms on the black horizon like an iron stain.

Susan stares at it for a moment, ignoring Salvatore's call.

"Susan," he insists. "We must take refuge for now."

"For now?" She turns on him, fists balled, anger dancing on her face. "And when does 'now' end? There is no time here. You said that before. And the Prince knows everywhere we go. The Prince *is* everywhere; he's the ground we walk on and the water that fills this swamp. What good will hiding do?"

"It is true. Time does not exist here. But it does exist in your world, the real world. And there are places in Abaddon where the boundary is thin. Places where time leaks through."

He gestures at a darkened thicket of swamp, an interstitial pocket amidst the floating, moaning souls and warped spire-trees. A place that had gone unnoticed to Susan before but now, as she gazes upon it directly, she can see.

"A cave?"

"A hole in the fabric of the realms. They are called Dream Caves."

"I've never seen one."

"You never knew to look."

"What is it?"

Salvatore motions for her to follow him, his spirit form wavering, both distinct and indistinct, lurching through space as he moves. "Dream Caves are very, very old," he says as he steps into the darkened grove and then vanishes from Susan's sight. She hears his voice still. "The oldest things in all of Abaddon. Come on, child. It's okay."

She follows his path and finds herself in a; a new memory returned to her by this most plain yet mysterious of locales, a memory of limestone caverns visited with her family as a child. Salvatore stands in front of her, silhouetted against the pitch black behind him, like the mouth of some giant beast threatening to devour him. Susan stares down the beast's gaping maw. "How can this place be *old*? There is no time in Abaddon."

"And that is why the Caves can remain old. They were here long before the Prince, long before Abaddon formed around them, like a tree that grows ever so slowly to encompass a stone." He gestures at the barren, rocky interior of the cave. "Time still moves here, though it is confused, distorted. But unlike the rest of the Realms of Shadow, the

Caves *were* and they still *are*. And that is why they remain." Salvatore sits on a nearby boulder, a collapsed chunk of the cave wall. "We should stay here and let some time pass, allow the Realms to flow by and with them, the hunters that track us. After they have moved on, we'll head for the *grigorim* city."

Susan ponders this for a moment. She cannot believe that the Prince might have aberrations in his perfect nothingness, his ever-changing wasteland. "How does the Prince permit this to be? Why does he allow these Caves in his realm?"

"He has no choice." Salvatore smiles, an expression that looks both eerie and grotesque on his protean face. "He can attempt to hide them, to obfuscate their locations, to forbid his minions from them. But he cannot remove them. His cyclones cannot sweep the Dream Caves away. Because they are not truly part of the Prince. He cannot sense them, cannot find them without sending his hunters to look. The Caves are anchors in the ocean of nothing, and at the end of their chain lies your world, the realm of the real."

Susan's eyes go wide. Can it be true? Do the Caves truly touch the real world, Trent's world? She longs to see him again, to touch his hand. She moves past Salvatore, deeper into the cave. She approaches the endless dark, lurking at the back of the cave, with nerves steeled and hopes afire, that they might light her way.

"Do not be deceived," comes Salvatore's voice from behind. "These Caves are but anchors, not doors. All you will find there are dreams of the real, momentary contacts with the other world. You are here now, Susan. You are dead. There is no journey to be taken beyond this place. Just memories cast as shadows against dark walls."

Susan says nothing.

The dark tunnel continues for some distance, deeper than Susan expects, deeper even than seems possible. As she descends, she only glances back once and notes that the light from the mouth of the cave, where Salvatore remains, has dwindled to a point. She steels her resolve and continues on.

The tunnel abruptly opens into something more. A cavern of sorts, with a mysterious dim light that radiates from nowhere; light that feels *old* somehow, and Susan shivers as the cold breeze in the cavern ruffles her hair and explores the folds of her dress. The air here feels thick, almost stifling, though there is no heat. It is as though time itself is sluggish in this place, and Susan can intimately sense its passage.

She moves about the unusual cavern. She runs her fingertips across the slick black rock, more glass than stone, like obsidian worn away by the motion of the air itself, carved into swirling and wraithlike patterns that dance in intricate whorls across the walls. She notes the smell of aged dust and strains to hear the faintest murmurs of voices, of birds and creatures, rushing water like white noise though there is no liquid nearby. She remembers watching birds from her apartment balcony, in a city whose name she cannot remember. And as the sounds grow louder to her listening, she begins to see that the walls are alive and beneath the glassy barrier move shadows, silhouettes trapped within the carved black, dreams dancing in the void.

"Susan," comes a voice and she spins to locate the source. But even as her sight falls on a dark pane, the shadows behind it twist and warp and become something other and the voice fades into unintelligible echo. Then, "Susan," again, louder this time, and she spins the other direction and sees a shape dancing in the dark and she rushes and puts her hand against the wall and sees the wavering silhouette of a shape she could never forget.

"Trent."

Her words ring out against the glass walls.

And as she thinks of him, as her thoughts turn to daydreams, the walls move with more purpose, the silhouettes writhe in more pronounced step and she realizes that the Dream Cave responds to her wonderings, to her thoughts. She focuses on Trent and watches his shadow slide across the black glass. She sees his past and his future. She cries.

"No. No, it can't be. Please, someone, help him. He's dying. Oh, God."

But God does not answer her, nor does anyone else and she watches, helpless, as her husband's silhouette crumples to a flat line beneath globs of shadow. She watches him struggling but failing and his shape becomes punctured by thin lines like porcupine needles jutting from every edge and vertex. She decides that something must be done.

There is no journey beyond this place. She remembers Salvatore's words, but she does not heed his warning, not anymore. She needs to see Trent, to help him, to banish the lightless assailants, and so she screams, at the top of her lungs, her throat raw and screeching and burning with pain and anger. "Let there be *light*."

And there is light.

A searing, blinding intensity breaks across the walls, scorching the black glass surface to white, like coal turned pale after a raging fire and the Dream Cave rings out with an ear-splitting screech. The walls crack. First, thin veins like a spider's web, spread quickly from the black where she had seen Trent's falling shape. Then, the lines grow thicker, denser, until irregular shards of smooth rock fall to the cavern floor, shattering like a black mirror, and in every one of them she sees a reflection of a woman in a billowing white gown, her face a mask of fury.

In moments, the walls are rough stone, unadorned by the mirror-like obsidian, and the floor is a ringing mess of shattered fragments and a thick grey fog begins to seep from cracks in the rock. The floor, the walls, the cavern ceiling. The fog spreads quickly and the cave rumbles and quakes. Susan turns and runs back the way she had come.

As she ascends the collapsing tunnel, desperately scrambling to reach the cave mouth, she hears Salvatore's voice ahead of her, both angry and terrified at once.

"What have you done, girl?" he shouts. "What have you *done?*"

6

"THOUGHT YOU'D BE RUSHING BACK to see your little girl," said Louis as his shovel crunched into the muddy ground. Light rain had descended on the region. Louis' t-shirt was soaked and his jeans and thinning hair were plastered down over his forehead. He kept blinking as water ran into his eyes. "This sucks, you know."

"Shut up and dig," snapped Trent. He glanced at the dead boy lying on the ground nearby, wrapped in his blood-soaked dress shirt. Rain trickled down Trent's bare chest, washing away the remaining blood. His skin ached, pocked with pinhole wounds. Every movement hurt, but he jammed his own shovel down into the mud just the same.

As he dug he wondered, for the millionth time that day, if he was being a fool. Was Louis right? He hadn't rushed back to the hospital after leaving the tunnels; hadn't rushed to check on Celia. Instead, he had recovered his bike (luckily the Metro hadn't connected it to the shooting of the officer, thanks to its distance from the crime scene) and then followed

Louis' ragged pickup truck to a secluded chunk of desert on the edge of town where they could give the boy a proper burial. He hated himself for it.

"Dammit," he said, as he sent the shovel squelching into the desert mud for the hundredth time.

"Hey, I didn't say anything. I'm just digging here."

"Not you," said Trent. "This fucking day."

Louis stopped digging and leaned on his shovel. He cocked his head to one side and gave Trent a sad look. "Hey, man. I'm not so bad, I swear. Lemme finish this up. I can do the burial and then meet you at the hospital. You go see to your kid, alright?"

Trent shook his head and stabbed the ground again, jamming the shovel down further into the mud with his boot.

Louis frowned. "Come on, Trent. You hang this heavy weight on your shoulders for what? You think the boy's gonna care which one of us buries him—?"

Trent cut him off. "Don't talk to me about heavy weights, you little shit. I'm carrying more than you can imagine."

"I know what you're carrying," said Louis. "I've been following you for years."

"What?"

A long silence passed, broken only by the sound of rain pattering against the hard-packed desert surface.

Finally, Trent broke the quiet with a hissed command. "You tell me everything, Mr. Bird. Now."

Louis grinned. "You think I'm some sort of villain. Like *I* made this happen." He pointed at the boy's corpse. "He's dead because that was his path—"

"He's dead because I got there too late, because I—"

Louis shot him the finger. "You, you, you. Everything's about you, isn't it? *You* need to save Celia. *You* need to be the big hero. *You* need to win at poker. *You* need to bury the kid. *You* fucking get to bring your wife back from the dead, even when nobody else gets that option. To everyone else on this planet, Susan Hawkins is dead. You hear me? Dead. Just like my little brother." He lifted the shovel and hurled it at Trent. It landed in the mud at his feet. "I can't go back in time. I don't get to go ask the Prince to give my brother a second chance. Susan is *gone*, Trent. Just like everybody else that dies. But to you it's... what? An inconvenience? Just an obstacle on your mindless goddamn quest?" He looked away, shoulders heaving. He stared out into the desert. "Fuck you, man."

Louis was a mouthy little jerk, but he was right. Trent glared and squeezed the handle of the shovel so hard he could feel wood splinters pressing into his palm.

Louis stared at the rain-shrouded city. "You wanna know about me?" he asked, without turning back around. "I'm your personal stalker. Paid to follow you and record. I know where you've been, what you've done, who you've talked to every day for the past five and a half years, since the day you fell out of that plane. My life for half a decade has been defined by yours. And you know what? You know what conclusion I've come to?" He looked back over his shoulder, his face sad, soaked with rainwater. "I think you're a selfish piece of shit."

Trent hung his head and stared at the boy's corpse in its dripping cotton-shirt shroud. He thought about Celia, about all of the people he had saved from Zamagiel on the night of the Blizzard. He thought about his wife. Dead. He sighed and released his shovel. It fell with a clang atop the one already at his feet.

"I'm gonna go see my kid," he said, and then turned and walked through the scrub brush until he reached his motorcycle. He climbed aboard, brought it to life, and roared off down the muddy path back into Las Vegas, leaving Louis Bird standing there in the mud and rain with two shovels and a little boy's corpse.

*   *   *

Gadreel tapped his cane in a steady rhythm on the sidewalk outside Obscura Books. His booted feet splashed through puddles of rainwater. He hunched slightly, keeping the brim of his hat low so that the pouring rain might run down off the front like a waterfall, through which he viewed the door to the small antique bookshop. He stopped at the threshold and made a small gesture with his hand. The doorknob turned and the door swung open with a bang. He stepped inside.

"Vretil!" A few people were in the bookstore, all of whom looked up at the sudden intrusion. When he heard no immediate response to his call, he said, "Or I guess it's Vladimir now, right? Ain't that what you're calling yourself these days?"

A thin, frail-looking man in an immaculate black suit stepped out from one of the aisles of shelves. He had a stack of books in his arms and a look of suspicion on his face. "Why are you here, Gadreel?" he hissed.

Gadreel took a step forward, extended his cane and pushed the stack of books out of Vladimir's grip. They tumbled to the floor. One of the spines cracked.

He made a grand gesture at the bookshelves around him. "You've filled these shelves with all sorts of pointless crap. Antiquities, you call 'em. But everything comes to an end, old friend." He smiled. "Our arrangement goes back a thousand years. But lately...? Hell, you couldn't keep the mortal in check for even six months." He shook his head.

Concerned, a woman and her young daughter shuffled past, toward the shop exit. Gadreel's cane whipped out sideways, blocking their path. He gestured with his free hand and they stepped quietly backwards, eyes wide, to rejoin the others watching from amidst the stacks.

Gadreel continued. "Let's call it what it is: you've failed." He poked Vladimir in the chest with the cane. "You failed to rein the man in, to keep him occupied. You think I wouldn't come for a visit? We had an agreement."

Vladimir narrowed his yellow eyes. "An agreement? Your agreements are as hollow as your soul, Gadreel. I did what you asked because I thought it was right. I set Hawkins upon the Shades. I've kept the Prince distracted for you and your ridiculous prophecy, just in case. You cannot suggest that I failed to do my part."

"He should still be out there, hunting. Now the Prince is chucking more of his scouts our way. And your boy has hung up his hat. It leaves me in an awkward position, Vretil."

"He was never my responsibility."

"I beg to differ."

Vladimir stepped forward and shoved away Gadreel's outstretched cane. "You think you can enter my domain and threaten me? Here? No matter how arrogant you've become, you still can't break the rules. No angel or demon has claim to destroy another. Not until the day of Armageddon. And even then, I can't see a filthy *grigorim* like you—one of the lust-fallen—laying challenge to one of us." He sneered. "I could turn you to ash where you stand. Get out of my shop!" He pointed an old, withered finger at the front door.

As if on cue, the door opened and the bell above it jingled. A wiry, bespectacled man stepped through, immaculately composed in a grey business suit and sky-blue tie. He closed and tied shut an umbrella as he walked in, and then looked up and smiled genially at the gathering of demons and mortal onlookers.

Gadreel glanced at him and then turned to look at Vladimir again. "Vretil, meet Edward Palisade."

Palisade walked calmly across the shop, stopped inches from Vladimir, and stared him in the eyes. The old man shrank back a step, as if retreating from the thin man's terrible gaze.

"Wha—? How—? I don't— I don't understand—"

Gadreel chuckled and placed a hand on Palisade's shoulder, whose gaze remained on the old man in the black suit.

"This is a fascinating man," said Gadreel. "And you know where I found him?" He patted Palisade's shoulder. "In prison. Can you believe that? A *gibbori* in prison. Been there since his eighteenth fucking birthday, multiple life sentences. Damn shame. Apparently, like his *grigorim* ancestors, Mr. Palisade had... well, let's just say he had desires that were out of step with refined culture... and a powerful gift." Gadreel chuckled. "That kind of power trapped in a jail cell? The empowered tied up by the ignorant. Wasteful, really."

Palisade advanced on Vladimir, who shuffled backwards and bumped into the end cap of a bookshelf. Dusty old paperbacks tumbled to the floor in a heap.

"But more important," Gadreel continued. "Mr. Palisade's gift is the most unique I've seen."

Vladimir snarled as the wiry man stepped closer. "This is enough!" he shouted and thrust a hand forward, palm open, fingers crooked like claws. Nothing happened. His snarl vanished, replaced by a mask of utter terror.

"See, old friend, this *gibbori* can deaden powers. And not just the weaker magicks. He can even mess up demons like you."

Vladimir, panicked now, tried to skirt around the bookshelf to his back, but slipped on a fallen book. He landed on his backside with a thump, then grabbed a nearby shelf to regain his standing, but only managed to pull the shelf from its moorings. A cascade of encyclopedic volumes collapsed atop his legs.

"Gadreel, you've lost your wits," he cried. "If he is what you say, then he's as dangerous to you as I. Call him off. You can't do this to me."

"We have an arrangement, Palisade and I. I keep him away from the law, give him the things he desires, and he does what I need. You had Trent Hawkins, but you failed to keep the War idling. You failed to buy me the leverage I needed. Now I've brought another gifted child to your doorstep to end you. We can't have the Prince finding out about us, can we?"

"Trent will come after you, Gadreel. When he finds out the truth—when he discovers who you really are—he'll show you no mercy. When he realizes you were merely using him to disrupt the Prince's plans for your own ambitions, he'll—"

Palisade glanced at his master and smiled as he fidgeted with his blue tie. Gadreel returned the grin. "He'll what, Vretil? Destroy me like he did Zamagiel?" He laughed. "I *expect* Hawkins to show up. I've made sure of that. He's gonna bring me Raziel's Book. And Edward here has already made sure that Trent will die, just like you're about to. After the Doombringer's mortal form goes cold, I'll find a way to extract that power of his. I'll take his strange power and regain my former glory. Then I'll end that stupid child of Zamagiel's too, and prevent whatever foul thing she's about to give birth to. The Prince will be forced to reckon with me, then."

"I beg you, Gadreel, stop this! No good can come of your alliance with the Prince. He cannot become a ruler of this world. He will not grant you what you seek. The Prophecy that *you* foretold, of which you could see only a fragment— You only saw the last piece. We have other parts, from Baraqel. The child must be allowed to live—"

Gadreel snarled. "I know more than you think. The kid's giving birth to one-third of the black trinity. The Prince's hunters have already started lookin' for Raziel's Book. Trent's the last third. I'd hoped to stave this off for longer, let the Prince think his plan was still in action, but because of you—" He poked Vladimir with the cane. "Our ace has run. He's off to find his own road to the Prince. But we're not done yet. The delay has made the Prince angry, made him desperate. Once I get the book and kill the mortals, the Prophecy will be broken. The Prince'll have no choice but to give me what I ask if he still wants his invasion. But..." he said, twirling his cane, "your role in all of this is done. You're no longer needed."

"No," said Vladimir. "Please, no."

But Gadreel ignored his protestations, turned his back, and walked back the way he had come. He heard Vladimir's screams turn to choking gurgles, then the quick snicking sound of Palisade's switchblade as it punctured the old man's throat. A murmur of blood, the quiet gasps and whimpers of the nearby onlookers, then the sound of Palisade's knife clicking shut.

"What shall I do with them?" asked the wiry preacher with a calm, pleasant tone.

Gadreel turned and surveyed the mortal bystanders, purposely avoiding any glance at the fallen demon's body. He waved a hand in a dismissive fashion. "Whatever you want," he replied. "But don't take too long. And don't let any of them leave here alive."

"Oh," said Palisade, his voice carrying an edge of malicious satisfaction. "I wouldn't worry about that." He loosened his tie, slipped it over his head and let it fall to the floor. He began to unbutton his shirt. "I'll make their deaths quick. Once I'm done with them."

Gadreel stepped back across the threshold and onto the sidewalk outside Obscura Books. The bell jingled as he carefully closed the door behind him, muffling the bloodcurdling screams.

*   *   *

Trent grumbled, and parked the Ducati on the sidewalk in front of the hospital Children's Wing. The rain had picked up and the streets ran with thin rivers that pooled in the low places, leaving deep puddles for pedestrians to slosh through. It didn't rain like this often in Las Vegas, but when it did, it pissed off just about everyone, Trent included. He shut off the motor, dismounted and stepped right into an oil-topped puddle.

He'd stopped by the house briefly to grab a shirt, since he'd left his dress shirt wrapped around the dead boy. The only thing he could find was a white t-shirt with some obscure band logo on the back. Now, after a twenty-minute ride across the city, his t-shirt was soaked, along with his grey cowboy hat, the brim crumpled from being sat on during the drive. His jeans clung to his legs like plastic wrap and felt about as comfortable. He'd also picked up a gun, an old Desert Eagle .50 he'd stashed under his bed for emergencies. He could feel the cool steel sticking to his wet skin where it was lodged in his waistband. In his left hand he carried the Book.

He walked through the sliding glass doors and into the Children's Wing. As he stood in the crowded elevator, water dripping from him into a puddle at his feet, Trent felt like he hadn't yet seen a light at the end of the tunnel. And to top it off, a strange warmth was emanating from the Book. It seeped into his fingers and travelled up his arm. He didn't like it. He'd seen the foul tome's contents once before and had no trust for the thing or what it contained. But he'd made a promise to Celia, and if this could bring her back....

The elevator dinged as its doors opened and he filed out with the others. He strode down the hall to Celia's hospital room and pushed the door open quietly and...

Nothing.

Empty.

A portly nurse making the bed looked up at him. "Help you?" she asked.

"Yeah," he said, his voice trembling with barely-controlled panic. "Where's the little girl that's supposed to be here?"

The nurse raised an eyebrow. "The teenager? Her grandfather checked her out. Said her father had found a private hospital in L.A. for her."

"I'm her father."

The nurse stuttered at first, then said, "Well, I... umm... I'm sure it's just a misunderstanding. You should..." She trailed off, confused.

"What's up?" said Louis behind him. The pudgy man walked up and stood next to Trent, still dressed in the same sopping mud-smeared clothes. He was carrying a gym bag.

"They lost Celia."

"What? How do you lose someone in a coma?"

"Ramón took her."

"Who's Ramón?"

Trent grabbed Louis by the shirt collar and led him away from the confused nurse to a secluded spot near the elevators. "You tell me, Louis. You've been following me all these years. Who *is* Ramón? Why's he run off with my kid?"

Louis dropped the duffel bag and knelt to unzip it. He produced a manila envelope full of photos and rifled through them. He pulled a photo from the stack and held it up for Trent to see: a picture of Ramón.

"This the guy you're talking about?"

"Yeah."

Louis blanched. "You haven't been trusting him, have you?"

"Who the hell is he, Louis?"

"Fuck, man, I thought you knew. That's the leader of the *grigs*." When Trent's expression didn't change, he added, "Gadreel."

Trent's heart leapt inside his chest. He staggered backwards and dropped into a chair. His thoughts swirled and writhed.

"I mean, you were at his freakin' mansion last night," Louis continued. "You tellin' me you didn't know him and your Ramón were the same guy?"

Trent's mouth hung open. *If Ramón is Gadreel, then he knows about the Medicine Man. He's been keeping me occupied. He set me up to lose the poker game. He set Palisade on me. And the fire-girl.*

"He's been playing me like a fiddle," Trent said, mumbling. "Holy shit." His eyes widened and his lips turned up at the corners into a grim snarl. He drew his Desert Eagle and headed for the elevator. The nurse let out a startled yelp.

Louis stepped between him and the elevator doors. "Whoa," he said, holding out his hands. "Hold on there, cowboy."

Trent shoved him aside and jammed the elevator call button with the barrel of the gun.

"Look, man," said Louis. "There's some shit you need to know about your buddy there. First off, he's got a chunk of a prophecy that we've been trying to get for years, decades really. And he's been trying to stop it, we think."

Trent looked up, brow furrowed. "Yeah, he's told me as much. Also said he was a prophet in Heaven, before he fell. A scribe."

Louis shrugged. "Yeah, probably. But most prophets never get the full story. They conjure up a piece of it and hope it's the right piece. Hell, the chunk we got is from a crazy monk in the fifteenth century who got kicked by a horse and wrote all this stuff down in a couple hours." A grin broke across Louis' face. "Died the next day. Actually, it's a funny story—"

Trent raised a hand to stop him short. "What's he doing with Celia?"

"That's why we need his chunk of the Prophecy." Louis frowned. "We don't understand half of what he's been up to. We just know what *you're* supposed to do."

"What's that?"

"Kill him."

Trent hung his head. "I can't."

"'Course you can. You took out Zamagiel, just like our prophecy said you would. Gadreel's next."

"I kill him, and then what?"

"Dunno. That's where our chunk ends and his begins."

Trent looked Louis straight in the eyes. "I can't kill him, Louis." He shook his head. "I can't."

Louis shook his head. "Why not?"

"He's got my soul."

"What?"

"My soul. When the plane crashed, he got my soul and I got his powers. If I kill him, I die."

"You sure that's where you got your powers? Prophecy doesn't say anything about—"

"Just quit it with the goddamned prophecy already!"

"Look, Hawkins. I'm not even supposed to be telling you any of this stuff. Hell, I'm breaking every rule of my order just by talking to you."

"Then why are you?"

Louis chuckled and stared at the ceiling for a moment. Finally, his gaze returned to meet Trent's. "Honestly? 'Cause I'm fucking tired of it. That fire-chick burned down my whole apartment. Decades of work gone, unique copies of ancient manuscripts up in smoke. I ain't got nothing left, man. If it'll make a difference, I'll help you with this."

Trent hung his head again. "How can you help me? You've already told me everything you know."

"Sure, everything *I* know. But I can take you to somebody who knows a whole lot more."

"Who?"

"Ever heard of the Medicine Man?"

"You've met him?"

"Well, no." Louis shook his head from side to side. "But I know *of* him. And I'm pretty sure I know where they keep him."

"They?"

"Yeah, the *cherubim*. Got him locked up tight, right here in Vegas."

The Medicine Man! If Louis was telling the truth, if he really knew where the Medicine Man was.... Trent shook his head. He thought again about Celia, lying there in the hospital bed. He pictured Ramón carrying her limp body in his arms, grinning maliciously, the giant cross tattoo on his forearm gleaming beneath his rolled-up shirtsleeves. "No," he said. "You were right before, back there in the desert. I've gotta rescue Celia. The Medicine Man can wait."

"But you said if you kill Gadreel—"

"If he does have my soul, if he's been telling the truth, then I die. But I'll take him with me. If that happens, you make sure Celia is safe. Protect her, Louis."

"I dunno, Trent. Maybe the Medicine Man can help—"

Trent shook his head. The elevator dinged as he popped the clip from the Desert Eagle, checked the bullet count, and then reseated it.

"Maybe you're right," he said. "Maybe the damn prophecy is right. I'll kill him, then you take me to see the Medicine Man. Maybe Ramón's been lying all along about my soul." He looked at Louis and smiled, then took off his grey cowboy hat, the hat that had once belonged to Ramón/Gadreel, before the Crash. "Demon named Ramón once gave me some good advice." He slicked back his wet hair. "He told me that demons always lie."

*   *   *

Fiamma's head ached like someone was pounding on it with a sledgehammer. She tried to make out her surroundings, but saw only fuzzy blobs. Her skin ached and every movement shot searing flares of pain along her nerves. She slumped back down onto the bed where she lay.

"Don't try to get up, not yet," came a sharp British accent.

A woman's voice. The woman in the red dress? A red blob moved closer, then reached out and touched Fiamma's forehead with something cold, wet. It dulled the pain a tiny bit.

"Time for more plasma," said the woman as she retrieved a straw-colored blob from what appeared to be a small table.

"Plasma?" Fiamma's voice was weak and her throat felt parched and burned. She broke into a series of hacking coughs.

"Your organs are flooded," the woman explained. "You burned through nearly all your blood proteins. Osmotic pressure is gone. This'll help balance you out."

A tube touched Fiamma's lips and she began to drink. She couldn't taste the fluid, but the oily consistency made her feel nauseous. She spit and turned her head away.

"Stop fussing" said the woman. "Your liver is nearly gone and you cannot produce enough of this on your own. You will simply have to bear with me here." She brought the tube back to Fiamma's lips. "You should be glad that you're so different from the rest of your kind. This wouldn't work for anyone else."

"No," whispered Fiamma. "No, I can't." Her vision grew a little clearer and she could make out the woman's features. Red, low-cut dress with ample cleavage. Blonde hair in a bob cut. A serious expression. The table next to the bed was covered in plastic bags filled with fluid, each bearing a drinking tube. Most of the liquids were yellowish but a few were a deep red.

"Blood?" she said as she looked at the bags.

The woman smiled and held up a finger. "Ah, ah," she said, like a mother scolding a child. "First, the plasma, then the blood. One thing at a time, my dear."

Fear ripped through Fiamma like a tornado and she struggled to pull herself from the bed, pushing through the agony that accompanied every muscle movement. She'd gotten halfway to sitting when something *caught*. She was tethered to the bed somehow. She couldn't move her head forward any further. She looked frantically at her arms, her legs. No shackles, no ties. She pulled again, tugging at the invisible cord that held her back. It wouldn't budge and she fought to turn her head, to see what was attached to it, but she couldn't even do that.

"What have you done to me?" she said, her voice wavering as she tried to achieve a yell.

The woman in the red dress frowned and retrieved something from the table of fluid sacks. She held it up in the glaring white light for Fiamma to see: a rusty nail with a blood-red hue. "I've used one of these to nail your shadow to the bed, my dear. I'm sure you have a terrible headache, and I apologize. But I couldn't have you running off on me."

"You're insane!" Fiamma struggled one last time before flopping back down onto the bed, eyes wide with terror.

The woman chuckled. "You should feel honored. I have only a few of these nails left and I chose to use one on you. Now lie back and relax."

"Who are you?" she whispered, as the woman moved closer to put the slippery tube into her mouth.

"You may call me Tricia," she answered offhandedly as she worked the bag of fluid, alternately squeezing and releasing in order to force Fiamma to drink. "That's a good girl. Drink up."

Fiamma's stomach lurched and convulsed, but with every gulp of plasma that sluiced down her throat, she felt some of her strength returning, though the headache persisted.

"You *nailed* my shadow down? That's not possible." Her voice had already gained some clarity and strength.

Tricia didn't look up from the small table, where she was preparing another bag of plasma. She nodded toward the nail again, its red surface gleaming. "They work on anyone or anything," she said. "Special nails, forged in Hell, back when the foundries were operating. They anchor your shadow to this world, to a single point. There were blades, too, but I haven't seen one in a long time. A shallow cut would cause pain, like the punishments of an eternity in Hell. A deep wound could banish any shade, angel, or demon straight back to Abaddon."

Fiamma blinked, barely comprehending this new situation. "What are you? A demon?"

"Succubus." Tricia winked. "But close. A daughter of Belial to be precise; a child of the last Lord of the Realms of Fury. Your kind calls it Hell." Her voice had suddenly taken on a tone of admiration.

She stared at Fiamma for a moment, smiling, then returned to her work with the plasma. "Last bag, and then we'll move on to the blood."

Fiamma sucked hungrily on the tube, the feeling of immediate recuperation buoyed her desire for the stuff.

"Good, good," said Tricia. The pink flesh of her breasts squeezed together as she leaned closer, and Fiamma couldn't help but analyze her form, the long eyelashes and blood red lips, the smooth curve of her waist, wrapped tight in the form-fitting dress. Fiamma caught a whiff of ash and kerosene as Tricia leaned in to kiss her on the forehead.

The kiss burned against her skin, but differently. This burn felt good. Somehow, she *remembered* the sensation, though she knew this woman—this creature—had never kissed her before.

Tricia moved away and prepared one of the bags of blood. "You're of rare lineage, my dear," she said, as she worked. "And this blood is quite unique, like yours." She cut open the top of the bag with a knife, and as soon as air had entered, the blood turned as black as molasses. Tricia looked up and winked. "Appetizing, eh?"

Fiamma hesitated as Tricia moved closer with the bag. The black blood had already crawled up the tube and a drop of it lingered on the tip. "Are you sure—?"

Tricia moved the tube close and put one hand behind Fiamma's head. The first gulp sent her into violent convulsions and dense smoke rose from beneath her as she drank.

"Drink of your bloodline, child of Belial," said Tricia with a soothing tone. "Drink and be strong. There is much still to be done. You'll be reborn soon."

Nowhere

Breathless, they run, with the Prince's hunters screeching in the distance, sweeping across the dead land, birds of prey with mouths full of razors and minds of eternal night, predators that do not rest, nor pause, nor have they ever given quarter to their prey. Behind them, the Dream Cave crumbles and falls, the first to be shattered by a mortal, and the Prince now knows that he must capture Susan Hawkins, for she is a powerful asset, and a powerful threat.

Ahead of them looms the Iron City, the City of the Dead, the place called Dis, and its metal walls seems to glow, even in the unending gloom of the Realms of Shadow. Susan knows that she must reach the city, for there the Prince's hunters have no sway. *But Lord Zamagiel knows his true name and so they are spared the Prince's wrath and hold a city of their own shaping.* She needs that name. With it, she will own power over the Prince. With it, she can help Trent.

"Run!" she screams to Salvatore. "Faster! They're catching up!"

And as they run, Salvatore gives her a plaintive look and she knows that his will is failing, that he feels the draw of the hunters as she does and that their screeching calls are slowing his steps.

"Don't give up now!" she yells, struggling to make her voice heard over the air-shattering shrieks of the flying hunters. "We're almost there!"

But her pleas fall dead and she watches in horror as Salvatore's steps falter and she passes him and looks back and sees him standing before the onrushing monsters, his back to her and the massive field of metallic spikes that stand between the shadow wilderness and the walls of Dis.

"Salvatore, no!" She watches for a moment, praying that he might regain his courage and follow her into the steel labyrinth. But he does not.

"I'm sorry, my dear," he says. "I'm too tired. I cannot outrun my fate."

"Your fate," she growls, "is your daughter! Remember her! You wanted to find a way to speak to her one last time. To give her your apology. Don't abandon her again!"

Salvatore whirls around and faces Susan, a dozen yards of blackened rock between them. Beyond his back, she watches the four hunters, their black shapes like gaunt silhouettes hanging limp in mid-air, claw-tipped arms reaching and jaws of white triangles like chomping machinery, bearing down on him with alien malice. "My daughter?" he asks, his face bearing a mask of confusion. "I... I had forgotten—"

But his words are cut short as the hunters rush up his back and the first one plunges its clawed arm through him. It bursts from his chest and his mouth falls open and his eyes go wide with surprise and Susan screams and runs for him, oblivious to her fear of the Prince's minions.

"No!" she yells, and draws the silvery dagger from within her dress. She reaches the fray and plunges the blade deep into the hunter's shadowy abdomen and it shrieks and recoils with pain and pulls its arm back, releasing Salvatore from the impaling spike. A brilliant glow continues to burn from deep within the gash in its ethereal flesh and it holds back with its companions. They face the woman in the white dress as she holds the limp body of the old man, and they show a moment of what she can only assume is fear.

And then, in sudden unison, they plunge forward, claws gleaming in the un-light, black spears of death diving for Susan's soul.

7

TRENT'S DUCATI HUMMED ALONG THE westbound highway out of Las Vegas. He passed the destitute suburbs and the rundown apartment complex he lived in with Celia. He passed the old air terminal, trying to keep thoughts of airplane crashes out of his mind. He passed out of the clanging bells and blinking lights, the noise and insanity of the City of Sin. Under the pale glow of dusk, he passed into the Nevada desert, mountains on the horizon and a raft of questions on his mind.

Things were spiraling now, coming to some sort of grand climax. He didn't suspect it would be anything pleasant, but anger had eclipsed his fear. Gadreel held the strings. Gadreel—Ramón—had always held the strings, he realized. The demon had played the game like a pro and had caught Trent in his bluff. He could only guess at Gadreel's motives, but in the deal of cards he felt a weakness. A bad hand lingered, still hidden in the deck. Maybe, just maybe, he had a chance to take the advantage.

The motorcycled bounced as it hit a large rock, causing the bag hanging from Trent's seat to clank against the tailpipe. Trent thought about the bag's contents and grinned. He might not have much of a chance, but he knew better than to sit down at a card table unarmed. Using one hand to steady the bike, he produced a small sheet of paper from his pocket, opened it and read:

Educational materials. Open when I retire.

The note had been taped to a large wooden crate that Charlie had sent to Trent and Celia's apartment a week ago. The old, quiet man who had dropped it off had made it clear that the box was to stay closed and hidden until Charlie retired, as the note indicated. No opening, no peeking. He hadn't said what 'retirement' meant for a Neutral. But now Trent knew. It had occurred to him shortly after leaving Charlie with Fiamma that that's what the angel had meant by announcing his retirement. He had abandoned his neutrality, had given up the one thing that defined his existence. Only the strongest of friendships can make a man change the course of his life. Angels lived forever, so it meant that much more.

Trent crumpled the note and tossed it into the humid air lingering above the damp desert. The paper hovered for a moment before whipping backwards and out of sight in the wake of the speeding bike.

Ahead, the western mountains loomed larger. The desert buckled and shifted form, becoming small hills and sharp inclines. The sides of the dusty highway were punctuated by cacti and scrub brush that thinned as Trent approached a small shack beside the road. A sign in front of the building read, "Buddy's Diner."

He throttled down and eased the bike into the diner's parking lot. He hopped off and slung the black duffel bag that Charlie had sent him over his shoulder. The items inside made a series of metal clanks as he walked up to the door of the diner.

Buddy's barely qualified for the term 'diner.' It had one cash register, five booths, and a dusty ceiling fan that looked like it had never been turned on. The floor was dirty wood planks. The grill sizzled with grease and bacon, attended by a scrawny, pale man that looked barely able to stand, let alone dish up edible food. The place was empty, though the jukebox filled the room with the voice of Johnny Cash singing *The Man Comes Around*, the somber tones contrasting strangely with the chintzy Las Vegas memorabilia that graced the dusty old walls.

The cook turned to acknowledge Trent as he entered. "Yeah?" he said, twisting his thin white moustache with his free hand. The other hand held a grease-soaked spatula.

Trent tried to order coffee and ask about the men's room, but the old man simply cupped his free hand to his ear. "Eh?" he said.

"Cup of coffee. Bathroom," said Trent, louder this time.

The old man pointed at a narrow door to Trent's right.

Trent smiled, hoisted his bag, and fished a dollar bill from his pocket. He smacked it down on the counter next to the register and then headed to the bathroom.

He emerged a few minutes later, still dressed in the jeans and white band logo t-shirt, but with some new accessories. He'd added a SWAT-style vest sporting a series of bullet magazines. In his hands he carried a matte finish black MP5 machine pistol. An ornate dagger hung from his belt, its metal blade gleaming with a subtle red hue beneath the diner's fluorescent lights. A lit cigarette dangled from his lips. *If there was ever a time for a cigarette*, he thought, and smiled.

He walked to the counter and set the gun down with a clack next to a saucer topped by a fresh cup of coffee. He rested the cigarette on the edge of the age-stained laminate top, downed the steaming liquid in a single gulp, and then returned the cigarette to his mouth.

"Thanks," he said, and turned to leave.

From behind him, he heard the old man's creaky voice. "Where ya headin' with all that?"

Trent didn't turn to answer. He said, quietly, "Gotta pick up my daughter from church."

By the time he'd made it to Gadreel's church at the base of the western mountains, the brief lull in the rain had ended and the night sky had become a maelstrom of distant lightning strikes fronted by a thick band of flashing black clouds that moved further eastward with every passing moment. Trent stopped the bike on the side of the dusty road and stared at the imposing church complex. A white-hot bolt appeared on the horizon, a flash that sent the fluttering church banner into silhouette. The air churned with gusts of wind. Trent ventured a thought about Celia but quickly banished it. He needed to focus now.

He knew that this was a potential suicide mission. Without his powers, he couldn't hope to charge in against armed guards and, based on his experience at Gadreel's mansion, he guessed there were plenty.

The church was a front for something far more sinister. If Gadreel controlled everything, then Trent could only imagine how many things stemmed from the massive, cross-topped chapel. Zamagiel and the Blizzard. The death of Celia's parents. The fire-girl and Charlie's murder. The theft of Trent's powers. Susan. Individual hands in a card game that had been going round for years. Maybe centuries. All because of some prophecy. And no one seemed to have the full picture.

A silent flash lit the night sky. He pulled a cartridge from his pocket, matched it to the base of the MP5 and then jammed it home, his action accompanied by a booming roll of thunder and the onrushing sound of a torrential downpour.

As he approached the church through the sparse line of trees and scrub, he could see two guards waiting at the chapel entrance and a few others moving about the campus. He paused beside a boulder, waited for a flash of lightning, and then used the darkness to make a sprint for some church vans parked near the entrance. He slammed his back against the side of one just as another peal of thunder shook the air. The driving rain played a deafening tune on the tops of the metal vehicles as Trent watched the guards' movements.

Without his ability to bring doom, a frontal assault had no chance of success. He wouldn't be able to avoid a hail of gunfire and he'd be riddled with holes in a second. But a quiet infiltration had prospect. He just needed to get past the guards and into the church, rescue Celia, and assassinate Gadreel. Without the demon gone, none of this would end. He had to kill Gadreel.

Another burst of thunder came right on the heels of a lightning flash. This time, the basso punch was strong enough to set off the vans' alarms and they screamed their displeasure like children woken from a nap. And that gave Trent an idea.

He waited for another flash and boom and when it came, he reached up and grabbed the door handle on the van and was relieved to find it unlocked. He slowly drew the door open and looked inside. He reached across the passenger seat, gripped the parking brake, and released it. The church parking lot was on a slight incline and the van rolled slowly backward. Trent dove to the ground and slid under another van.

There was a chorus of shouts from the guards and he could see legs and feet converging on his position.

"Get it!" yelled one of the guards.

"Damn parking brake went!" shouted another.

The feet splashed past Trent's hiding place and went after the rolling van, giving him just enough time. He scrambled to his feet, and sprinted to the unguarded church.

Even with the outside guards delayed, there were bound to be more inside the front door. Instead, he veered around the side of the building, tromped through a waterlogged flowerbed and then came to a crouch, back against the brick wall beside an ornate wooden side door. He glanced around, saw no guards nearby, and opened the door with a soft click.

The chapel was dark. It was more than a chapel really. The mega-churches that Gadreel controlled were enormous affairs whose 'chapels' were merely the largest of several buildings that comprised the church complex. The construction and interior styling reminded Trent of a high school. The laminate tile floor gleamed with polish beneath the red exit sign and dim night lighting. The walls were cinderblock, painted a pale shade of green. Obviously not the ceremonial wing, Trent thought.

He crept past the water fountain, bathrooms and a glass bulletin board papered with flyers for church activities and after-school programs. His boots squelched wetly with every step as he approached a 'T' hallway intersection.

He straightened up against a wall, trying his best to find a pool of shadow in which to hide as a man in fatigues appeared in the hallway, carrying an assault rifle. The man's phone rang, which he answered.

"Come again?" he said. Then, after a moment, "Understood. I'll keep an eye out."

Trent figured they'd caught up to the van and discovered that the parking brake was fine, just depressed. Now they knew someone was around. He'd have to be even more careful.

The guard replaced his phone and checked the ammo cartridge on his rifle. The metal and plastic click of the magazine echoed in the empty corridor. The guard grunted, dropped his weapon to his side and moved on.

After the guard rounded the corner, Trent stepped into the intersection. He had to find Celia; had to make sure she was unharmed. He no longer trusted anything about Ramón—about Gadreel, or whoever he was. He was a demon, and he had lied, and that's all Trent needed to know. He'd lost his friends, his supposed allies, his wife, his adopted daughter, everything. Even Snake, who'd filled Trent in on the realities of the dark underbelly of the world over the past few months, had been notably absent as of late. Everything had led up to this.

He cupped a hand to his ear and tried to listen for sounds beyond the splashing rain and thunderous booms. He listened for human sounds, voices, cries of any sort. He listened for Celia.

And he heard her.

A high-pitched murmur through the air vents, intermingled with the humming A/C. She was alive. One floor up. Hurt, maybe? What did Gadreel want with her? Trent reached behind him and ran a finger along the edge of the leather-bound manuscript in his back pocket. Without the Book, she was nothing, a scared little girl with a handful of magical gifts. She could freeze water with a touch. She could make things cold and brittle, broken when enraged. But compared to Gadreel? Trent didn't understand. He wondered again if there was something more to her, something he didn't know.

He gripped the machine pistol tighter and headed down the hallway until he found a door to the stairwell. One last glance around for watching guards and then he opened the door slowly, quietly, and slipped inside.

Down or up? Apparently the church had a basement. He'd heard Celia's voice upstairs, but maybe Ramón (Gadreel, he corrected himself) rested below, huddled in the bowels of religion like the monster he was. *No*, he decided. *Celia first. Then Gadreel.* He slipped quietly up the stairs.

The stairwell opened into a second floor hallway, a long corridor flanked on both sides by doors. No guards nearby. Trent thanked God for that, then wondered why he'd bothered. God hadn't helped him yet, as far as he could tell.

It didn't take long to find Celia's room. It was sparsely furnished, originally a classroom of some sort that had been cleared out, save a lone chair, an old teacher's desk, and a trundle bed that had been pushed up against the wall beneath a small window. Above the window, parallel to the concrete wall joist, was taped a long banner of Mark 9:23, printed in cursive: *Everything is possible for him who believes.*

Trent checked for guards and then, after seeing none, removed his heavy SWAT vest and rushed to the small bed, to Celia's side. She lay on the dingy mattress without sheets or blankets, eyes closed, brow furrowed. Quiet moans escaped her lips at regular intervals. With each moan, her body convulsed and she curled into a semi-fetal position before relaxing again with the accompanying exhale. Her fingers gripped at her stomach like twisted claws.

Trent watched her for a moment, mystified by her pain. He couldn't bear to see her like this, but couldn't bear to look away, as if maybe his mere attention might ease her torment.

He reached out and brushed back the fine blonde hair from her eyes and caressed the lone clump of strands that she had dyed black without his permission, an action he had chastised her for but secretly loved. Her eyes popped open, wide and terror-filled.

"Trent?" she said aloud, and he quickly responded by covering her mouth and putting a finger to his own.

"Shhh," he whispered. "I'm here for you, kiddo. But you gotta be quiet."

She took a long, ragged, body-trembling breath, and then looked at Trent. "It hurts, Trent. Please, help me."

She had never called him 'Dad,' not once since the night
of the Blizzard, when the demons had arranged their current
relationship. It was a reality that left Trent both saddened and
relieved. On the one hand, he wanted to be a father, a good
father, and with it, he thought, should come the title. But on
the other hand, the lack of that parental title gave him
breathing room, space to be someone else, to be the monster
he'd become since the Blizzard and Zamagiel's death. He
didn't want to be a father *and* a killer, even if his targets were
monsters. He wanted her to have a real father, and he didn't
feel like one. But now, watching her shiver with pain, his
desires became immaterial. He wanted to be whatever she
needed, whatever would save her from this madness.

"What's wrong, Cee? Do you know? What's hurting
you?"

"My stomach," she hissed, as another wave of pain swept
over her. "Oh, God it hurts."

Trent moved closer and put a hand on her forehead. She
felt cool, extremely cool, in fact. "What did he do to you,
Celia? Can you remember anything from the hospital?"

"The hospital?" She gritted her teeth. "Who?"

Trent realized she'd only just now woken up. Was it his
presence that had roused her? Or the pain?

"Trent," she whispered. "I'm sorry."

He put a finger to her lips. "No, not this again. It's fine,
kiddo. I don't blame you."

"But I've been lying to you," she replied, her eyes like
white orbs against the dark of the thunderous night. "I... I
haven't told you everything about... about that night. About
the Blizzard."

Trent frowned. "What? I don't... Celia, what haven't you told me? What does it matter now? I'm gonna get you out of here and then we can talk, okay? You have to be quiet now. Listen to me—"

"No," she said. "You listen to me for once." She gritted her teeth again and writhed as a wave of pain rocked her. Her voice came out in gasping croaks. "I killed all those people," she said. "Those police. I killed them all. And then I swallowed that thing...." She trailed off as another wave hit. Lightning strobed, illuminating the torrents pouring down just outside the small classroom window.

"What thing? I don't understa—" And then, suddenly, he knew. The Bringer of Nightmares. He'd never fought it. He'd assumed it had gone away with Zamagiel's death, or had vanished into the dark places of the world. It was a powerful creature. How could a girl, even a *grigorim*-child, how could she have...?

"You *swallowed* it?"

She clutched at her stomach, rolling on the dingy bed and letting out an agonized moan. Blood oozed from between her clenched teeth.

"I'm sorry," she replied. "I should have told you. I saw Susan. I saw her. I know where she is in the darkness. I can feel her—"

Trent put his hand over her mouth. He shook his head. "Susan's gone. This is about you and me now. I'm gonna fix this. Gonna get you somewhere safe first, then we'll talk about Susan. But we've gotta go *now*."

Tears burst from between her clenched eyelids and when she opened them again, Trent saw that the whites were gone, replaced by solid black, like ebony marbles in the sockets. "Oh, Jesus," he said.

"She said not to tell you," said Celia, though her voice dropped in pitch with every word and by the end of the statement had become more of a hoarse moan than a sentence. Her lips went pale and, in the next flash of lightning, Trent saw that her whole body had gone white, drained of pink, like a bloodless corpse. Her arms shook as she sat up. Then her hand shot out, clawing for his throat.

Trent stumbled, landing on his backside next to the small bed. "No."

"Give it to me," she said, her voice lower in pitch now than seemed possible.

And he knew that she meant the Book. And he knew that she had crossed a line, had become something new and that he was suddenly in great peril. But still he resisted.

"No," he replied, voice loud, unafraid of who might hear. "No, goddammit. I won't let this happen. I'm not losing you, too."

He moved into her embrace, wrapped his arms around her and tried to ignore the sound of her hissing demands, the pain as her fingers clawed at his back. "No," he said, tears forming at the corners of his eyes. "This is not happening. I'm taking you away from this."

He stood then, struggling to carry her fourteen year-old frame toward the door as she clawed him and bit at his shoulder. He could feel her thin blonde hair against his neck and he hated himself with an intensity that he had never felt before. "It's my fault, Cee. I'm taking you now. I'm taking you—"

"Put her down, son." Gadreel/Ramón stood in the doorway of the tiny classroom, blocking Trent's passage. "There's nothing you can do now."

"Fuck you, Ramón. Gadreel. Whoever you are. You've taken everything from me. You're not taking this." With his free hand, Trent pulled the red-hued dagger from his belt and thrust it forward. For a moment, he had forgotten that Palisade had sapped his powers. For a moment, he had believed that he could change Gadreel's fate, could force reality to find a place for the dagger in the demon's flesh. He was wrong.

Gadreel moved quickly, a sudden still life against the flashing lightning. His hand shot forward and, in a second, Trent's dagger was in Gadreel's hand. The old man sneered and tossed the blade aside.

"Put her down," he said, reaching for the girl. "And then we can end this, just you and me."

"No," said Trent, backing away. He shook his head. "She's my daughter."

"She's lost to you, Trent. You've run out of cards. You don't have a play here. Not anymore. Time to pack it in."

"It's not over!" He took another step backward. His legs backed against the side of the bed.

"Where are you gonna go?"

Celia let out a long, animalistic howl—a powerful cry of fury and anger as one of her hands gripped the Book and ripped it from Trent's rear pocket. Gadreel, startled, took a step back and grabbed a rifle from a guard standing behind him. He brought it forward and pulled the trigger. The blast eclipsed a simultaneous crack of thunder. There was a burst of blood from Celia's chest. She flew backwards, out of Trent's grasp. Her thin body crumpled, crashed through the glass, and fell out the small window. The Book, dislodged from her grasp, dropped to the floor with a thump.

Trent looked over his shoulder at the bed, the Book, the broken glass, and his world slowed. A look of sadness passed over Gadreel's face. Trent screamed. Not an intelligible yell, or a curse, or anything of this world, but the scream of a father destroyed, a friend abandoned, a husband ruined. A scream, pure and simple, and he dove for the fallen dagger. Gadreel didn't move to stop him as he snatched up the blade and scrambled to his feet.

A moment of rumbling thunder passed between them. Gadreel stood silent as Trent brandished the red blade. And then Trent rushed forward, dagger squeezed tight in his grip, point gleaming in the aftermath of a lightning flash. He charged Gadreel, his enemy, his ally, his friend, his curse, and he no longer cared about his soul. He only wanted revenge. Death be damned.

Gadreel lifted his arm. In the still frames between lightning strokes, Trent's sight locked on the giant cross tattoo on Gadreel's forearm. He felt the dagger twist in his hand, pivot down, slice the flesh of his own fingers, until it changed direction entirely, stopped in mid-air. Trent could not change his momentum and ran onto it, piercing his breast.

Shock overtook fury. He stumbled forward and landed against Gadreel, who reached out and held the younger man in his arms. Blood ran down Trent's torso, forming a puddle at their feet. His hands clung desperately to Gadreel's shoulders.

"Why?" he gasped.

Gadreel leaned in close, his voice a whisper. "It's over, Trent. Your role in this is over. You were just a pawn, a distraction. Sorry, Trent, but you should have listened to my advice. I gave you a chance to do the right thing. Your job was to keep the Prince busy. But now it's time to clear the decks."

He rubbed Trent's back affectionately and then shoved the dying man backwards where he collapsed onto the classroom's tile floor, a bloody streak connecting him to Gadreel's feet. He looked first at the old, scarred Mexican, then down at the dagger protruding from his own chest, its blade gleaming red. He grabbed it, shaking, trying to pull on the handle, a desperate attempt to save the life ebbing away in red rivers.

Gadreel shook his head. "I was the leader of all the *grigorim*. I taught your kind to forge a blade, to wage war with sword and iron. You can't bring mortal steel against me. You should have known that, but you never did the research, never asked the right people. All you cared about was your damn wife, even with a war coming. Now you've paid for it." Gadreel's face betrayed a quiet anguish. He stepped towards Raziel's Book.

Trent held the blood-slicked hilt of the dagger with one hand. With the other, he flailed backwards, his hand seeking something to hold on to, something to give him the leverage necessary to free the blade from his chest. His hand landed on the Book and curled his fingers around it. He sucked in one last breath of air and used it to mutter, "Not... mortal... steel...." And then he slumped to the floor, dead.

The old Mexican stopped then, looked quizzically at the lifeless body and bent down to examine the dagger. The red metal gleamed in the storm-light. He reached out to pull it from Trent's flesh, but then thought better of it. He stared at it through a long flash of lightning.

"I see," he said.

When the next flash came, he was only partly surprised to find that Trent's body, the dagger, and the Book had all vanished.

8

THE THUNDER OUTSIDE THE CHURCH could barely compete with the old Mexican's furious roars. Palisade stood quietly nearby, fidgeting with his tie as he watched Gadreel pace in front of the altar, waving his fists.

"Dammit! Where did he get Hellforged metal? Who gave him that? It's been forbidden in this world for an eternity."

Palisade said, quietly, "Perhaps it was that Neutral, Charlie."

Gadreel stopped mid-pace and marched up to Palisade, causing him to take a nervous step backward. "It *was* that Neutral," said Gadreel, a finger pointed at Palisade's face. "That little rat. Smart little bastard. Clever last mistake." Gadreel stepped away from Palisade and began pacing again. "But he was a damn fool. He's undone everything. With both Trent and Raziel's Book now in Abaddon, the Prince has got everything he needs. The Prophecy's coming true. The invasion is on the way, Edward."

"But we killed the girl, right? Celia died. Won't that—"

Gadreel cut him off. "They're still looking for her. She... survived somehow."

"I thought you shot her?" Palisade raised an eyebrow.

Gadreel spun on his heel. "Don't you dare question me, you filthy little shit. All the guards could find was some bloody grass and footprints. A few took off down the mountain to look for her." He turned his back on Palisade and walked down the long corridor between the pews, his hands resting atop the benches. "Bring Fiamma to my study. I'll get her to find the child and wipe her out, if the guards can't find the kid first. Either way, the Prince's son won't be born. He might have Trent and the Book, but we'll deny him the black trinity at least."

"I lost her," replied Palisade, his voice wavering.

Gadreel stopped in the middle of aisle, his back still turned. "What?"

"I... I lost Fiamma. Someone dragged her from a convenience store, on fire, after she killed Charlie."

The thunder rolled. Rainwater ran in intricate lines down the faces in the massive stained glass window that took up the bulk of one wall of the chapel. Gadreel laughed. It started quietly, growing to a crescendo before stopping abruptly. He was leaned against one of the pews with both hands, his head down, silent. He looked up and stared down the aisle at Palisade, who stood fidgeting, watching.

"Goddammit, then *you* find her," Gadreel said. "Find the child, and kill her. She's too powerful for me, now. She's too close to the end of this. But for someone with your gift..." He straightened up and walked the remainder of the aisle, letting the heavy chapel doors slam shut behind him, leaving Edward Palisade alone beneath the open arms of a wooden Jesus.

*   *   *

Celia stumbled through the trees and scrub, rain beating down upon her, cactus spines tearing at her exposed flesh. Every drop of rain that slid against her skin burned like a white-hot flame and her fine blonde hair, limp and matted against her scalp, felt like a hornet's nest of pain atop her head. But she knew the pain was indication of her survival. As the water washed over her, so did the pain in her chest, where the bullet had entered. The wound healed quickly. It had been months since she'd manifested this level of magick. It scared and delighted her.

Despite the pain, she kept one hand clamped across her lips. Even against the thundering fury of the summer sky, the hunting dogs could pick up the slightest noise. As if in response, a dog's baying emerged from a rolling thunderclap, spurring her to keep moving.

She could hear shouts, too. The guards were relentless in their search and Celia knew that if they found her, they'd bring her back that strange old Mexican with the scarred face and the tattoo on his arm. She had no desire to see him again.

She could still hear the voice of the Book with each passing footfall. She could *taste* the dust-strewn pages of the ancient manuscript. And she longed to touch it again and at the same time lamented what she had done to Trent. She tried to push the thought from her mind, lest his demise dampen her instincts and ruin her chance of escape. She needed her wits about her, and it was hard enough to concentrate with the pain of every raindrop, the ache in her chest, and the shuddering, convulsive stabs coming from deep within her gut. But she had heard the shouts, had heard the gut-wrenching sound of blade through flesh in a rare moment of quiet betwixt the thunder.

Tears burned as they streamed down her face. She crouched behind a boulder and cried, her chest heaving and stomach lurching with alternating waves of grief and stabbing pain. *What have I done? What have I done?*

Another howl, closer now. A bolt of lightning arced across the sky, a sudden jagged tether between the black sky and the glowing city of neon beyond the mountains. She needed to get back to Las Vegas. She could find help there. She'd go to the Inferno. She'd make a deal with Jack Mars.

The solidity of a plan gave her strength despite the constant barrage of pain and sorrow. Trent died trying to protect her. She only had Trent before and now, because of her, he was gone and she had no one. Fury burned in her now-healed chest, bringing back long-repressed memories of the Blizzard, of the horrors she had witnessed, of the police station, the fight atop the Luxor, the deranged men assaulting the nurse in the snow and what she had done to them, the horrors she had committed. Her fingers trembled and magick surged along her spine, making her muscles quiver. She'd spent months subduing the urge to use her powers. She'd promised Trent. A distant voice in her mind, a voice she had struggled for what seemed like an eternity to ignore, said *But Trent's not here now, is he? Not anymore.*

Celia burst from her hiding place and sprinted through the trees as the storm battered her and soaked her clothes. She had no shoes on and her feet stung as she swished through the underbrush and stumbled over cacti and scrub. She did not see the sudden decline and tumbled down the hill, slamming against rock and scraping across thorns. Finally, she came to a stop and lay there a moment, taking inventory, hoping she had not broken anything.

She lifted her head and was relieved to see a road a few hundred yards from where she lay. The lights from a roadside diner cut through the night. She could maybe reach it if she kept running. Maybe there would be a car and she could hitch back to the city....

She pulled herself up, groaning, and took a few tentative steps. Her hip ached, but it was nothing compared to the pain in her stomach or the burning of the rain. *At least the bullet wound has healed*, she thought. She stumbled forward a few more steps and then, out of the night, stepped a man, only inches from her. A guard. He grabbed Celia by the throat, grinning. "Gotcha, kiddo." He chuckled.

She was paralyzed, the man's fingers choking off her air supply with his strong grip. Righteous purpose glowed in his eyes. He was one of the church guards, come to bring her back, and beyond him the lights of the diner wavered, beckoning. Tingling energy danced along her spine.

"You can't call me that," she said. She felt her fingers melting, liquefying, and reforming into something colder. The foul smell of ash lingered around her. With what little strength she had remaining, she thrust her arm forward, into the guard's gut. His eyes went wide. There was a squelch, and warmth spread along her frozen arm. A wicked icicle burst through the guard's back, red, glittering with every flash of lightning. The guard gurgled and his grip relaxed. He fell backward as Celia stepped away, her arm coated in slick, crimson warmth. The thing in her belly kicked, hard.

Anger replaced fear. Nightmare replaced reality. She stepped out into the road, her mind now filled with a terrible sense of purpose. She walked along the rain-soaked asphalt toward the diner, her ears ringing with the roar of rain against the pavement. In her nostrils lingered the twin smells of wet desert and fresh blood.

*   *   *

Fiamma writhed amidst the bed sheets, stained red by the overflow running down her cheeks as Tricia forced her to drink from the plastic pouch.

"I'm sorry, gorgeous, but your timeline went awry a while back." Tricia threw empty pouch to the floor, grabbed another, and slit the top open expertly with a razor-sharp fingernail. Again, blood headed down Fiamma's throat. "This will help remake you, strengthen your blood for what comes next. But a friend of mine will have to iron out your past."

Fiamma's fingers gripped the mattress, white-knuckled claws that squeezed and relaxed with every shuddering wave of pain. Her skin burned with every movement. Her lungs screamed with every breath.

Teeth clenched, she managed to say, "Please, stop." But Tricia ignored her.

"You never should have gotten that call," said the succubus. "Never should have been talked down like that. Someone was messing with your fate. Someone powerful." She smiled and threw away the empty plastic pouch. "There," she said, "last one." She stroked the side of Fiamma's face and made soft, cooing noises. "Quiet. Just try to relax."

Fiamma struggled, her vision dimming, sounds dropping so low that she could barely understand any of Tricia's motherly reassurances. She managed, finally, to ask, "What are you doing to me?"

And Tricia replied, with a sad smile, "Killing you, my dear. You're supposed to be dead." She shrugged. "I'm sorry to say that what's coming is not at all a dream. But you're lucky, in a way. He doesn't do this for just anyone, you know."

Fiamma's mind succumbed then to the impossible fever and she descended into herself, walking within her memories to a heartbeat of distant, soothing sounds from the woman administering her torturous demise.

She fell into a dreamscape of pain and fire.

Her eyes opened. Flames danced along her bedroom walls and she knew that she was ten years old and terrified.

Chemical fumes and the overwhelming stench of burning carpet filled the air. The roar of the fire, the cracking of sheetrock and ceiling joists. The collection of stuffed bears atop her dresser smoldered and dripped, soft fur turning brittle, hairs twisting and waving as flames colored their bodies black. Their eyes oozed out one by one; glass and plastic marbles dripping down the stuffed animals like globs of molasses.

She tried to scream, but no sound came out. Ash and smoke filled her lungs. Her whole body buzzed and the air around her warped with heat. The sheets tucked close against her body smoldered. The window frame sagged and broke, shattering the glass. Her mother screamed through the wall behind her head and she squeezed her eyes shut, crying, as the heat enveloped her like a womb.

Soft lips touched hers. Fiamma was fifteen. The other girl, Megan, was sixteen. They were alone together along the wooded path upon which the high school cross-country team practiced. Fiamma opened her eyes to see the pale girl's lips slide against hers. And then Megan opened her eyes too and the stare that lingered between them fanned the flames. Megan pulled Fiamma close and they hungrily took from each other. Fiamma's body buzzed and her skin tingled and she felt sweat through the back of Megan's jersey and wondered for a moment why *she* never sweated. And she wanted so desperately to be naked against the other girl and feel that sweat between them, slick and cool....

Then Megan's hands started to claw at her and Fiamma felt the fingernails tearing at her flesh, but she couldn't bear to pull away, couldn't stand the thought of ending this perfect moment. So she kissed feverishly, pressing herself closer, even as the older girl squirmed in her grasp.

Finally, Megan tore herself away, her eyes wide with shock and confused anger. A hand went to her mouth where blisters had formed, but she never broke gaze with Fiamma. Her cries started first as a shout, a terrified guttural yell that belched a cloud of smoke. Fiamma stumbled back, tripped, and landed amidst a pile of oak leaves.

Megan brought her fingers to her own lips screaming with each touch as her pale fingers traced over the swollen burn blisters, which bubbled and oozed clear fluid. Leathery black crusts formed beneath charred patches of flesh.

Megan fell to her knees, hands still on her face, tears running from her eyes, chest heaving with strained gasps. A jagged red line traced down her neck and disappeared beneath the collar of her yellow running jersey. She looked at Fiamma, face mutilated, burned, and awash with panic and betrayal.

Fiamma leapt to her feet and ran, her own tears steaming as she wept, legs churning like she might never stop and instead simply run, run, run as far away from the swirling fear and emotions as she could get, run, run, run until the nightmare ended.

"Hey, lezzie," came the voice to Fiamma's left. A teenage boy had come up next to her on the track as she jogged her solitary laps. She insisted on running alone. She was eighteen, but still as thin as when she was twelve. "Bite any faces today?" Steven snapped his teeth together in mockery, and then laughed.

She hated him. He insisted on tormenting her. The whole class knew she was gay, and most kids had heard about the incident with Megan a few years back; the older girl had spent weeks in the hospital before her family abruptly moved away. But Steven insisted on tormenting her daily. Fiamma's foster parents had said that both girls had gotten what they deserved for being sinners. Fiamma hated them too.

She shot Steven the finger and picked up her pace. He chuckled, caught up with her, and gave her a shove that knocked her out of her lane. She stopped and turned on him. "Fuck off, Steven!" She shoved him back.

He stopped running and stared her down, his devious smile intact. "What's your problem, bitch?"

Her narrow frame trembled with fury. She didn't know what to say or do. Anger consumed her; it seared up through her core.

"Ooh," he said. "Now you're angry, huh? What are you gonna do? You gonna kiss me too?" He made a 'V' with his fingers and stuck his tongue through it and waved it lasciviously. "Nah, you don't like guys, do you?" He laughed. "You sick fuck."

Images of burns and blistering skin consumed her and fury threaded its way down her spine. She leapt forward, hands ready to choke the life from the boy, but he saw her coming.

Steven dodged her and she pitched forward, staggered by her own momentum. He stepped behind her and shoved again, much harder this time. She lost her balance, fell, and hit her forehead against the rubber track surface and twisted her wrist. Her ears rang and her skin became clammy and cold and hot all at once.

"Everybody hates you, you know...." His voice was distant, receding, with a singsong quality, like her mother's when she would sing in the bathtub. Her mother...

She blacked out.

Fiamma pulled the Black Flag t-shirt down past her face, over her shoulders and smoothed it out. She didn't bother with bras anymore. Her breasts hadn't filled out; she was thin as a stick and she didn't really give a fuck what other people thought anyway. She lit a cigarette and exited her tiny New

York apartment for the last time. She left the door swinging open.

The taxi ride to the Empire State Building was short and the cabbie didn't appear to speak English, but that was fine with Fiamma. She didn't want to talk. Talking made her think, and she definitely didn't want that.

She slipped by security like one of the shadows she hunted daily. Normal people were easy to move around, as though her world didn't interface as tightly as theirs. In hers, she was queen. She rode the elevator to the 86th floor observation deck, her mind blank as the lift hummed upwards, spewing quiet, non-offensive jazz.

She walked out to the deck and stood alone in the night, watching New York twinkle and the yellow and red streaks moving along the black roads that from so high up resembled veins and arteries carrying a colorful, glimmering fluid. She had a distinct sense of standing outside herself and couldn't resist the urge to look behind her.

She expected to see a security guard or bum that had found his way up here. But instead, it was a man in a fine suit jacket with a tan dress shirt beneath. Bistre slacks topped polished brown shoes. He wasn't attractive, and didn't look like he deserved to be in the tailored suit, even if the fit was perfect. A wispy collection of strands were pasted down with sweat atop his balding, pale scalp, and his mouth held a collection of pointy, scraggly teeth framed by too-thick pink lips. A patch of thin fuzz covered his chin. But his eyes... his eyes were a perfect, brilliant blue that seemed almost to glow in the midnight dun. Those eyes held Fiamma immobile for a moment, until she saw the face of the boy beneath.

"Steven?"

"Fuckin' right." He smiled.

"What the hell are *you* doing here?"

He winked and pulled an apple from his inner jacket pocket. He bit deep and a trickle of juice ran down his chin. "Now I should be asking *you* that," he replied, talking with his mouth full. "And my friends call me Snake now, by the way."

Fiamma shook her head. "No, it can't—" She pivoted on her heel and looked back out at the city as if it might provide her some answers. Then she turned back to Snake. "It's been—"

"Coupla years." He finished the sentence for her. "I bet you still hate me, huh?"

Fiamma gritted her teeth. She was dimly aware that she had balled her fists, too. She remembered the boy's—the man's—face as he looked down at her, calling her 'lezzie', 'dyke', 'whore'. She narrowed her eyes. "You the best they could find to come up here and talk me down?"

"Nah, I came on higher authority than your people." He chuckled. "You know what's funny? After all those years I tormented you, you're gonna hate me even *more* after tonight."

"Yeah," she said, eyes narrowing. "Why's that?"

"'Cause you're starting to think I'm up here to talk you down. Hell, you were probably *hoping* someone would come. They *did*, the last time you tried this shit. Maybe a security guard or you got a phone call or something like that. But here's the thing: I'm not here to talk you down this time. I'm gonna finish this apple...." He rubbed the red apple against his jacket collar, and then took another bite that snapped in the quiet night calm. His mouth stuffed with fruit, he mumbled, "And then I'm gonna make sure you jump."

"Fuck you," said Fiamma, with a snarl. "It's people like you that put me up here. People've treated me like shit my whole life. Teachers, friends, even those monsters I work for." She punched a metal girder with her fist and a small puff of acrid smoke rose up from the point of impact. "Well they can all fucking go to Hell. And you too. I don't care what kinda shit you're trying to pull. You want me to jump? No fucking problem. Just wait and watch."

"Monsters you work for, eh? Yeah, they're rotten sons of bitches." He took another bite of the apple. Some bits fell from his mouth as he chewed. He shrugged as he ate. "Never trust demons."

"Wait—" Her voice wavered, confused. "You— you know about them?"

"Sure. We work together from time to time."

"Who *are* you?"

He frowned. "Why does everyone always ask me that? You people always have to know who, what, when, where. Hell, you know half of those things aren't even all that real, right? Can't you mortals just learn to take some things on faith?" He took another bite of the apple and rolled his eyes. "Fine, let's just say I'm a messenger." He chewed while eyeing his piece of fruit. Only a few more chunks hung from the core.

"Demon or angel?"

"We're all the same, dumbass. Some of us just traded our halos for pitchforks." He chewed thoughtfully for a moment, looking off into the New York distance. "Matter of miscommunication, the way I see it." He winked at Fiamma.

"You think the Fall was a *miscommunication?*"

Snake pulled off the last lingering chunk of fleshy fruit between his teeth. "Let's get down to business," he said, and began to advance on her. With a flick of his wrist, he raised a palm and the iron anti-suicide bars behind her creaked loudly, snapped loose and shot off into the night.

Fiamma watched the chunk of fence spiral down. She wondered who it might hit. She looked back up at Steven (Snake?). "No," she said, eyes wide. Something had gone wrong. She *remembered* this, somehow. This wasn't how it had happened. Not in her memories. Her father, Salvatore, had called her before, his voice straining with sobs and heartfelt apologies. She'd told him off, cussed him out and hung up the phone before spending the night on the observation deck floor, crying and listening to the coos of the pigeons. She pulled the cellphone from her pocket and stared at its impassive digital face. Dismayed, she dropped it to the cement. It clattered and the plastic broke.

"Ahh. No call this time, huh?" Snake whipped the apple core out into the night. "Pity ole Gadreel put your Pops up to that last time around. Like I always say, never trust demons; especially demons fucking with prophecies. They always get it wrong. Every time. Meddle around, and end up making it come true anyway. Or they break it, only to cause something worse."

"I don't— I don't understand—" But Snake moved closer and she edged backwards towards the hole in the fence. "No— wait—"

"Sorry, babe," he said. "Told you this would piss you off. But hey, it's been fun reliving life with you." He grinned wickedly.

She backed right to the edge and felt her heels hanging over nothing. She gripped the remaining bars on either side of the opening. "No!" she yelled. "This isn't how it happened! I never died! I didn't jump!"

Snake's pink lips glistened. "Of course not, stupid." He put his right palm on her breastbone. "Didn't Trish tell you? This isn't a memory."

He shoved. Smoke burst from her fingers as they dug molten tracks through the bars of metal. And then her fingers came free and Fiamma Cortina fell into New York's sea of lights, screaming.

*   *   *

He passed through blinding white, then black, then white again, and with a buffeting slam found himself plummeting through the viscosity of an alien atmosphere, a moment eerily reminiscent of his plunge from the airplane so many years before. His chest burned and he screamed out into the starless black. His hoarse cries grew in strength as he discovered a depth in himself that hadn't been there before. His bellowing roar shook the air, sending thunder rumbling through the atmosphere and across the grey, dust-swept wasteland. The Realms of Shadow trembled.

Trent hit the ground with a sickening thump and as he lay there in the dark sand for a time, listening to his cries echoing across the landscape, he realized that the pain in his chest was abating. He could *feel* this new world moving around him, bustling in its own unfamiliar way. He could hear winds howling, dust scraping against dust, distant cries. He felt his body being moved, and then the ground beneath him went away and came back as something more solid.

He opened his eyes.

He saw walls of darkened wood, gnarled and knotty, and an odd assortment of things that he recognized: old toys, broken machines, ruined artwork, all remnants—though none whole—of the mortal world. A swirling oily black pool, its edges lined with junk objects. And though the things and the walls remained still, the air itself buzzed violently and a shape moved impossibly fast amidst the detritus, alternately watching and tending to him, poking and prodding and making strange noises. With every passing second, his awareness sharpened, and the motions seemed to slow. The world was slowing; the train of the mortal realm had run ahead on its temporal rail, leaving Trent behind, though a part of him still felt the inexorable passage of time even here, in this nowhere land, where time has no meaning.

*   *   *

The buzzing has stopped and the person dancing about him moves at a normal pace. There is no past tense anymore, only present. And yet, with every passing moment, he feels as though he has aged a year or more, and the pressure of time upon his soul is suffocating. He tries to make out the features of the person looking down at him. His eyes focus. Blonde hair. White gown. Thin and lithe in her movements. A woman.

Susan.

And she looks at him and smiles, her fingers tracing the weathered green surface of the Book.

Nowhere

BLACK SHAPES POUR DOWN UPON Susan as she clutches at the limp, wavering body of Salvatore. She raises a hand to defend herself from the creatures' terrible onslaught. But she does not close her eyes, does not turn away, and she is surprised when the sky above her and beyond the hunters vibrates suddenly and a black cloud, even darker black than the charcoal-grey horizon, breaks across the canopy of the world. And with its sudden arrival comes a roll of booming noise, a sustained, ground-rattling thunderclap. The rumble shakes everything. The hard-packed dirt floor cracks in places. Spires shatter and crash down to the wasteland surface, glassy black fragments sloughing off the main mass before the rest crumbles and collapses. And for a moment, the hunters pause.

A moment is all she needs.

Quickly, Susan draws the silvery dagger from the dress sash tied around her waist. She drops Salvatore's body to the ground and leaps forward, bare feet leaving the dust for a moment as she plunges the blade into the center of the first of the shadow creatures. It lets out a hideous screech, high-pitched treble and low bass notes combined into a horrible, discordant death cry. The thing evaporates in an instant, as though it had never existed in the first place.

The other three hunters, shaken from their thunder-induced trance, let out screams of anguish and swoop forward, long-clawed arms waving and piercing as they come on. Susan holds her ground and grits her teeth, feet firmly planted, blade-point smoking.

The first of the remaining creatures lunges at her and she narrowly avoids one of its seeking claws. She takes a measured swing with the dagger. The claw snicks off and disappears in a rain of black dust. The creature comes in at her again as its two companions circle around to her back. She stabs and misses, feints, then dodges another advance. A duck and a quick slip to one side, but not quick enough. Claws rake lightly against her torso, tearing jagged lines in her white gown. The Shades move too fast for her. She took the one by surprise, but she cannot hope to defeat them all. She squares up and surveys the fight, looking for any exit.

One of the Shades is coming on fast, swooping in at her with claws extended. She looks past it and sees the maze beyond, and she makes up her mind. With a ferocious slash, she throws all of her fury against the onrushing shade. Her blade dives deep but she does not slow her step, and as the thing bursts into dust, she has already passed through its remains, leaving whorls of dense smoke in her wake. She sprints for the iron-spiked maze, never looking back even as the two remaining Shades scream and roar behind her.

Her bare feet slap against the dusty ground as she approaches the entrance to the metal labyrinth. For a moment, she laments leaving Salvatore behind, but knows that if she stops, if she even falters for a split-second, the hunters will destroy her. She plunges into the maze, passing beneath an ornate iron arch as she dives to the ground, hoping the creatures cannot pass.

For this is the labyrinth that stands before the *grigorim* city of Dis. This is the gateway to their land, the oubliette that guards their domain, and though she fears what may lie inside, what horrors might serve as their guardians, she knows that she cannot stay behind, or the Prince's hunters will surely rend her to nothing.

She looks back and is relieved to see the hunters waylaid in their approach. They swirl and swoop above the archway, letting out howls of fury, but they do not advance within. This is a place where the Prince's jurisdiction ends and they cannot enter. It is a place created and named.

The Iron Labyrinth.

9

CELIA'S MIND SPUN WILDLY, CONCOCTING scenarios, reliving long-repressed horrors, fantasizing about revenge. Her thoughts always settled on vengeance. *They killed Trent.* She loved him. She knew that, though it seemed a different sort of love—a love she couldn't place. Not romantic love, nor the love of a daughter for a father, though that's what she expected to feel. No, it was something else. Something foreign to her. A burning desire to keep him safe, and now that he was gone, a stinging sort of pain that called out for blood. She felt far older than her fourteen years.

She staggered through the skin-searing rain toward the poorly lit diner. A single pickup truck sat empty in the lot, rain pinging in the metal bed. Celia didn't know how to drive, but figured the truck's owner could be persuaded to take her to the city.

The gravel hurt her bare feet and she knew that the flimsy hospital gown no longer concealed much, especially soaked with rain. She fought back her embarrassment as she pushed through the diner's front door.

The diner was mostly empty. The television in one corner babbled on, with a reporter interviewing a convenience store owner about some woman that had trashed his store. The grill sizzled and Celia smelled fatty bacon and fried eggs, but she wasn't hungry. She didn't feel much of anything in her gut except the constant stabbing which had grown more intense after she stepped in out of the rain. The old cook looked up at her from the grill as the door smacked shut.

"Raining, huh?" he said, with little apparent concern. "Take a seat, little lady. Anywhere's fine."

"Who drives the truck?" she asked and glanced around the small diner. She didn't see anyone else.

The old cook didn't respond.

"I said, 'Who drives the truck?'" she shouted, this time.

The cook put a hand to his ear. "Eh?"

"*Goddamit, who—?*"

The bathroom door opened and a big, grizzly-looking man stepped out. He had a week's worth of stubble and a few decades' worth of beer belly. "Whaddya want, kid?" he grumbled, cutting her off. He zipped up his fly and walked toward her.

"Drive me to the city."

The fat man glanced outside. Then he chuckled. "Yeah. In this rain? Can't hardly see past my headlights." He shook his head and took a seat near Celia at the counter. As soon as his butt hit the chair, the old cook dished up a plateful of bacon and eggs and poured out a giant cup of coffee. "No," said the fat man, "probably best to just wait this'n out."

Celia walked over to him and put her hand on his shoulder.

"What did I say, girl?" He pointed a stubby finger at one of the empty booths. "Now you just go over there and sit. I'll take you in after the storm passes. Shouldn't be too—"

Celia's countenance darkened and she lowered her head ever so slightly. Her hand remained on his shoulder. Her other hand went to the back of his head. The thing in her gut kicked hard. The steam lifting off the fat man's food stopped abruptly, and the plate cracked down the middle, the two halves sliding apart, dropping an egg onto the dirty countertop. He looked at her with panic plastered across his face.

"N-n-no," he mumbled. "I didn't mean to, I swear. That girl, she just, well you know, she just looked so pretty standing there. I didn't mean— I never was gonna— But then—" Tears rolled down the big man's cheeks. "God, n-no, please. Don't make me see it again. Don't make me see it—"

Celia had never been able to summon up the kind of magick that could force people's hands, could change their minds. Magick that could *command*. The thing inside her was growing stronger, and she liked it. She stared into his eyes with a powerful intensity. "Now," she said.

The haggard truck driver sobbed all the way to the city. Celia paid him little mind. The pain in her stomach had grown more intense, and she clutched at herself with both arms, frequently doubling over in pain. The man refused to look at her as he drove. He just kept muttering about the 'pretty girl' and 'all the blood'.

After an intense wave of nausea that forced her to vomit out the truck window, Celia looked up through the mud-stained windshield and saw the lights of The Strip a few blocks ahead. But she didn't need to go quite that far. Her destination was off-Strip.

"There," she said, pointing at the Inferno Casino, a red and orange two-story with neon flames above solid black double-doors.

The man, sobbing, pulled the truck over and let her out. As soon as she had shut the door, he peeled off down the street. She suspected he wouldn't last the night. She didn't care.

She gritted her teeth against the constant, burning rainfall and the pain in her belly, and strode up to the front doors of the casino. She needed revenge and she knew of no person— no entity—in all of Las Vegas more suited to its foul deliverance than the one named Jack Mars, the owner of the Inferno Casino. She slicked back her hair, attempted to cover herself with the flimsy hospital gown, and pushed open the doors.

*   *   *

"Welcome back, gorgeous." British accent. Lips brushed across Fiamma's forehead, then down over her brow to kiss the tops of each closed eyelid.

Fiamma blinked, and then opened her eyes. Her back ached as though she had fallen a great height. She remembered Steven—Snake?—pushing her off the Empire State Building. A dream? Her arms and legs felt sticky and she glanced down to see them covered in blood. Her leg was twisted at an awkward angle and she realized she couldn't move it. Her lungs hurt.

"Wha—" she gasped for air. "Wha—"

"Shh." Tricia put a finger to her lips. "No need for panic. You fell off a building, once upon a time, but you'll be fine soon enough."

Fiamma tried to lift her head but remembered her tether. "What happened to me?" she whispered.

The woman in red smiled sadly. "You died, gorgeous. Committed suicide, I'm afraid." She shrugged. "Or close enough, at least. I apologize, but we had to be more direct this time. We didn't want you to make that same mistake again."

"I don't understa—"

Tricia shook her head. "Shh. It's okay. Time and memory aren't as related as you mortals think. It'll make more sense later. For now, just lie back." She adjusted Fiamma's pillow, Tricia's breasts brushed across her face. Then she stepped away from the bed and took a seat. "I want to tell you a story. Listen, while your body heals. It won't be long now before you're up and walking again."

After high school, Fiamma had worked for Gadreel, hunting Shades in New York. She'd seen bizarre, horrifying things. But the current situation had no comparison in her memories. She felt as though she were being tortured and seduced.

"There's a reason I brought you here, Fiamma. A reason I saved you. And a reason for the change you're about to endure."

"What—?" hissed Fiamma, but Tricia raised a palm and shook her head.

"Just listen," she said. "Gadreel played a trick on you. Played a trick on us all, I'm afraid. A trick that began thousands of years ago."

"In the early times, after the Lightbringer divided Heaven from Hell, a post was created in the latter; a throne, of sorts. In the mortal tongue, the post was called 'the Satan', the adversary. The demon lords of Hell needed a ruler, a representative to marshal the creatures that had fallen, powerful and base alike. And Hell needed a representative to this world, the world of man.

"Many demons filled the post of *ha-satan* over the centuries. Satanail was the first and the one for whom the post is named; then Samael, Azazel, Duma, Mastema, and eventually the one you know as Gadreel. And then, as your kind entered into its golden age, as the Israelites were escaping across the sands, Hell too underwent a great revolution. The greatest lord Hell had ever seen, Belial, gathered an army and deposed Gadreel, and all of Gadreel's network crumbled, from his lords and holdings in Hell to his influence here in the mortal realm. And Lord Belial took the throne."

Fiamma's extremities tingled. Her fingers trembled, burned. Her fingernails suddenly peeled back, though without pain. In their place, yellowing, pointed nails reformed.

Tricia continued her story, apparently unconcerned by the sudden transformation. "As punishment, Lord Belial cast Gadreel into the Realms of Shadow, a gift to the Prince. He could not have known that Gadreel—once a great prophet in Heaven—had foreseen these events and had arranged his own escape.

"For centuries, Gadreel had seeded the demonic host with notions and select information. And when he reached the throne of the Prince, he had all he needed to make a bargain. He struck a deal that let him return to the mortal realm, to take human form and begin to construct his alliances anew, and the Prince in turn received prophecy that had been withheld from him for millennia. And in a thousand years, Gadreel had everything in order. He only needed to lift a finger.

"Belial's downfall came suddenly. I watched him dragged from the chamber of the *ha-satan*. I was his second-in-command, though I knew better than to wear my role like a badge amidst the fiends. I'm the daughter of Lilith, from before she died. I'm not a demon, not exactly. Though fallen, the demons were angels still, and insisted upon their hierarchies. My discretion saved me. I slipped away, even as the great city fell.

"Of the glory that was once Hell, only the city of Dis remains, perched on the edge of the pit, now sealed, at the border between Hell and Shadow. Below, what was once the Realms of Fury became only the Realms of Ruin."

Fiamma's back arched as she cried out in pain. Anger and hatred and malice rushed through her veins, washing out every other emotion. The sticky blood that had pooled around her dried, hardened, and then cracked, birthing smoke. She found the strength to tear her head away from its unseen tether and heard a quiet, metallic clang as the small red nail bounced into a dark corner. The broken bones of her leg snapped back into place and her spine reshaped itself at the same time her jaw popped back into alignment. She exhaled thick, black fumes. She glared at Tricia beneath her lowered brow, eyes half-lidded.

Tricia looked back at her, lust dancing in her eyes.

Fiamma sat upright and stretched her neck, tilting it in each direction until the vertebrae let out a crack. "Why are you telling me all this?" she asked.

Tricia grinned. "Because, my love, war is on the horizon and Hell is in ruins. We need an army and a new Lord. And with your bloodline, you're next in line for the throne."

"What if I don't want to fight your war?"

"You don't just fight it, daughter of Belial. You *start* it. And if you don't, Trent Hawkins will give the Prince everything he needs to destroy all of the Realms, including this one."

* * *

The inside of the Inferno bore little resemblance to the outside. Where the exterior sported neon flames and gaudy signage, the inside screamed class and money. Every wall was paneled in dark wood, like an enormous Victorian study. The black marble floor gleamed under the ornate chandeliers. The smells of gourmet food from the kitchens drifted lazily between the poker and blackjack and baccarat tables. A roulette wheel clacked loudly against a backdrop of murmurs from the players gathered around it, murmurs that made way for cheers and polite applause each time the wheel stopped. Celia could not spot a single slot machine or any of the normal accoutrements of the more tourist-friendly casinos. The Inferno catered to a higher level of customer, as evidenced by the array of designer gowns and expensive suits.

Celia, shivering with pain and very aware of her near-nakedness, stood in the marble atrium, dripping rainwater, clutching her stomach, saying nothing. Just watching.

One of the bouncers came over, frowning. "Sorry," he said, "No one under twenty-one."

Celia didn't notice or hear him at first. Her brain reeled with thoughts of vengeance and her feeling of exposure. "What?"

The bouncer gestured his bald head toward the door and jabbed a thumb in the same direction. "Out," he said. "You're too young."

"I need to see Jack Mars."

The bouncer raised an eyebrow. "Yeah? And why do you—?" He stopped midsentence and raised a finger to his plastic earbud. He glanced out across the casino as he listened. His expression changed. He looked back down at Celia and shrugged. "Your lucky day. Boss'll see you. Follow me."

Celia staggered after him. Convulsive waves from her stomach threatened to send her to her knees with every step.

They entered an ornate elevator that had only two buttons inside. They rode it the short distance to the second floor and exited into a long hallway, which was carpeted in a rich, deep red and lit by electric wall sconces that mimicked flickering flames. The big bouncer strode the length of the hall to a door at the end—a thick wooden affair, with carved panel inlays and a gilded handle. The bouncer knocked quietly, then listened. After a second, he nodded and pushed down the handle, gesturing for Celia to step inside.

Jack Mars' office didn't mimic the casino's more expensive themes. It looked instead like the office of a corporate executive, simple and unadorned, but marked by carefully selected furniture and a few expensive paintings. A large mahogany desk dominated the room, topped only by a small flat screen computer monitor, a keyboard, and a phone. A neatly arranged stack of books and papers graced one corner of the desk and behind it, in an immaculate grey Kiton business suit, sat Jack Mars.

He looked up over his wire-rim glasses at Celia. "My dear, this is most unexpected." He gestured for her to sit at the visitor's chair opposite him and motioned for the bouncer to leave.

Celia sat in the overstuffed leather armchair, a deep blood red like the carpet in the hallway outside the office. She felt tiny.

Jack removed his glasses and smoothed back his thin, short-cut black hair. He lifted a coffee cup to his lips, sipped, and placed it back down. "You look... uncomfortable. Are you alright?" He had a piercing, almost hypnotic gaze.

"It's just my stomach," Celia said quietly. "I'm okay."

Jack nodded. "I hear differently. From what I've gathered, you swallowed a Bringer of Nightmares last year. That must be awfully painful."

The revelation stunned her. Not even Trent knew that until tonight, right before he... she banished the thought.

"Did you know," continued Jack, "that there have only ever been *two* of those Nightmare-Bringers in existence at any given time?" He tapped a few keys on the keyboard and then reached over to switch off the flat-panel monitor. "Fascinating, really. The Realms of Shadow are filled with bizarre creatures and nearly infinite numbers of some of them.

But the Bringers of Nightmares? Only two. And you swallowed one of them." He chuckled. "I certainly don't envy you. There are only a few creatures in all of Abaddon that can bridge the mortal world and the shadow world as they do. Dreams and nightmares are unique in that way. To have one inside you...." He gave her a serious look. "You've become a gateway, child."

"Help me," she said, gathering courage. "I want revenge."

Jack nodded in approval. "Against Mr. Gadreel, I assume? The man who owns the church up the mountain?"

She nodded.

"And this would be because...?"

"He killed Trent," she replied, teeth gritted against a wave of pain from the thing inside her belly.

"Do you think—" Jack paused, frowning. "Do you think you'll survive that long, my child? Celia, isn't it?"

"I don't care." Celia shook her head. "I just want Gadreel dead."

"And why then, did you come to me?"

"I've heard the stories," she answered. "Trent told me what you used to do to people, the ways you'd make sure a cheater never cheated you again. Help me, please."

Jack smiled. "You flatter me, Celia. But I'm not that sort of demon anymore. Just a respectable businessman now. I have a casino to run—"

"I think Gadreel's trying to take over the world—" she blurted out. "I heard him talking, when I was lying there in his church."

"Ahh," Jack replied, tapping a finger against his temple. His expression implied mockery.

"You've got to help me," Celia pleaded.

"No, I think not." Jack picked up his glasses and perched them on his nose. He tapped a button on his cellphone. "I'm sorry, but this is much larger than your petty quest for vengeance."

The cold welled up inside her. Jack's intransigence and mocking tone made her feel worthless, and a part of her rebelled against the idea of weakness. A familiar voice resurfaced in her mind. She stood and slammed her hands down on the desk. The wood cracked. Ice crystals formed along her pale arms and fingers.

Irritated, Jack pressed the button on his phone again.

The door behind her opened and she felt drained and tired. Even the pain in her stomach began to subside. It felt good.

"I'm doing you a favor, Miss Celia," said Jack, a tone, derision in his voice. He walked around to her chair and grabbed her by the throat. With a quick shove, he slammed her back into the chair.

Footsteps and then a pair of slim hands landed on her shoulders, holding her in place. The touch felt comforting and deadening at once. She looked behind and saw a thin, wiry man with round glasses and short blonde hair. His grey suit was damp with rainwater and his sky-blue tie was slightly unknotted, but he was smiling nonetheless.

"Celia Cagill—" Jack bent at the waist to look Celia in the eyes. "Or do you want to take 'Hawkins' now?"

She sneered.

"Celia, meet Edward Palisade. He and I are both good friends of Mr. Gadreel. I'm afraid you came to the wrong place for revenge." He chuckled. "But I'm not a terrible man—"

"You're not a man at all," she said.

"I'm leaving you in the care of Mr. Palisade here. He can help to... remedy... that pain you feel. And he'll make sure you're just a normal, pleasant little girl from now on."

She struggled in the chair, but Palisade's held her firm.

"After all," said Jack, smiling. "Your last father just didn't cut it, did he?" He caressed Celia's face with the back of his hand and brushed a few strands of white-blonde hair back behind her ear. "I'm sure Edward will be much better suited to the task."

Nowhere

"SUSAN? WHAT—?"

She puts her finger to her lips and hushes him. "Quiet, my love. It's alright." She moves forward to comfort him, but Trent backs away, scrambling like a crab until the back of his head clunks against a small table. A metal object falls off the table and lands point-first on the floor an inch from his leg. The red-hued dagger wobbles slightly. Trent looks at it for a moment, then back up at Susan, and then he grabs the dagger and aims the point at her.

"Stay back! Who are you?"

She looks at him with an expression of sadness and pity. "Trent, baby, it's me. Susan."

Trent shakes his head. "No— No, Susan's dead. I don't believe you—"

"It's me, Trent." She frowns, stroking the cover of the Book.

"Then put that down. Throw that fucking thing away."

Susan looks down at the Book as if noticing it for the first time. "What? This silly thing?" She looks at Trent and raises an eyebrow. "No, I think I'll hold onto it. To protect you."

"Drop the Book, Susan. It'll destroy you, like it did to Celia. Just drop it."

"No." Her lip turns up into a snarl. She narrows her eyes. Her voice is nearly a hiss as she says, "It's mine."

Trent glances frantically around the small room. It's a cabin of some sort, a tiny hut, sparsely decorated. An old wood-burning oven stands against one wall and beside it is a small porcelain sink. The air hangs with a thin layer of wood smoke and smells strongly of cooking meat. He spots steaks sizzling in a pan on the stove.

Calm returns to him. And though he feels like he should be gasping with the weight of some invisible force upon his psyche, at least now he knows one thing for certain, and that emboldens him. "Too bad," he says. "It was a nice try, but you missed something."

With a sudden flick of the wrist, he whips the dagger forward at Susan's hands. Instinctively, he blinks and searches the darkness for reality variants, and he is startled to find that his power has returned. Hovering in the dark recesses of his mind are a hundred layers of possibility, floating and moving in and out of one another like ethereal shreds of image and sound. For the first time in the years since the Crash, he feels absolutely in control of the power. He can move and separate the possibility fragments with ease, and he carefully selects one and wills it into being.

Susan's eyes widen and she moves quickly to one side, but she can't move fast enough. The tumbling dagger's hilt smacks against her wrist and her fingers involuntarily splay and the Book drops to the floor with a heavier-than-expected thud.

"Susan doesn't eat red meat," Trent says, grinning.

The woman screams then, and as she does, her face twists and her skin slides against itself in impossible ways. The whole of the cabin changes; melts and transforms into less picturesque. It is a small cave, walls of unhewn, heavily knotted black-and-green wood. Junk rests against every surface, on every small, crudely made table, against every wall, stacked in some places to the ceiling.

Then the creature before him reveals itself—grey and sagging flesh, naked and covered with patches of sharp black hairs. Breasts like empty husks sway grotesquely as the thing shuffles backwards away from Trent. Its visage is a hideous array of skin folds and sallow bags, like a person that has aged—and starved—for a thousand years. The thing opens its mouth and bares its teeth, yellow and brown spikes, jagged and misshapen.

"You do not treat us this way," she whispers. "You are transgressing."

"Who are you?"

The thing issues a high-pitched howl that forces Trent to squint in pain. The creature rushes at him, yellow-clawed hands reaching for his neck. He sidesteps and deadens the creature's luck. A misstep and the monstrosity places a foot on a piece of junk, slips and pitches backwards, striking its head on a table before collapsing into a pile of old diapers and rusty tin cans.

In a flash, Trent drops to one knee, grabs the red dagger, and advances on the monster, placing the edge of the blade against the thing's neck.

"Talk!"

"We are the Shadow of Lilith, the dark hag, the forgotten Shade-Queen," she hisses. "You will pay for your insolence."

Trent shakes his head. "I doubt that." He presses the blade in closer, until he can see the edge depressing Lilith's flesh. She reeks of rotting meat and shit and only Trent's fury prevents him from retching at the smell. "How did I get here? Where am I?"

Lilith grins, her pointed teeth dripping with grey, mucosal saliva. "For questions, we ask a boon."

"A boon?" Trent pushes the blade further into her skin, threatening to split it open. Grey tears stream down her pallid face. "How 'bout I *don't* stab you with a knife forged in Hell?" Trent says. "I hear this metal does fun things to monsters like you. How does that sound?"

She snarls, but nods.

Trent pulls the dagger back an inch. "Gadreel stabbed me. How did I end up here?"

"This is the Realms of Shadow," she says. "A part of you is always here, *Trent*," she spits out his name like a curse. "The shadows are your alpha and your omega." She gestures toward the small opening leading out of the cave. "We find you in the black desert." She glances at the dagger in his hand. "We find you with *that* in your chest. As you say, weapons made in the demons' forges banish the Shadow-kin from the mortal realm. You must be one of us if it sends you *here*."

Trent shakes his head. "I'm mortal." He gestures toward the Book with his head. "Must've been that. What exactly is it?"

"Raziel's book," she says. "It is a part of him, a part of the Prince. He is Raziel and Raziel is he and the Book and this place all at once and separate. You should not bring it here."

The suffocating pain slams against Trent's psyche again. He winces and doubles over, though the knife remains level with Lilith's neck.

"What's happening to me? Why does this place hurt so much?"

Lilith raises an eyebrow. "You are still connected? You are here, in Abaddon, but some part of you remains there, the God-given part, in His jurisdiction. Time moves differently here: there is no past, just what *is* and what *will be*. The longer you remain here, the older your soul becomes, until it is nothing but dust, just like your wife, just like me."

"Where is she? Where's Susan? Take me to her—"

"Susan is dead." Lilith giggles, a malevolent flare in her eyes.

"If this is the Shadow Realms, then she's here." He presses the dagger into the flesh again, and has nearly made a cut when Lilith stops him with a howl.

"No," she says. "You cannot cut one of our kind, not here. Not with that. A deep wound and we will cease to be, removed, unmade from all of existence."

Trent considers that for a moment. It's a strong card, stronger than he had expected. With a quick motion, he draws a fine, superficial line in her skin with the edge of the blade. Black fluid wells up.

"Where is she, then? Tell me or I'll cut deeper."

Lilith howls again. "No more, no more. Please! We send her to her demise," the old hag says, pouting. "We send her to the *grigorim* city, to see Zamagiel." Lilith grins, despite the tears running down her ancient face. "But we tell the *grigori* after we get our boon. Zamagiel will rend her to dust."

Fighting back revulsion, Trent reaches out with his free hand and grabs Lilith's arm. He pulls the hag to her feet. She scratches between her legs, though remains stiff in posture.

"What will you do with us?" she asks.

"You're coming with me," Trent says. "You're gonna take me to the *grigorim* city."

"To Dis? It is too far."

"Time moves differently here, right? I'll bet you know a shortcut."

Lilith shakes her head at first, but Trent advances with the blade again. She snarls, and says, "There is one, but—"

"I don't care," replies Trent, interrupting her warning. "I'll face anything to find her before she reaches Zamagiel. I won't let him destroy her." He looks deep into the hag's eyes. "But if you betray me... if you fail to get us back to the mortal realm, I'll destroy *you*."

She ignores his threat. "Oh, you can't go back," she says, her face a grotesque mask of mockery. "You're in Abaddon now. You've always been here. And you always will be."

Trent snorts and shoves the hag out of the cave and into the dim, dust-strewn wasteland of the Realms of Shadow. At the last second, he remembers the Book and reaches back inside to take it with him.

*   *   *

The labyrinth's iron walls stretch hundreds of feet above her and she feels a twinge of memory, a sense of moving beneath the skyscrapers of New York City on a visit there once; steel canyons suffocating and hemming her in, herding her along their arcane and pointless paths. She runs a hand along the cold, rough metal to ward off onrushing vertigo.

It is as though she has been walking for a hundred years and knows that, in some sense, she has, for there is no past here. It may take her a minute or a millennium to reach the end of the maze, but when she finally does, she will be free of it, and there will be nothing that came before. The notion comforts her, even with its alienness.

She wonders if Zamagiel will recognize her. If his memory remains intact enough to remember when he encountered her in the hospital, when he killed all those people in his brutal attempt to kidnap a terrified little girl. She wonders if Zamagiel remembers her husband, the man who sent him here and saved the mortal world. *Trent.* She likes repeating his name. She doesn't want to forget it.

She walks, her mind running through memories of her past life with Trent like an erratic, frame-jumping home video.

After what seems like an eternity or a second, Susan stops. She looks around. The iron maze appears much the same as it always has. She feels no progress. Hope dwindles.

"No," she says aloud. "I will find my way out."

She looks at the sky as she walks, wondering about the dark cloud that appeared while she fought the Prince's hunters. It had long since dissipated, returning the sky of

Abaddon to an unchanging charcoal grey, but flakes of ash now fell like light snow, and she wondered if this new weather was somehow related.

She stops again and looks ahead. The rusted walls stretch on forever into the distance, turning sometimes at ninety-degree angles, sometimes at forty-fives, and sometimes even doubling back on themselves in wide, sweeping circles. She does not feel lost, not quite. She feels abandoned.

She sits upon the ashen dust, her brilliant white gown twitching with an imperceptible breeze. She plays with the fabric as tears form at the corners of her eyes. Despair sets in and she begins to cry, softly, distraught with the frustration of failure, of knowing that she has the ability to make choices, yet none of them effect change in this place.

Change?

Her tears dry and she grips the hem of her dress, analyzing it as though it might contain some great secret. A smile breaks across her face. *Change!*

She stands and walks to one of the iron walls. *I am different*, she thinks. *This maze is to keep the wild Shades out, to protect the city of Dis from the things that roam the shadow wastes.*

She places both hands on the rough metal surface and feels the crevasses and pocks with her fingertips. "But I am not a thing of this realm," she whispers. Then louder, "I am Susan. I have a name." She concentrates and iron shifts and buckles beneath her palms. It lets out tortured, metallic shrieks. "I can shape things here!" she yells. "And I want a Door!"

The labyrinth wall convulses and shudders, and the ground rings as the metal stresses and cracks. And before her, now, stands a crude door, cut flush into the iron surface, with a square bar for a handle. She gives the door a hard shove and it swings open on invisible hinges. Beyond, she sees the first new thing she has seen for what seems like a thousand years.

Iron towers, black and foreboding, most crumbled into ruin, stand on the horizon across a great empty plain, surrounded by labyrinth for as far as Susan can see. Amidst the towers hulk inactive foundries and massive, complicated monstrosities, titanic siege machines now become monuments of a time past, and she knows that this is a mote in the Prince's ever-changing eye, a static place amidst the unending chaos. A place with a past. It is the City of Dis, the *grigorim* stronghold, the frontier outpost of the once-powerful empire of Hell. And even in ruin, it remains a sanctuary for those within, a contained fiefdom beneath the iron hand of Lord Zamagiel, who has the answer Susan has come to find.

10

THE DAY HAD GONE FROM bad to worse. Louis sat in the cabin of his old pickup truck, listening to the rain tap-tapping on the metal roof and watching it run in rivulets down the cracked glass windshield. Beside him were all the possessions he had left—a handful of crinkled old manuscript pages, a jacket with a scorched hole in it, a gym bag with a handful of files that he had saved from the fire, and some yellowing bank ATM deposit envelopes he had found in the truck's glove compartment. Beyond the rain-dappled side window, he kept a wary eye on Trent and Celia's apartment, hoping that one or both of them would eventually show up. He tried to fight back the notion that they wouldn't. He closed his eyes and leaned back against the torn-vinyl seat.

Guilt washed over him like the rain washing down the windshield. In the distance, a quiet roll of thunder. He'd told Trent too much, some of it even true. He'd pushed him too far, revealed too many secrets, and now the man was gone, off to exact revenge on a creature that Louis suspected would be too great of an adversary even for the Doombringer. And what of Celia, lost to that demon? Could he have prevented that? Should he have?

His faith in the Prophecy had been deeply shaken. It might even be broken. Many prophecies never came true—it stood to reason that perhaps the course of things could be altered. Where did that leave him, a scholar, a seeker of truths, if the truths he sought had gone sour, in part by his own hand?

A sudden banging on the driver's side window ended his ruminations. He opened his eyes and looked out expecting to see a vagrant or a cop. He saw a thin, black-haired woman instead, fury in her eyes. His heart raced. "Shitshitshit!"

He wrapped his fingers around the keys, already in the ignition. One turn, a grumbling and grinding, but no spark. Another turn, same thing. From outside, Fiamma's voice.

"Open the door, Bird. We're goin' for a ride."

Louis ignored her, frantically trying a third time to start the truck. It finally grumbled to life. He yanked on the parking brake lever and heard the metallic pop as the brake released. Then he fumbled with the automatic shift and ground it noisily into 'D'. But before he could hit the gas, there was a bright flash to his left. He looked and, to his horror, Fiamma's entire right arm had burst into white-hot fire. She slammed it through the truck door, ripping through the metal like a bullet through paper and her glowing fingers appeared inside the cab. Then, with a powerful motion, she tore the entire door off its hinges and tossed it into the street.

"Move," she said. "I'll drive." Louis obediently moved over and she climbed inside, arm cooling to normal, her shirtsleeve now little more than a collection of smoking threads and fluttering, ashy scraps.

As they barreled down the highway, *sans* driver-side door, Louis found himself pushed up tight against the passenger door, hoping that the lock wouldn't give way. Sometimes it popped open when he made sharp turns and he didn't want to end up deposited on the road at high speed.

"The Medicine Man," she said, as if the question were implied.

"Yeah?"

She turned on him, smoke wisps curling from her nostrils. "Where?"

"You're driving," said Louis, a faint spark of courage dancing in his chest. "You figure it out."

The smoke from her nose grew thicker, blacker. Her eyes glowed fiery orange and her veins glowed yellow beneath her skin.

"Okay, okay!" he said, putting his hands up in defense. "*Cherubim* have him. He's heavily guarded. On the Strip."

"Where?"

"Silver."

"What?"

"That new casino. The really swank one they just built. Called 'Silver.'" He took a deep breath, steadying his nerves. "Pretentious fucks," he said. "Fucking *cherubim*." He hoped the dig would curry some favor with his captor.

She didn't seem to notice. "Why is it kept in a casino?"

Louis shrugged. "Why not? Best security in the country, the world maybe. This whole city is a fucking police-state in disguise. Did you know when you get off a plane at McCarran, the big casino-hotels can be automatically notified of your arrival? Then the cameras everywhere, they track you from your first step on Nevada soil all the way to the bathroom in your suite. And then, if you try to cheat a game—"

Fiamma turned the wheel sharply to the left, launching the old truck onto Las Vegas Boulevard. Sure enough, the passenger side door popped open. Louis scrambled for purchase on the fabric seat, but felt his legs slip further out the door as the truck bounced over a curb. He cried for help.

Fiamma straightened the vehicle, grabbed Louis by the collar and pulled him back into the truck. The door clanged shut as the vehicle rocked.

"Why is it kept here?" she repeated.

Louis gasped for breath, his chest heaved and head bobbed with fear and exertion. "He— umm— he—"

Fiamma made a 'hurry it up' motion with her finger.

"They— they— this, Las Vegas valley, I mean, this is an old place. I mean really *old*," he said. "Haven't you ever wondered why so many groups of people wanted to put down roots in the middle of a goddamn desert? There's something under the dirt here, and I don't mean Mafia bodies."

Louis took another deep breath and tried to ignore the fact that Fiamma ran a red light without hesitation. Cars honked and screeched behind them. "The— the Spaniards named the place at the turn of the nineteenth century. Mormons founded the original city fifty years or so later. Leave it to religious zealots to sense a weak spot in the fabric of reality and decide to start a fucking colony there." He fidgeted in his seat, paused. "You gonna kill me?" he asked.

"Maybe."

"Umm..." He trailed off. Then, "Turn right."

She spun the wheel again and he dug his feet into the floorboards in order to keep from sliding into her lap.

She straightened out the truck and turned to look at him. This time, her eyes were normal. "Look," she said. "Things have changed. I've changed. I'll kill you if I need to, but right now... I don't need to. So relax. I just need to see the Medicine Man. Does it speak English?"

"I dunno. I've never met him."

"What is it, exactly? Who is it?"

Louis shrugged. "Everyone just calls him the Medicine Man. I've always pictured an old Native American dude."

"You watch too much television."

"Probably. Well, I did... until you melted my TV."

"How do you know all this shit?"

"Freemason, remember?"

She turned and eyed him suspiciously. "Why do I think you're lying to me?"

Louis smiled weakly.

"You're not coming in with me," she said. "This is between me and him. I don't care where you go, but I'd recommend you get un-involved with this whole situation real quick. Things are not going to go well after what I'm about to do."

Louis stared blankly out the window.

Ahead, the gorgeous façade of Silver came into view. It was a thoroughly new casino-hotel, with unusual angles and modern, sharp lines, punctuated by the oddly-complementary ancient-looking decorative touches: lines and tiny circles, arched doorways, angelic script carefully inlaid as modern art, though to Louis' eyes, the hand of the *cherubim* was obvious. Unlike many of its neighbors, its neon focused only on white and faint blue. Even in the rain-dimmed midnight dark, the cylindrical hotel tower gleamed white.

*   *   *

By 3:00 AM, the thunderstorm had become an ominous beast growling and rumbling as it loomed over Las Vegas. Quiet flashes of lightning lit the horizon frequently, sometimes straying closer, sometimes accompanied by a low roll of thunder or a short, loud bang. The rain pelted the roof of Palisade's car as he drove through downtrodden West Vegas, passing myriad homeless and tired, sickly squatters and deviants. They all watched the lone car splash down their garbage-littered streets. Celia remained silent.

His mere presence made her feel good in a way that she had never felt in her life. It made her feel normal, quiet inside; his glances quelled the whisperings of the Nightmare Bringer in her gut and the voice at the back of her mind that compelled her to do the things she hated. But Palisade's deadening effect also made her feel empty. Dead inside. And his desires made her feel sick. But something else lingered deep inside her, something strong enough even to resist Edward's deadening effect....

"We're here," he said, in his quiet, perfect, accentless tone. He parked the car and got out. Celia refused to budge from the passenger seat, so he came around and yanked her to the ground.

The Lucky Lady Motel. The irony was not funny at all. Edward Palisade had told her most of the horrible things he had planned for her on the way to this motel on the edge of urban squalor, a place that people came to for only a handful of reasons, none of them pleasant.

He pulled her to her feet and dragged her to a ground floor room, keyed in, and shoved her inside. She stumbled and fell to the floor. He shut the door behind them and slammed the deadbolt home.

"On the bed," he said, pointing.

She didn't move.

"Now," he said and narrowed his eyes.

"No."

He walked over to her and kicked her hard in the ribs. "On the goddamn bed!"

She wouldn't move, he kicked her again, harder. She felt a rib crack. Her breath came in gasps, but she wasn't about to obey his orders.

"Fine," he said, and pushed up his glasses. He tossed his sky-blue tie onto the bed and unbuttoned his shirt. "We'll do this your way, then. On the floor, like animals."

"You're sick," she said quietly.

He smiled and tossed aside his shirt. "Clothes off," he said. "Sooner we're done here, sooner I can end you." He chuckled. "Gadreel would be terribly angry if he knew I was delaying for… this. But it can be our little secret, can't it?"

She gave him the finger.

Furious, he reached down and hoisted her to her feet. Tears rolled down her cheeks as she struggled to maintain her steely expression. She met his gaze and refused to look away.

"I said..." He grabbed the front of her hospital gown, preparing to tear it off of her.

But then her fear and despair vanished, and the voice from the back of her mind welled up like blood from a sudden and unexpected cut. The voice whispered at first, but grew louder with every passing moment. Its insistence girded her courage. With an anguished cry, she kicked Palisade in the groin.

He shrunk back from her, clutching at himself. His face reddened and as he rocked in pain, he shouted, "You little bitch! I'm gonna fucking kill you!"

Celia ran for the back of the motel room, hospital gown flapping. She entered the bathroom and slammed the door shut, just in time to smack it against Palisade's face. She turned the lock and jumped back from the door.

"You goddamn *whore!*" he screamed. "Where are you gonna fuckin' *go*, huh!?"

Every time Palisade slammed against the door, her courage intensified and the voice grew louder in her mind, eclipsing her fear. Cold pain seeped back into her arteries and she could sense strange and fell energies surging along her spine, fighting against Palisade's deadening effect, and winning. The thing in her stomach kicked again, harder than ever before.

She rushed to the sink first and turned on all the water, then did the same with the shower. Palisade continued to rattle the door in its frame.

He swore over and over as he punched the wood. Then his pounding stopped. Celia knew he was listening, trying to figure why she had turned on all the water. Then the realization would come. Gadreel had told him about Celia, had explained her lineage. It would suddenly hit home.

She heard him shout, "Oh, shi—"

The door burst outward in a spray of wood splinters as a thousand gleaming, crystalline shards pierced the painted surface, skewering Palisade's flesh like the closing lid of an iron maiden. His arms flailed and twitched as he fell to the floor amidst a splash of water, the spikes having returned to their natural form. Blood pooled on the cheap green carpet.

Celia stepped out of the steam-filled bathroom, her hospital gown clinging to her thin form, sheathed in sparkling ice. Water dripped from the hem of her gown as she stepped over Palisade's bleeding, gasping body. She didn't look back as she unlocked the motel room door and walked out into the dirty streets, cloaked in early morning darkness.

A light rain continued to fall, turning the dusty streets into corridors of trash-laden mud. She sloshed through it, barefoot, ignoring the blood and pain. A single thought occupied her mind, a thought that, for now, kept the entity in her belly quiet and still.

She thought about the Book. *I hear you, my angel.*

Vengeance consumed her.

Now it's my turn. Raziel will teach me. She could hear him now, through the thing inside her, speaking from the world beyond, as though his voice were channeling through the darkness at her core. She could hear the dark angel's voice echoing from within the pages of the Book, somewhere in a distant place, calling to her, drawing her ever closer to that impossible realm. He waited for her there. He promised her unbridled power. She would finally be able to channel her own powers and control the Bringer of Nightmares that lurked inside her, to use its power as her own.

I will become a queen of ice and fear, an unstoppable force. I will build an army of believers, and nothing will ever hurt me again.

She moved through the dark and fetid underbelly of the Las Vegas wasteland. Her bloodied feet kicked through trash and filth on the dirty streets. She passed the dead husk of a defunct liquor store, drawing puzzled stares from the two bums lying propped against the graffiti-stained exterior. The grizzled old men watched her as she passed.

A thin veil had sprung up around her, tendrils of black mist darting and swooping through the air, surrounding her like an indeterminate shroud. She felt the presence of the Book and knew the whispering came from it, through her, through the dark creature at her center; whispering, calling, Raziel's distant voice filling the night with a siren song that hung invisible in the dim light. It was a call to arms, but she did not yet know to whom it was calling.

And then the pain in her gut came back, suddenly and with more ferocity than ever. She tumbled to the asphalt in the parking lot of an abandoned shopping mall. She screamed in pain, pressed her palms against the ground, leaving icy handprints in the puddles of rainwater. The wave of pain subsided and, crying now, she struggled to her feet.

The mall, she thought. For a while, I can rest. Decide what to do.

She stumbled toward the mall entrance, one hand clutching her aching belly. Her knees trembled, threatened to collapse. Without a thought, she placed a hand upon one of the locked doors, transformed it into ice, and then shouldered her way through with a spectacular crash that sent her reeling to the dust-covered floor inside, surrounded by glittering shards.

When she next opened her eyes, a strange calm descended on Celia. She was soaked through, lying in a pool of ice-cold water just inside the entrance to an abandoned shopping mall. It might have been seconds or it might have been days, for all she knew, since the last time her eyes had been open. Her thoughts, her memories, seemed *fuzzy*. The only clarity was the growing realization that something was *coming*, something new and terrible and different, and she would be its beginning and its future. She would birth it and be it. Stinging pain pounded her insides.

She climbed to her feet and shuffled a few feet into the mall. The nearest entrance was to an old theater. When the mall had closed they hadn't even bothered to tear down the posters and it still proudly advertised some movie about a happy, smiling couple, another featuring animal cartoon characters, and a modern western. The poster featured a man in a grey cowboy hat set against a backdrop of flame. A memory stirred in Celia's brain, rattled around for a while, and then died, unrecognized. She passed the poster and ice-smashed her way into the theater.

The place looked as it must have the day it closed, except for a heavy layer of dust on everything. A black faux-leather bench rested against a nearby wall. Dusty red velvet ropes divided the lobby into lines.

Celia made her way wearily towards the bench, knocking over a stanchion in the process. It clattered to the ground with a loud, metallic bang.

She fell onto the bench, clutching at her heaving gut. She let out a bloodcurdling scream, scaring even herself. And another as the next wave of pain outdid the first. "Oh, God," she said aloud, "What is happening to me?"

And then she blacked out in the dark theater, the air around her growing colder by the second.

NOWHERE

TRENT FEELS A STRANGE SENSE of belonging as he moves behind Lilith, a sensation that nags and eats at him, like a word at the tip of his tongue, nearly remembered. And when he looks at the shuffling hag, her darkened form seems familiar, as if she were the shadow of a long-forgotten friend, cast upon the rock walls of the cavern. He can't help feeling like they'd met, once before, in that other world, where time has sway.

His gaze darts constantly from black, looming spires to the strange, diminutive shadow creatures scampering across the dusty plain, to the charcoal-grey sky and its unending rain of fine, drifting ash. But despite his wavering attention, his arm remains outstretched and his hand holds steady at the back of Lilith's neck, red-hued dagger gleaming dully in the interminable dusk. He will not have her divert him. He has promised to slit her throat at even the slightest whiff of betrayal, and the comingled fear and lip-curling anger that dances across her face convinces Trent of her understanding.

He looks out at the horizon, the thin grey line separating black plains from the ashen sky, and he prays that Susan still lives—prays that he is not too late.

"Is in here," the old hag says. She has stopped and points into a narrow canyon, barely four feet wide in most places, hemmed in by enormous rock walls, like endless ebony skyscrapers. Even the dim light of Abaddon has difficulty piercing here, and the canyon is swathed in deep shadow, pitch-black in places.

"What is this place?" Trent asks.

Lilith smiles, showing her crooked, mucous-laden teeth. "It is one of the old places, from before Creation. One of the dreams buried in Abaddon. The Satan made it once, and so it stands. Only the Satan may be its unmaking."

Trent pulls the knife closer to the hag's throat, and as he leans in to whisper into her ear, he smells the stomach-churning odor of rotting flesh mixed with an almost heady perfume of sex and sweat and he winces, but holds firm. "Why have you brought me here? Where is the shortcut to Dis?"

Lilith raises her hands in defense, back arched to maintain a precarious position between the blade and Trent's grip on the back of her neck. "This is it," she says, waving her hand at the dark corridor. "The Black Canyon. At the end is the *grigorim* city. Much shorter than walking the wastes."

"What's in there?"

Lilith snarls. "The Black Canyon is nightmares. Is mortal dreams, stories, myths, horrors, tragedies." She looks Trent directly in the eyes. "Is the beginning and the end of all that you know and want and believe."

Trent shakes his head and lets out a quick snort. "I've faced worse things than nightmares. Let's go." He pulls on Lilith's arm, still holding the blade to her throat.

"No, no, no!" she shrieks. "I cannot go to Dis! The Prince will destroy me."

"Either he will, or I will. Your choice."

The old hag glowers at him and then turns away and shuffles toward the canyon opening. Trent jogs to catch up and then follows closely, his blade still pressed tight against her withered, sagging throat, and Raziel's Book still burning cold against his lower back.

*   *   *

In a sense, she has made it, she has reached her destination, and yet Susan's heart is heavy for she stands before the gates of the Iron City, Dis, the outpost perched upon the edge of the black pit, the gateway to Hell. And she remembers reading Dante in college and is startled to see his insights incarnate. Above the sky-piercing iron doors, above the rusted, inlaid caricatures of mortal faces, screaming in fury and anguish and horror, above all of this looms words in a language she does not know, but can read, raised metal letters, rounded and worn from countless eons of Abbadonian cyclones sweeping across the gates:

Abandon all hope, ye who enter here.

She stands before the massive, closed doors, and listens to the wasteland winds as they howl across the iron wall that rings the city. The inlaid faces and wicked carvings catch the breeze and turn it to horrible music, screeches and high-pitched, ear-splitting whistles that rise and dim again without warning. And always a low howling, a dark keening—despair as song.

Susan falls to her knees. "Oh, God," she says, and can think of no words of greater dismay, for she realizes in that instant, truly and completely, for the very first time, that she is dead.

A sudden rumbling fills the air and the iron doors begin to open, the crack widening as the portal grinds against the dirt at its base. Guards pour through the crack, their forms like things from ancient woodcuttings, tall and perfect in shape, but horrific also, with gaunt, sagging skin and bat-like wings of immense width folded against their backs. Each of them carries a metal spear. They rush to Susan where she kneels and grab her and lift her and take her back inside the doors, which have already begun to close again.

And she cannot stop crying as they carry her into the Iron City, her bare toes dragging limply through the black dust.

*   *   *

"Reality—your mortal reality—is the best of a set of nightmares. Your world is created by God, but the darkest events stem from here, from the Realms of Shadow. It is a womb, birthing tragedy."

Trent shoves the hag, who had begun to slow in her steps. "Keep walking," he says. "Find the exit."

As they move through the narrow canyon, the walls seem to press in on them, making Trent nervous. He's never thought of himself as claustrophobic, but now he wonders. He wants out—the sooner, the better.

"Look," she says, pointing at the glassy black wall of the corridor. "There's a tragedy *you* might remember."

Trent can't help but look and sees the shadows dancing in the black glass. Shapes that at first seem unfamiliar, but then horrifyingly real. He sees himself in shadow. And Susan. The doctor is approaching them. This is the second time they've been here, the second time the baby has come entirely too early, in a wash of blood and quiet. The doctor shakes his head slowly....

"No!" Trent averts his gaze, a lump forming in his throat and a pit in his stomach. He shoves Lilith even harder, forcing her to stumble forward. "Keep moving," he mutters through clenched teeth.

She lets out a hideous cackle. "And you think you'll walk in ignorance to the end?" She makes a *tsk tsk* sound, a mother scolding a child. "No, no. You'll not make it through like that. You must see where you are going, Trent Hawkins. And you *must* see where you've been." She cackles again.

"Why does this place exist?" Trent whispers, still trying desperately to fight the urge to watch the terrible scenes playing out behind the gleaming dark. "Why would Satan put it here?"

"Hard to say." The old hag shrugs. "The dark hag only knows of its beginnings and its ends. In one way, the way we came, and it ends in Dis, where the pit Sheol stands as the edge of Hell. But in the other way, from Dis, and it ends in dust. It is the last walk for ruined angels. A judgment in the Iron City and then a walk into nothingness. Banishment not only from God, but from all of existence. Enter that way, and you cannot turn back. Perhaps the first Satan feared an eternity here. Perhaps he fashioned himself a permanent escape. Or maybe he made his own punishment. And none after him had the courage to unmake it."

But Trent is only half-listening. Beyond the dark hag's ramblings, the walls echo with human tragedy, and so many of them speak directly to him. He sees the men and women stabbed or shot to death by drug dealers empowered by his own dollars. He sees children worked to death for the diamonds he had bought with his gambling wins, diamonds he had given to her, to Susan, in hopeless attempts to make up for his cheating, for his drug habit, to placate her cries in the middle of the night as she clutched her distended belly that no longer moved. Tears roll down his cheeks as he pushes the dark hag along the canyon.

She cackles and claps gleefully as she shuffles along the dusty canyon.

11

THE PICKUP TRUCK'S TIRES SQUEALED as it sped away from Silver. Fiamma didn't blame Louis for that. She had tortured him and burned down his apartment and most of his life's work in the past twenty-four hours alone. *Sure*, she decided. *Guy has a right to be a little pissed.* But in the back of her mind, somewhere very far and very deep, a low, powerful voice rose up. A voice that demanded an extermination of weakness. A voice that insisted upon a lack of pity for others' worthless emotions. A voice that gave Fiamma pause.

She hadn't meant to pause, as she stared up at the gorgeous, ornately-modern façade of the Silver casino-hotel. She'd expected constant determination to carry her through what she was about to do. It worried her that that determination had faltered.

There is no faltering, came the deep, powerful voice. *Only rage.*

Fiamma felt heat spreading through her limbs. The acrid twin smells of sulfur and ash surrounded her nostrils. She looked around the Strip, the city of Las Vegas, the world in which she stood, and realized with a tiny flicker of dismay that she was no longer part of it, in many ways. She was something *else* now, a thing that could not smell the baked goods in the nearby patisserie, a creature that could not smile at a nearby couple, kissing beneath a rain-dappled umbrella. She had become a monster.

I've always been a monster, she thought, knowing that this was her own voice, even as she heard the sentiment echoed by the deeper, nastier voice.

She balled her fists, producing thick black smoke that curled up from the cracks between her fingers. Eyelids half-lidded, she lowered her head. Raindrops sizzled as they turned to steam upon the exposed skin of her neck. Her thoughts, her emotions, her hopes for a normal life, turned inward, and then faded to black and red.

Her confident strides carried her across the threshold of the casino's main entrance. She wondered, with a tinge of malicious excitement, what the operators behind Silver's security cameras thought of her, a skinny woman in black pants, torn black shirt, tattooed, with dense black smoke curling in her wake. Did she look like a monster yet?

As soon as she stepped into the lobby, she knew that security was already on to her. Men in their crisp all-white suits and white-corded earbuds came towards her, each with a finger pressed against the device in their ear, listening to the orders from on high. She smiled.

The casino's main lobby, except for the touches of angelic script and art-deco flourishes, was like any other: bank after bank of ringing, clanging, flashing slot machines stood in rows like grocery store isles, food for the weak and desperate. Beyond the slots, various related video games, and beyond those, table games. A glittering gold ball that bounced around a silver roulette wheel, from slot to slot, as players watched intently. At several craps tables, gamblers alternately cheered and groaned. To the right, was a walled-in poker lounge and next to it, the cage, where white-clad casino employees traded shiny metallic chips for dollars. All around, men in white suits observed. Drifting between every chaotic node of luck and wealth were the waitresses, gorgeous women in diaphanous silver-and-white gowns. Fiamma noticed silver faux-tattoos of angel wings on each of their shoulders.

She sneered, muttering. "The *cherubim* have fucking lost it."

And then she began.

The first two men to reach her were a pit boss and his muscle; a heavyset, boxer-type with a mean scar that crossed his cheek and dug into his left ear. Both men, of course, had one blue eye and one green.

Fiamma nodded, smiled at the men as they approached, and then set them aflame with a touch.

She couldn't believe how easy it was. The power that pooled within her now, deep in her core, seemed almost endless in its depth, and entirely summonable at her briefest whim. The unpredictability and struggle to keep her powers in check had been replaced by a feeling of absolute control. Now she felt the energies' ebb and flow, a natural movement from her core to extremities and back again. Merely a touch, the tiniest bit of contact, and fire rushed up the front of the two men, catching in their suit fabric, white-hot, faces of concern blackened by flame and panic. They fell to the floor, screaming.

Heads turned, women screamed, men cursed in surprise. Sudden bursts of shouting, commands and orders were barked from all over the cavernous space. A few seconds of shocked silence made way for terrified panic and bloodcurdling shrieks, as gamblers clawed over one another, heading for the nearest exits.

Fiamma closed her eyes, tilted her head back, and felt the wonderful, terrible warmth wash over her. She felt calm, comforted, and purposeful. She knew she was a thing of beauty.

Her arms shed white-hot light, with fiery orange veins glowing beneath her rippling skin. Wicked yellowed claws had replaced her fingernails. A waitress ran past her, shrieking.

Fiamma grabbed the woman's throat with her clawed hand and effortlessly tossed her thirty feet through the air, where she smashed into a slot machine. Blood flowed down across a line of three cherries and intermingled with the coins spilling from the shattered device and collecting in the waitress' motionless lap. A flicker of pity rose in Fiamma, but she fought it off and turned to face the approaching trio of security officers and their guns.

The trio of *cherubim* fired upon her. Fiamma did not flinch, or duck, but watched as the lead slugs approached and summoned a wreath of flame to surround her. She felt the molten lead splatter her skin and drip off onto the floor. She smiled at the security officers and walked towards them.

"No! No!" shouted the one in the middle, firing his gun over and over, to no avail. The slugs vaporized, splattering lead on the slots nearby.

Fiamma grabbed the guy to his left, and hurled him across the room. The angel struck the metal bars of the cage and fell to the floor in a smoldering heap.

"What are you? What do you want from us?" said the *cherubim*. He dropped his gun, blubbering.

The guard to his right came at Fiamma and she grabbed his balled fist, which blistered, then bubbled and smoked. It cooked to a black, wretched eschar that crept up his arm to the elbow, then the shoulder. The angel passed out and slumped to the floor.

Mortal bodies, she thought. *Angels strike a balance with their hosts. Consensual possession.* One of the first things she had learned when she started working for Gadreel was that angels and demons still lived within the corpse, even after the human soul had shuffled off. But fire complicated things. Fire ate the body, cleansed the flesh, and sent the angel packing to the Shadow Realm. The only true way to remove them from this world. She watched as the unconscious guard smoldered and burned and she willed the fire atop him to a greater burn, only half-listening to the terrified babbling of the remaining security guard.

"We're doing the work of the Lord here. Why would you want to do this?"

Fiamma turned on him then grabbed his suit lapels with both smoldering hands and brought him close. The flesh of his face blistered in her radiating heat.

"The Medicine Man," she said, whispering. "You have him. Where?"

Resistance flickered in the angel's blue-and-green eyes. Thousands of years of service and loyalty, never broken, never compromised. But there was, Fiamma knew, a price to be paid for co-possessing a human body. Unlike demon possessions, the angelic ones never had entire control. The man glanced down, if only for a second.

"The basement," she said, smiling. "Of course." And then she lifted him off the ground and hurled the *cherubim* through the window of the poker lounge. He crashed through the glass and then lay, unmoving, amidst glowing curls of green felt, melting poker chips, and a snow-like cloud drifting ash and bits of burning cards.

She headed for the elevator.

Halfway across the now-emptied casino lobby, the sprinklers switched on. Cool water stopped inches from her skin, vaporizing to steam. By the time she reached the elevator bank, she knew that they were inactive. She heard more guards shouting beyond a white-painted door labeled "Stairwell".

When she opened the stairwell door, her immediate presence surprised the tangle of security. They all backed up a few steps as she stepped in among them.

Fire burst from her then, engulfing the small stairwell chamber, peeling the paint from the walls and setting the railings to shrieking with heat-borne metal fatigue. The concrete floors cracked and popped and groaned. A strange mélange of smells assailed her—burning hair and clothes, vaporizing chemical volatiles from within the metal and concrete, cooking meat, and the ever-present odor of ash and sulfur. The light from her own heat was so intense that she could see nothing for a moment. And then, the light died and the smoke cleared.

The pile of carnage that lay at her feet smoldered with bits of singed fabric, molten metal and plastic. Flames danced and licked the unrecognizable mess of cooked flesh and charred, blackened bone. The floor, once white concrete, was a yellow-brown mess of gooey, coarse muck. Gleaming from within the pile of charred skin and bone was the hilt of an angel's knife. Higher-ranking *cherubim* often carried them. She remembered the one Trent Hawkins had wielded against her, remembered it piercing her flesh, judging her, showing her terrible images of what she might become... what she now was. She picked it up and stowed it in what remained of her smoldering waistband and belt. Then, she extracted her boots from the molten goo, allowed her ambient temperature to drop to a lower burn, and headed down the stairs towards the basement.

As she descended, she heard more men shouting from up above and booted footsteps clattering on the concrete stairs, metal railings ringing. Then, the anguished shouts when they reached the mess of their cooked associates, and the redoubled orders to "Get her! Stop her!" But none of this worried her in the least. Her powers were beyond them now. These *cherubim* were but minions in a multiverse in which she was now a lord. The Lord of Hell itself. She tasted the name on her tongue as she traversed the stairs. It seemed so unlikely, so altogether mythological, and yet... She glanced at her hand. The skin boiled and danced with white-blue flame like that of an acetylene torch.

Who but a Lord of Hell has ever commanded such power?

The voice, she knew, was not entirely her own, though the two had become more difficult to separate in her mind now. That realization sent a spark of terror and revulsion coursing up her spine, but the fell energies rippling through her blood quickly swept it away.

When she finally reached the sub-basement door, she found it, unsurprisingly, locked. Without a second thought, she ran a finger down the length of one side, neatly melting through the internal hinges until the door fell off under its own weight. She walked into the dark, quiet concrete hall beyond, then placed the door back in its frame and welded it back into place. She wanted time to deal with the Medicine Man, whoever he or it might be. She didn't want *cherubim* buzzing around her like flies.

The long, dim hall, unmarked in any way save simple fluorescent safety lights every few feet along the wall, led finally to a single, steel door. In front of it stood two more security guards, eyes wide, machine pistols raised in defense.

"Back down!" one of them ordered.

The other shouted, "Step away!"

Surely they knew the futility of their current position. *Cherubim*, she thought then, countering herself. *Ever faithful. Someone important is behind this door.*

She did not stop. She made no attempt to dodge the hail of gunfire that did little more than dapple her skin with molten grey. She gripped each guard by the neck and stepped *into* the metal door, dragging their bodies through the groaning, melting mass. Her body flowed through, unmolested. Theirs did not. When she reached the other side, she dropped what remained of them and stood, staring, mouth suddenly agape, at what could only be the creature everyone called the Medicine Man.

* * *

Celia opened her eyes once more to the dim, miserable light of the abandoned mall theater. Her initial gaze fell upon an old poster, a movie about a serial killer that she had heard about a year or so ago, before the Blizzard, before her parents' deaths, but she had not been allowed to see it for its 'R' rating. A part of her laughed at that now, the strange impossibility of a life so mundane, so ordinary, with parents that cared for her, that protected her, that set rules and boundaries to keep her away from people like Edward Palisade. Parents that constructed a life for her, saved her from the madness of fallen angels and supernatural monstrosities.

She had wanted Trent to be her father, of sorts, after the Blizzard, though her feelings for him were stronger than that; an intensity that worried and delighted her, even as he failed her over and over. In what way did she love him? She had been confused about that for so long, but he was gone, dead, and now....

She lifted her head from the black faux-leather bench. The pain in her stomach had subsided some, at least for the time being. Everywhere seemed so still, so utterly dead and devoid of activity, and yet... there it was! A movement in the corner of her vision! She snapped her head around and fixed

her gaze on the thing, but there was nothing there. Except...
again! Against the wall behind the ticket counter.

She sat up. "Who's there?"

But no sound. Only stillness.

Then another shadowy flicker in her periphery.

And another.

And yet, with every one, she was unable to train her sight
upon the source of the distraction. She leapt from the bench,
afraid, wincing at the sudden, knife-like pain in her stomach,
and rushed to one of the big glass windows that looked out
over the mall parking lot.

"Help!" she screamed, pounding on the window with her
fists, though she saw no one outside that might hear her.

Dark shapes flitted about to either side of her. She could
sense their presence, even though she struggled to see them.
There, in the parking lot! A dark *something* appeared beneath
the light of a flickering sodium lamp, and then was gone.
There, another! And Celia then realized that whatever these
things *were*, they were descending upon her, massing. They
were coming to see her, though she could not see them.

And she panicked.

She would hide in a theater; wait for the things—
whatever they were—to leave. Her bloodied, sore bare feet
ached as she crossed the lobby. She gripped the theater door
handle and veins of ice burst from her fingers, covering the
door in a web of frozen strands. She yanked.

She expected to see, beyond the open door, a dark, empty
theater. Instead, gaping at her, stood a grey, swirling portal.
Beyond it stood a nightmarescape of jagged, obsidian spires
aimed at a black, starless sky. And traversing this nothing-

world, a multitude of shadowy *things*, not distinct and yet not indistinct at the same time, some with white, eye-like spots, others spider-like, or even humanoid, lurching with impossibly thin arms and legs across the barren landscape toward her, toward the swirling portal, toward her world—

Celia slammed the theater door shut. She rushed to a different theater, marked by an old poster for a movie about fighting robots. She noticed idly that ice was creeping from between her toes, travelling in spidery wires along the walls around her. The air had grown cold. She wrenched open the theater door.

Another vision of that same dead world of grey ash and dust. In the distance, a single human-like form, tall and thin and black, with a white spot where a face might be. It moved in fits and starts across the world, never traversing the space between its points of rest, and then it was closer, and then closer, and Celia saw its face; a simple, smooth mass of white, like a ceramic mask, with a single, razor sharp slice down the middle, from which oozed trails of red blood that moved out to the sides, as if the creature were perpetually facing a driving wind. Where eyes might be were two simple, round holes, and the blackness within stretched to the ends of time—

"No!" she yelled, and threw the door closed in the thing's face.

She staggered backwards, clutching at her chest and gut, which pounded now with a ferocity that matched each of her faltering steps. She sensed movement all around. She could *feel* the things lurking behind those doors. More shadows moved across the parking lot.

Celia stumbled back to the bench and fell upon it, sobbing. Just beyond the glass, snow was falling instead of rain. Icy frost crept in from the corners of the window frame. The walls around her cracked and popped with the ever-increasing cold. Shades danced in the corners.

"No, please," she whimpered, remembering the day of the Blizzard, the day that the fallen angel Zamagiel had tried to turn her bloodline to dark purposes, to death and destruction. She remembered swallowing the Bringer of Nightmares. She felt the kicking inside her belly now, growing in intensity with each passing second. Her eyelids closed with the pain.

A sudden nudge knocked her from her dream state. She looked into the face of a woman she recognized, but how? A woman, pretty but not striking, in a dazzling blue evening gown that glittered and sparkled, even here in the dim light, the sheer *blueness* of it reflecting in the ice that now covered every surface nearby. And behind the woman, past her wide-eyed, terrified face, a slavering mass of shadows danced and lurched.

"You!" said the woman, in a strangely awed tone of voice. "You see me!"

"What—?" Celia managed to say.

"You see me! You see me! You know me! I ate your apple! I ate it! My name is Anna! Please, I want to help you...."

But her voice trailed off into the black as Celia passed out, terrified and cold and suffering a pain that she had never once encountered, not in all of her fourteen years. The strange woman shook her, said something that Celia couldn't hear, and then Celia realized with dismay that her labor had begun;

the birth of the impossible child, lonely and scared and immensely powerful.

*   *   *

Fiamma recoiled at the sight of him—of it—or whatever it was once and had become now. Shock rippled through her, dampening the fires that burned from within, setting off a quiet transformation that made her a person once more, wings gone, claws become fingers, half-naked, draped in the scorched remains of her clothes. Her breath caught as she gazed upon the creature before her.

The angel—for he could be nothing else—sat, head bowed, upon a simple, metal folding chair in the center of the nondescript, white-concrete room. His pale, bare feet rested on the polished cement floor.

His body, or what she could see of it, looked frail and withered, the translucent skin sucked back against bone, pale as paper, through which Fiamma could see blue veins. Emaciated. Ruined. Draped in what she mistook, at first, for a strange cloak of some sort, until she realized with horror and revulsion that it was not clothing at all; the angel wore a robe of a thousand tubes and wires and multicolored lines of fluid so numerous that they blended together into a solid mass that shifted and swayed with even the subtlest movement. His pale skin quivered at regular intervals and his flesh had been broken in innumerable places to make way for the tubes and lines and catheters and wires, all pulsing, twitching in time to some rhythmic, silent beat, a chemical heartbeat that sent fluids sluicing into the figure's body. In some, the fluids moved quickly and in others, they seemed not to move at all.

But they were moving in, not away, and the machines and IV stands and cylindrical tanks lining the walls of the concrete chamber hissed, chirped, beeped, pumped their contents into the angel, all of them connected to the multitudes of tubes snaking across the floor in every direction.

His head bore a mass of stringy, lifeless blonde hair and he lifted his gaze to watch her approach. Unlike the rest of his body, the angel's face was beautiful, impossibly so, unmarred by whatever wasting disease had ravaged him, and his eyes were two glowing, golden-ringed orbs that seemed in that moment to bore straight into the center of her.

Fiamma took a few tentative steps forward.

The angel rose from his chair at her approach. The languid motion with which he did so suggested that this was not a movement he had made in quite some time. As he stood, the tubes lifted with him, still ferrying their contents into his form.

His voice came out pleasant, almost quiet, and with a calm that belied thousands of years of contemplation. "Come closer, child of man," he said, gesturing with his right hand, an action that caused a curtain of a hundred thin wires to sway beneath his arm.

She walked a few more steps, stopping at the edge of a mass of tubes upon which she dared not tread. "You're the Medicine Man."

The angel raised a golden eyebrow and gestured at her with his index finger, adorned at the tip with a thin, clear wire that ran back along his arm and disappeared into the mass of its kin. "You," he said, slowly, "are not Trent Hawkins."

"No."

A pulse set the tubes twitching again and the Medicine Man closed his eyes for a second and shuddered. "Something has changed."

"What *are* you?"

The long pause that followed was broken only by the whir and click of chemical pumps. "I am Michael," he said, finally. "The second-made."

"What have they done to you?"

"My *cherubim* have done nothing to me that I have not asked." He made a sweeping gesture that elicited a swishing sound from his cape of wires. "I am the representative of all of mankind to the heavenly host. What you see before you is what you have become, what your kind has become. I am you."

"That's insane."

"I am ruined. Every chemical, every drug, every electron, every communication, every thought and deed and desire and hunger, everything that man has become dependent upon, I am fed. I absorb all of this so that I might understand, so that I might share in man's sorrow. And it is only in this manner that I can find the strength to remain in this world, to live amidst that which humankind has made of God's creation."

"And you told the *cherubim* to do this to you? To string you up with permanent chemical drips? Why not pull the plug and end this?"

Michael took a shuffling step forward, the tubes sliding across the floor all around him. He stopped a mere foot from Fiamma.

She thought at first that she might back away from this strange, once-powerful being, but that deep voice rose up inside her and she held her ground. Fiamma did not back down, nor cower, nor avert her gaze.

To her surprise, Michael leaned in and smelled her with his perfect, unblemished nose. Then he stood straight again and locked his eyes with hers. "Why do you disturb me today, daughter of Belial?"

"The Prophecy is unfolding," she said, her words punctuated by a hydraulic hiss from some unseen equipment beneath the floor. The next words came natural and calm; she had practiced them over and over since leaving Tricia's bed. "I come seeking passage to Abaddon, so that I might set the sides to balance before the battle."

Michael stared into her eyes without speaking. Finally, he said, "You ask a great deal of yourself."

"I ask for passage," she repeated.

"And why do you believe that it is my charge to grant you passage to that place, that realm outside the jurisdiction of God Himself?" Michael leaned even closer, until his forehead nearly touched hers. "Do you truly know of what you ask, child of Hell?"

"I *ask*," she said, "for *passage*."

The archangel straightened up suddenly and his overwhelming presence set Fiamma's heart pounding. The voice from the ruined angel's lips came out strong and powerful. "You ask for my demise. There is only one way that I may enter the Realms of Shadow, and it is the only way that I might grant passage to another. That journey begins with my death and ends with my undoing. Is this what you ask of me? Ask yourself, Belial-kin: can you kill an archangel, even broken as you are?"

A tear rolled down Fiamma's cheek, but her impassive expression remained, her lips unwavering, her hands clenched tight. "Yes," she said.

The angel's countenance softened. He turned away from her and shuffled slowly back to his chair. The tubes pulsed rhythmically as he seated himself once more. "Then so be it," he whispered. "The covenant will be broken. Now an aspect of Belial, your murder of an archangel will begin the Great War. You understand this?"

Fiamma nodded, quietly sobbing, She walked to the seated angel and placed her hands against his temples. She leaned in and kissed his forehead. Tears fell from Michael's beautiful, downcast eyes. Her body shuddered, mirroring the pulses that rippled through his. Then they embraced and she kissed his head again, heat waves lifting from them both. Holding his head with one hand, she used the other to reach behind her back and retrieve the angelic dagger.

She brought it forward.

Michael closed his golden eyes.

She drove the dagger home.

She tried not to listen to the lamenting cries filling the room like an extended echo, and then ended, just as suddenly.

The room stood empty, save for a mass of untethered tubes, contents oozing together and casting up fumes that might have smelled like sorrow and death and ash.

NOWHERE

WITH EVERY STEP, TRENT HEARS his name whispered, screamed and yelled. Black images within the walls dance and gyrate, all competing for his attention, and he is forced to avert his gaze lest the nightmares he witness send him to the ground in despair. On more than one occasion, a sidelong glance nearly does just that.

"You cannot look, you cannot look," says Lilith in a singsong voice, goading him with delight. "The dreams haunt you even now. How can that be?" She giggles. "Your kind has strength in the land of the real, but cowers in the face of dream. It terrifies you, worries you, makes you wake up in cold sweat. And every journey between nightmare and real is a journey to this canyon and back. In the belly of nightmare we are. In the belly of horror."

"Shut up!" Trent growls. "Just show me the way out."

Lilith laughs, long and high-pitched, her body shaking with glee.

After her chortling dies down, she whispers, "I'll show you the way out. I'll show you your precious Susan."

They shuffle along in the black dirt for what seems like hours to Trent, or maybe decades. His grasp of time fails him. He feels, with every second, as though he needs to rest, needs to sit and think for a while, needs to let his problems and his thoughts and his memories and his identity slip away, and he knows that if he does stop, even for a moment, he will become nothing. Just another shade in the Prince's realm, lost and unaware of anything beyond the nonexistence of Abaddon. Only the constant thoughts of Susan keep him moving. Only the picture of her face in his mind keeps him alive. Only the memory of her touch prevents his heart from growing cold and dead.

And then, between one moment and the next, the canyon changes, and he sees her. There, ahead, beyond Lilith's hideous form, silhouetted against a strange backdrop of iron towers, he spots Susan.

Lilith turns to look at him, grinning, her blackened lips curled up a horrible, strange rictus, a mockery of pleasure. "I told you I would show you Susan. I told you I would take you to the end of the canyon."

But Trent is not listening. His heart has stopped at the sight of his lost wife. He feels nothing but love, overwhelming, burning, painful love. He can think of nothing but having her in his arms and telling her he's sorry and that he loves her and....

He takes off at a sprint, his feet barely touching the fallow dirt as he lopes through the canyon. Lilith steps aside to let him pass, laughing maniacally. The canyon opening grows larger as he approaches and then he sees Susan turn and look away, back toward the iron towers, and he wants to regain her attention. He can't bear the thought of not seeing her eyes, her smile, her face. He yells her name.

*   *   *

Near the edge of the city of Dis stands an ancient thing, an archway of fused black glass and stone that faces the Nightmare Canyon, which itself stretches away from the city. The arch is crumbled and worn and cracked throughout, but still it stands. Susan has her back to it as she stares into the canyon mouth, tears dribbling from the corners of her eyes. The rebel leader Zamagiel and his minions stand nearby, seething, waiting, and ready for Trent's arrival. It is an ambush and Susan has unwittingly become the bait.

Her body shakes with a mixture of anger and terror and grief. She clenches and unclenches her fists. She wants to fight, wants to tear into Zamagiel and his kind. They are horrifying in visage and carry rusted, tarnished metal spears, but her courage has begun to seep back in.... And yet she knows that she cannot take them all. There are hundreds of them, and perhaps a thousand more moving about the iron city; gaunt, terrible figures of broken, sallow white flesh and brutal orange eyes that burn with malice and lust. They are the *grigorim*, the lust-fallen, cast down from heaven for their transgressions against mortal women. And they are massed here in Dis, on the edge of the iron-sealed pit, Sheol, which leads to Hell, as a bird might perch on the fence around a slaughterhouse.

Susan watches Trent run, watches his stride as he moves through the canyon toward her, and she sees the determination on his face. She sees the love propelling him forward and it makes her want to cry even louder, makes her want to warn him, but she cannot, because she knows he must continue forward. For if he turns back, he walks down the long path into demise. Wracked with guilt and anguish, she turns away, averts her gaze and looks instead at the crumbling arch, a focal point for her mind, and she is startled to see it change.

Within the airy confines of the inside of the arch, blackness has formed. It spreads slowly at first, then quicker, until it has become like an amorphous gel moving within the stone frame. She remembers Lilith's pool and wonders. And then there is a massive, thunderous boom.

The archway shatters, throwing chunks of stone and glass in every direction. At the center of the explosion is an incredible, pure-white flash and then nothing. Upon the ashen dirt of Abaddon, in the midst of the iron city of Dis, there stands now a young woman, her arms entangled in those of an old, wire-thin man.

It is a mortal woman, of that Susan is certain. A young-looking girl, maybe in her twenties, with black hair and tattered, burned clothes and pale, tattooed skin. She is crying, as is the gaunt, strange figure in her arms, naked and pink. The young woman drops the wasted figure to the ground, where he manages only to prop himself up on his elbows. He grasps at an angel's silver-and-white dagger, embedded deep in his chest, but even as he does, the dagger dissolves to ash beneath his trembling fingers.

Immediately, Zamagiel's guards descend on the surprised duo. As the first guard reaches the young black-haired woman, she grimaces, extends a hand, and the guard recoils in sudden and terrible pain. Three others reach her then and she turns her head only slightly to look at them. Her eyes glow a deep, blood red. The *grigorim* burst into flames, screaming and dancing wildly and contributing their own ashes to the dust of Abaddon and then they are no more. The other *grigorim* cease their advance and look toward Zamagiel, waiting for orders.

The young woman steps forward, leaving the gaunt figure behind her on the ground. "I claim this city in the name of Belial, the rightful King of Hell, ruler of all the Fallen. Lower your weapons now, or face his wrath."

"I know you," says a voice from Susan's left. It is Zamagiel. He speaks as he steps forward, pointing at the young woman with a withered, bony finger. "You're Fiamma, the little brat that old man Salvatore sired."

Fiamma? Susan is startled to hear the name. *This is Salvatore's daughter? The child he mentioned?* She thinks about Salvatore then, lying broken upon the grey field before the iron labyrinth, swarmed by the Prince's remaining hunters. She remembers how he saved her from her own demise.

Fiamma's eyes narrow. "Salvatore?" She says it as if the name were a curse. "I have no father save Belial."

Zamagiel grins. "No, no," he says. "Your father was Salvatore. You are Fiamma. I know your name. Bow before me, mortal. This is my city, not yours."

"No!" Fiamma shouts, but Susan can hear her voice wavering. The mention of her father, of her own name, is swaying her resolve. Zamagiel wields immense power in the

Prince-given city, and with the girl's true name, Susan knows he will bring her to her knees.

"Yes," says Zamagiel with a hiss. "You're above your head, dead-child. The old man sired you, then left you and your mother to burn. You're no leader, no ruler. You cannot claim Dis in Belial's stead. You're just Fiamma. That's all."

Fiamma's lip quivers and Susan knows that she is on the verge. Zamagiel's assault on her memories is taking its toll.

"He never loved you," says Zamagiel, quietly.

The young woman crumples and the *grigorim* soldiers are upon her. A hand encircles each arm and they lift her to her feet as Zamagiel strides over. From within the shadows cast upon his back come sudden, huge wings, dark and tattered like those of a dying blackbird. He walks up to Fiamma and wraps first his arms and then his wings around her as she begins to sob. "There, there," he says. "I will be your father now. I will love you as he never did."

Susan watches all of this with increasing dismay. Fiamma was, for a moment, her only chance. She glances back at the canyon mouth, where Trent's shape has grown larger. He is nearly to the mouth of the canyon, nearly through into Dis. Several of the *grigorim* guards have moved closer, waiting for Trent's first step into the city.

"No!" shouts Susan, loud enough to startle the *grigorim* near her. Zamagiel's turns his head to look at her. "He loved you," she says. "He saved me from the Prince. And he loved you more than anything. I left him to die." She buries her face in her hands. "I'm sorry, Fiamma, I'm sorry. Zamagiel used him, and I left him to die."

At the mention, Fiamma shoves Zamagiel away from her, breaking his embrace. She glowers at him. "How did you meet him?"

"No," says Zamagiel, shaking his head. He turns and casts a terrible glare on Susan. "Shut your mouth, woman, or I will torture Trent until the end of time." And then he turns back to Fiamma. "She is lying, she doesn't know—"

Fiamma lowers her head and her mouth turns to a frown. She steps forward slowly, advancing on Zamagiel. "You used him?" she asks. "You made him leave us? You made him leave my mother? *You* were the 'god' he was serving?"

She raises both of her hands. Zamagiel stumbles backwards. His wings fold up and disappear back into his shadow. He holds his hands out in defense. "He was weak. He asked for a way to help God."

"You're not helping God," she says. "You destroyed my entire life." She looks past Susan then, and past Zamagiel, and sees Trent, nearly at the mouth of the canyon now. "And now, you're being used by the Prince of Shades. This is a trap for all of us."

"You can't possibly understand." Zamagiel sneers. "This is necessary. Trent *must* be delivered to the Prince. It is all part of the plan. It has always been part of the plan."

"Well you won't be here to see it." She sprints at Zamagiel, hands covered in white-hot flames, eyes glowing with a blinding light.

"Kill her!" Zamagiel screams as he stumbles further backward, stopping when his back strikes the edge of a long-dead machine of inscrutable purpose. "Destroy the girl."

Buoyed by their master's command, the *grigorim* rush forward and block Fiamma's passage. She throws them off with ease and they burn and scream and writhe in pain like moths come too close to the flame. But the onslaught buys Zamagiel enough time to grab a nearby metal spear, the blade tinted red. He jabs at Fiamma as she pushes through the mass of swarming *grigorim* and approaches.

"One nick and you'll be begging for me to stop. One deep cut," he says, leering, "and you'll be unmade, Belial-kin. Never more than ash on the ground." He jabs again and Fiamma dodges.

The young woman turns her head to look at Susan. "Stop Trent," she says, quickly. "You can't let him come through here."

"But how? How can I tell him?"

Fiamma dodges another powerful swipe of the spear and dances backward as Zamagiel comes on strong. "Just make him stop."

Screams echo throughout the city of Dis as more of the Fallen pour from their hiding places. They converge on the battle and swarm around Fiamma and Zamagiel, a sudden and informal arena as the two weave and dodge, avoiding each others' quick strikes.

Susan turns her attention back to the canyon. Trent is nearly in Dis. She rushes to the opening and he sees her and she begins to scream, as loud as she can and with all of the energy and emotion and power she can muster, she screams for Trent to stop.

But either he cannot hear her, or he has misunderstood, for he continues onward, rushing as if into her arms.

"He won't stop!" Susan yells.

"If he comes through—" Fiamma ducks as the *grigori's* spear pierces the air above and clangs against an ancient piece of metal machinery. Three of the *grigorim* charge into the circle to take advantage of her sudden opening. She ducks a long-clawed strike from the first of the attackers, then jabs him in the throat. Her leg comes around in a solid kick that sends the second *grigorim* tumbling into the third. She squares off against Zamagiel again and glances at Susan. "The Prince is coming. Trent, the Prince, and the Book will become one." Zamagiel lunges and cuts the cloth of Fiamma's pant leg, barely missing her flesh. She rolls away from the strike and hits the ground near another spear. She grabs it and lifts it just in time to block a downward slash. "They are all three pieces of the same," she says, gritting her teeth, as she fights to throw Zamagiel back. But his strength matches hers and they are, for a moment, deadlocked. "The Father, the Son, and the Ghost. You have to stop him, Susan, or—" She rolls as Zamagiel's spear tears into the dusty ground beside her head. "—or Raziel, the Prince, will be reborn from that damn book, and everything will die in shadow."

Susan turns to the canyon for the final time. She knows what she must do. She glances back at Fiamma, fighting for control of the Iron City. The *grigorim* have massed in the hundreds around them. Susan can no longer see Fiamma amidst the fray. She does not know if the young woman will survive the onslaught. But for now, the Fallen are paying little attention to Susan, save one or two that have noticed her and are pulling away from the main battle. They advance upon her. She must do this now, or never.

She gathers her courage and then, with a powerful push, throws herself into the canyon opening, taking that step that leads down the long walk into demise, that step from which one cannot ever turn back, the Angels' Walk into nothingness.

As she bursts through, Trent's eyes widen and his hands come up as to stop her, but he's already too late.

"No!" he yells. "No, Susan! No!"

She silences him with her embrace and buries her head in his shoulder. It feels as though she has waited for this moment for an eternity, and she knows then that she has. "I'm sorry," she whispers. "I'm sorry."

"No," he says. "This can't be. It can't be like this. Not like this. Lilith—She was lying, she must be lying—"

Susan looks up and over Trent's shoulder and sees Lilith advancing on them, furious, balled fists shaking at the air. "No, no, no!" screeches the hag. "This is not how it goes. This is not how it ends. Prince Raziel is reborn and my reward is given. I want to live again. I don't want to be only the shadow. I want to be Lilith, a queen among men. No, no, *no!*"

Susan pulls herself from Trent's embrace and steps away from him, advancing on Lilith. The old hag looks confused as Susan approaches, but her confusion is broken by Susan's fist. A solid right hook catches the hag in the cheek and sends her into a downward spin.

Trent's jaw drops. "Baby, what have you done?"

"I'm teaching this old bitch a lesson," Susan replies. Then she looks down at the writhing, hissing hag. "I gave you a boon. I allowed you to bind me to this place that I might never return to the world. But I've found a loophole."

"You can't do this," Trent says. "Not after what I've gone through to find you. I was coming through the canyon. I was almost—"

Susan turns on him, angry. "This isn't about *you*, Trent Christopher! This is about more than you, and more than me, and more than her." She points at the fallen hag, mewling and crying on the ground. "I had to stop you. This was the only way."

"Stop me?!" Trent is panicked and exasperated at once and raises his arms in supplication. "Why would you want to stop me, Susan? Why? Goddammit, you *can't go back*." He balls his hands into fists and punches the black rock of the canyon wall. "Why the *fuck* did you need to stop *me*? I don't understand...."

Susan walks to him, wraps her arms about his chest and buries her face in his neck. "It was the only way," she says. "You're more important than this. More important than us. More important than me. You're all they have left."

He strokes her hair and feels tears coming to his eyes. He is confused and shaking with frustration and anger. "There's nothing more important than you, baby. Nothing. *Who* am I important to? Goddamn it, tell me what's going on."

She pulls her head from his neck and looks him in the eyes. "You're part of the Prince of Shadows, Trent. You're his son. And he needs you back. If I let that happen—"

"—the world will end in black." The voice is Michael's. Both Trent and Susan look up to see him shuffling through the canyon mouth. He is emaciated, weak, and bloodied, but he is moving toward them, taking the Angels' Walk. His last act as an archangel. "You are the Son of Shadows, Trent Hawkins. You cannot deny that."

"Who are you?"

"I am the archangel Michael, once the guardian of mankind. Now I am but a forgotten creature."

Trent shakes his head. "No," he says. "That can't be. How can I be the son of the Prince of Shades, the son of Raziel? I just— No, I don't believe it—"

Susan puts a finger to his lips.

Trent tries to speak, but she gives him a look that makes him know that she is right, and serious, and not interested in his arguments. He tries a different tact, his countenance brightening.

"Maybe there's a way out, a way to get you out of this canyon." He glances around frantically and analyzes the black rock walls, swimming with painful images, then at the squirming Lilith and finally at Michael, still moving quietly, slowly towards them, his gaze downturned. And then Trent pauses and remembers the Book. He rips it from its hiding place in the back of his waistband and flips it open. "The Book," he says, excited. "There's gotta be something in here. Some spell, some way out. Maybe Michael can—"

"You're meant for something more than this, Trent," says Michael, quietly, as he stops next to them. "You were once meant for something horrible. And now there is a chance to turn that around. There was never supposed to be a plane crash. The Prophecy never foretold that. It was... an aberration. And now, the darkness of that foretelling may be altered." Michael turns his gaze on Lilith, who is sitting up now, snarling at them all. "*They* will continue to conspire against you, but you now have a choice to make. Your wife is a Shaper, Trent, a very rare sort of being in Abaddon. She can send you back to the material realm. Or you can stay here and walk with us into nothing, and leave the mortal world to die. It is your choice."

"But if I stay here, if I die here, the Prince won't ever find me. The Prophecy will still be broken."

Michael shakes his head. "Raziel has a great deal of power. Even if you and the Book—" he points to the green journal in Trent's hand, "—are both destroyed, the Prince of Shadows still has an army, and soon a portal through which to send it. And without you, the mortal world stands no chance. They will all die, and the world will be overrun."

Trent turns his gaze to the dusty black sand at his feet, tears dripping down his cheeks. "Then how does it matter?" he says, shaking his head. "Humans are doomed either way." He looks at Susan. "And I can't just leave you here. I've searched so long for a way to save you. What's the point if I go back?" He looks at Susan and locks his eyes with hers. "Everything I've done to save you—"

"Has led you to this," she says. "Everything you've done has given the world one last moment of hope. People die every day and no one has the choice to bring them back. People grieve, and people move on and do great things, even alone." She grabs Trent's hands and squeezes. Tears are streaming down her face, too. "You've always been there to protect me, baby. But you have to let me go. You have no right to pull me back; no more right than the Prince had to send me here. But now it's done. And you stand on the brink.

You can turn your back. Or, you can choose to go back and help them."

"Goddammit," Trent says. "*They* don't matter. *They* are a planet of six billion worthless people that are just as likely to wreck their world as Raziel is. Name one person who truly matters."

"Celia."

"She's dead."

Susan shakes her head. "I'm not so sure of that." She turns to look at another scene on the opposite wall of the canyon; a scene of a terrified young girl, lying on a dusty floor, a blonde woman in a blue dress hovering around her as the young girl screams and claws at the floor.

Trent watches the scene for a moment, then turns and looks into Susan's eyes for a very long time, and in the timeless Realms of Shadow, it might be seconds or it might be an eternity. And then, finally, he nods, still frowning, eyes wet.

She gives him a pained, simple smile and again watches the walls of the canyon. They ripple and flash with dancing shadow imagery and one scene quickly drowns out the others, rising to the foreground. An airplane, passengers seated quietly, a young man listening to music a few seats behind a man with a cowboy hat perched atop his head. "Gadreel lied to you, baby. He wasn't there hunting any Shade. He was there to stop you—the Shadow you—because the Prophecy had led him to the moment that you would die, the first death, and he wanted your power for himself."

"I don't understand—"

But Susan ignores him and turns to the scene on the wall. She presses her palms against the black-glass surface and squeezes her eyes shut and focuses on the imagery dancing before her.

Trent watches as the wall comes to life with terrible scenes. He can hear sounds, though it's unclear from where they emanate. He hears the metal of the plane hull straining against the rushing winds outside it. He sees the passengers eating, talking, moving. He can even feel emotions now, their private fears, their joys, their anxieties. And he can feel the weakness in reality at this moment. With a bloodcurdling scream, Susan shapes a Portal.

The image of the airplane lurches and shudders and there is a black-on-black explosion, and chaos fills the wall.

"This is where you were broken." Her voice is ragged now with the effort of Shaping. "I've seen your past, seen it on the walls of a Dream Cave. And I've seen your future, or what might be. You never survived that crash, Trent. No one did, except Gadreel and your shadow-self, the son of Raziel. The mortal you, *the you with a soul*, died like everyone else." Susan screams again and an explosion rips through the cabin of the plane.

The glass wall suddenly spiderwebs with cracks and huge chunks fall to the floor, leaving behind a swirling black, smoky mass of air. Through the vortex they can see the chaos inside the plane.

"I don't understand. How will this bring me back?" Trent struggles to be heard over the cacophony that has filled the canyon. "Where did I get a Shade version of myself in the first place?"

Michael answers him, his back now turned to the couple as he continues his Walk. "You, like every mortal, are the child of your mortal father and mortal mother. But there is another *you*, a shadow *you* that can only be the offspring of a mortal mother and a very powerful creature from this place." Michael gestures around at the black canyon, but Trent knows he means Abaddon itself. "This place *is* the Prince. *That* makes him *your* father. Reality—your world—always attempts to heal itself. This moment," he gestures toward the scene playing out on the canyon wall, "is the aberration that ruins the Prophecy. Your soul can't leave this place, but the shadow creature inside you still can. How that thing came to be there at all is a mystery that still remains to be solved. There must be a mortal mother out there, a woman giving birth to something impossible, something that gets tied up in this moment, your shadow self and her child, one and the same, birthed from her womb into that crash, where it finds your body to give it substance. And when you wake, you will be where you last were, before the blade sent you here, mortal body whole, shadow-self restored along with the gifts of your father's lineage."

"But my soul...?"

Michael stops and turns, sadness in his eyes. "I told you it was a choice, Trent. You are whole here, in Abaddon, soul and shadow intertwined. But you died in that world, once. Nothing will change that, not even this. Your soul stays here."

Trent stares at the swirling vortex, watches the screaming people and the violence and sees himself, his mortal self, rise from the airplane seat and scramble over the back, confused and terrified. He sees Gadreel—Ramón the old Mexican—rise from his own chair, calm and steady. He sees the old man draw a thin, gleaming blade.

"You have to decide," says Susan, quietly. "In a few seconds, Gadreel will kill the mortal you and this possibility will be lost. You will never have come here in the first place. The shade that inhabits your flesh now will instead be captured when it arrives, and Gadreel will reign over the world with an iron fist, changing fate as he sees fit. This is the choice you've already made once, Trent, but you can change it if you wish. Step through, so that you can fight on. Or turn away. Alter fate. Doom the world. So long as you take the Walk with us; don't give yourself unto the Prince and let him win."

Trent points at the imagery playing out on the canyon wall. "You can come with me! Susan, this is your chance—"

Susan shakes her head and puts a finger to Trent's lips. "No," she says, and turns to watch the impending disaster in the plane cabin. "I gave Lilith a boon. I'm bound here. And even if I could, no one survives that crash, baby." She looks deep into his eyes. He can see the tears building at the corners of hers. "Not even you," she says.

Trent turns from her gaze. He can't bear to see her cry. He watches the horrifying scene and then looks down at the Book in his hand. He can feel immense power coursing out of it, power that a part of him wants to control. He looks at Susan again and then holds out the old, leather-bound journal. "Take this," he says, calm restored to his voice. "Take it with you on the walk. Raziel can go fuck himself if he wants that piece back."

Susan grins, sniffles, and Trent watches a tear trail down her cheek. She walks to him and puts her palms against his temples and smothers his mouth with hers. Their kiss seems to both of them to last forever, and in a certain sense, in the timelessness of the Realms of Shadow, it does.

She finally pulls herself away. "I love you, Trent," she whispers.

Trent smiles. "I love you too, baby. I always will." A moment of doubt flashes through his mind. "I can't do this."

"You can," she replies, still smiling.

He leans in and kisses her again and feels her body against his and he shudders with the pain of imminent loss.

"But you don't have to remember," she says into his ear. "Once I walk down that canyon, I'll never have been in the first place. You'll be a hero. I won't haunt your memory anymore. Be what the world needs, Trent. Be the hero you always wanted to be."

He forces a withered smile. "I don't want to forget you, hon."

She turns away and begins her walk down the long canyon, toward the blackness that waits at the other end, the void that will swallow her entire existence, from beginning to end. She clutches the Book in her arms as she goes. She is shaking.

For a moment, he watches her as he hovers on the edge of the swirling portal. He thinks about running after her. He considers for a moment that possibility—walking into nothingness with Susan, arm in arm, and leaving the wretched, broken world of man to its own demise. But as he watches her go, he's pretty sure he sees her shake her head 'no'.

He turns back to the portal and the madness in the smoke-filled airplane cabin, and he takes that fateful step through, a *real* smile on his face, even as his heart breaks.

12

THIS, MY DEAR, CAME THE voice from deep within her blackened, ash-filled dreams, *is your destiny. This is what must happen, what must be, and what will be. It is what already has been.*

"What are you doing to me?" she screamed, shouting into the pitch-black darkness. She could not tell if she was standing or lying, conscious or otherwise. Maybe she was dead, she thought.

We are making you better, said the voice. She knew now that it was the voice of Abaddon, the voice of the Prince of Shades. *That foul thing—our child, my dear—will leave you soon. And then, you will be a queen, and it will be my son, to bring about my glorious resurrection.* There was a long pause; long enough that Celia thought for a moment that the voice had gone. And then it said, *you will become a queen of ice and shadow, and you will stand above this world, above these worthless named creatures, a queen at my side, ruling over all that you have ever known.*

Somewhere distant, she felt immense pain. A rippling tremor of agony shuddered through the nothingscape around her. Torturous waves of impossible labor. Beyond the pain, a voice cried out, "Girl! Girl! Wake up! Please, wake up!" She focused on that voice as it guided her through the darkness.

No! shouted the voice. *Do not turn away from me, mortal! This is your fate. You cannot escape it! Come to Abaddon. Have your child here, where it can be safe, protected. It should not be born in that world. It is not a thing that should exist there!*

But she continued to move—to drift?—through the darkness, toward the voice, pushing back the pain, ignoring the voice.

And then her eyes opened, suddenly, with a ripple of fear that made her body tremble. She looked into the face of the nurse to whom she had given Snake's apple, so many months ago, at the apex of the Vegas blizzard. The woman wore elaborate eye shadow, tinted blue, and a glittering blue evening gown, torn and threadbare in places, but still stunning; a thousand-dollar dress. She had no shoes. Her forearms and hands wore matching blue gloves. Her necklace sparkled with diamonds.

"You see me!" exclaimed the woman in the blue dress. "Do you see me now? I'm here, I'm here for you. I can help you. I'm— I'm a nurse."

"Anna," said Celia. The word dropped from her lips, dead of emotion, an utterance without meaning. Even as she said it, her brain struggled to assert its relevance, to *remember*. Something about an apple, given out of pity during an unholy snowstorm.

"My name!" said the woman. "You remember! I remember it too! No one has remembered in such a long time!"

Celia sat up, arms crossed over her aching belly. Around her, the abandoned theater was transformed. Where velvet ropes had stood, now gleamed horizontal bars of crisp, clear ice and hanging icicles below. The walls, carpeted in deep burgundy and gold, were now coated in frost and glittered in the dim light. There was a fog in the air around them, and Celia realized that it was from her own breath. It seemed like too much for one person. A thought nagged at her. Had there been someone else here, only recently?

And then her shoulders were gripped by Anna, the nurse. When had she arrived? Had she always been here?

"Don't look away from me," she said. "Please don't forget. When you look away, you forget. Everyone always forgets. Ever since I ate that apple you gave me."

"I— I don't understand." Celia fought through the contractions to summon up the words. Even then, they came out weak, ineffective.

Anna shook her head, diamond necklace swinging. "Everything has changed. Everything goes away, even while I stay with it. You can't go away. You can't go to that dark world."

"What do you mean?"

"The doors. Never open the doors. Never close your eyes. Never dream. That's where it is. The thing with the white face and the bloody line. That's where it waits. Behind the doors, inside the dreams. Every time I open a door, every time you open a door, it might be there, the black world, and *it* might be coming. I've been avoiding it for so long. Running from it. Closing the doors when I see it...." Her voice faded to nothing.

"You're insane," said Celia, though with a tinge of regret. She'd seen the portals behind the doors, the black world, the thing with the white, ceramic face. She'd heard its voice....

"Can you walk?" asked Anna. "Can you come with me? We should go where it's safer. Away from the windows. They hide out there, just outside the lamps. I won't let them hurt you. I won't let them take your child. It should be born here, in the light, not there, in the dark place where *it* can take it from you. Your child should choose its own fate."

"My child?"

"You're in labor aren't you?"

Celia had avoided thinking about it for so long, for so many months. This was not something she wanted, not an event she had foreseen when she decided on that snow-filled night to swallow the Bringer of Nightmares into her body and soul. How could she be having a child? What could that child be? A monster?

"I'm Celia," she said, finally, saying something, anything, to avoid further talk of the impending birth. "That's my name."

"Celia," said the woman in the blue dress. "Thank you."

"For what?"

"For seeing me. For remembering."

"No one sees you?"

"Not since the apple." Anna turned away, looked out the window at the parking lot. Her shoulders tensed and she turned back, gripping Celia's hand hard in her own. "We've got to go," she said, breathless. "We have to get away from them, move to where I have my lights, to where there are no doors, only light, only color."

With a deep and painful groan, Celia let Anna pull her off the leather bench to her feet. She looked out at the parking lot and felt alone, so utterly alone in this icy place. Shapes flitted about beneath the yellow sodium lamps, coming closer with every lurching motion. Her chest pounded. Why was she here? Why was she so alone? Where was Trent?

Trent was dead. She had heard his yell after falling from the window at Gadreel's church. Trent Hawkins was gone.

Her belly heaved with a sudden pain and nausea. Hands gripped her then, hands she recognized immediately, hands that some small part of her mind told her had been on her shoulders all along. She cried in confusion.

"Don't cry, don't cry, not now," said a woman in a blue dress. Celia remembered then that her name was Anna. She had eaten the apple. Had she been here all along? Why couldn't she remember?

"I told you not to look away. Never look away! Eyes on me, Celia! Don't open the doors!"

Anna held her, and Celia could smell expensive perfume, could feel the cool touch of diamonds against her skin. She never wanted to forget this person, this saint that she had doomed with the gift of an apple. Why did she keep forgetting?

"Come on," said Anna, and led her away.

With intense concentration, Celia focused only on Anna and her blue, glittering gown, as they moved together through the abandoned theater, toward the exit back into the mall. The door was clear glass, frosted with ice and old dust.

"I opened it to come in," said Anna. "I had to open it twice. Sometimes, if you open them twice, the doors are normal again— I didn't want to scare you."

"I— I don't—"

Anna wrenched a dusty old cash register from the ticket counter and clumsily hefted it across the few feet to the door. "I'm not opening it again," she said and with all her strength, sent the register hurtling through the frozen glass door. The crash rang out like a bomb going off in the destitute mall. "Come on," said Anna, and they stepped gingerly through the jagged hole into the mall.

They shuffled barefoot together through the mall, past shuttered kiosks that once sold knock-off sunglasses, perfumes, useless kitchen tools, and past boarded up stores, proclaiming that something else was "Coming Soon" though they knew it never was. An old toy store, still with leftover, damaged inventory strewn about the cleaned-out interior, possibly because the owner had abdicated, leaving the cleanup to the mall ownership, stood open and dead. And Celia, still a child at heart despite the terrors that had befallen her, couldn't help but look....

Black shapes danced about in the toy store beyond the dusty glass. Not merely shadows anymore, these shapes had physicality, *substance* of a sort that let them move, bump, and even pick up the toys. They seemed to be inspecting the items and the world around them. They were *curious*. Celia's jaw dropped. They were not monsters, but lost children, creatures from another realm given no purchase in the real. Creatures abandoned to Abaddon. And now, with her help, they were here.

She moved towards them, towards the door of the shop. She would encounter them, be among them, her friends now, her *subjects*. She was, after all, a queen among Shades, right? Her hand reached out for the door handle—

A shrill cry broke her reverie and she recoiled from the door. She turned to look at the source of that voice, a woman in a blue dress, a woman she suddenly remembered. A woman that had been with her recently?

"Anna?"

"I told you not to open the doors! I told you not to look away!"

"I—I'm sorry. I'm so sorry." Celia felt shamed, though hardly could say why.

Anna frowned at her. "Come on," she said, and grabbed Celia's hand.

"Not everyone remembers again," she explained as they hurried away from the toy store. "Not everyone sees a second time. You're different. You see me over and over. Few do."

Celia watched Anna's blonde hair swish against her back as they walked. She found herself gritting her teeth in an attempt to maintain her focus on the odd, beautiful woman.

"My fiancé forgot me in only two days. My parents, a week."

"Didn't they have pictures? Letters from you? Emails?"

"They were confused. Then they deleted them. I stopped existing. They couldn't see me anymore. They never knew me at all."

"I'm so sorry, Anna." And then a contraction sent Celia to the floor, doubled over. But she refused to turn her gaze from her savior. She would not let go of Anna's hand.

Anna turned, bent down, and lifted Celia to her feet. "Don't worry," she said. "It's not much farther now. Soon we'll be safe and I'll help you through this." She put an arm around Celia's shoulder. "Just watch my face. Watch me talking. I'll help you. Tell me what's wrong."

Celia knew then what the answer was. It was a truth she had been avoiding, but could no longer. "I'm pregnant," she said. She barely managed to choke out the next part. "I'm gonna have a baby."

They stopped when they reached a luxury-clothing store called *Barrister's*. In its front display, mannequins in pricey evening gowns stood in awkward poses. The glass doors, like the theater, had been crudely smashed open. Inside, the lights were on, an intensity that had become so alien to Celia that she squinted, averting her eyes, until Anna interposed, walking backwards and holding the sides of Celia's head.

"Come on, Celia," she said, "don't look away. Just come inside with me. You'll be safe here. Your child will be safe. So much light. So much color in here."

And Celia followed as Anna backed her way into the clothing store, knocking aside a rack of designer belts, and led her to the back of the room, near the checkout counter; an area that Anna had surrounded with dresses, shirts and expensive business suits of every color and style. It was a raucous, mismatched collection, but it was bright and colorful, and the farthest thing from the swirling black-grey of the shadow portals that Celia could imagine. They sat down amidst the colorful racks, upon a makeshift bed of folded cardboard and piled clothes.

Celia wondered why this store had retained its inventory when all the others, except for the toy store, had been so thoroughly cleaned out. She was interrupted by another wave of horrendous pain in her gut, and then another, even worse than the first.

She groaned.

"Shhh," said Anna, rubbing her face. "Just lie down. Lie down, Celia."

And so she did.

Anna was smiling, though behind that smile Celia could see fear, lingering panic even.

"Relax, Celia. This is going to hurt. But you need to relax. I'll do everything I can—"

But before she could finish the sentence, it began.

Celia felt waves of cold begin pouring from her. Anna recoiled from its intensity. She mumbled something but refused to let go of Celia's hand, for which she was thankful.

Another contraction sent ice burning through her veins. Deep black spots filled her vision, danced, swarmed, coagulated, blocking out more and more, but she sought Anna's face between the ever-growing patches of blind nothing.

"Please..." she groaned. "Please don't let go."

"I won't let go, honey. I'm not going to let you go."

Anna squeezed tighter on Celia's hand. Another burst of pain. A scream. Her own? And then, with limited vision, she saw smoke tendrils lift from her in coils between her and Anna's shocked face. Cold escaped her mouth. Her heart beat an impossible rhythm. Somewhere, someone laughed. Acrid smoke in her nostrils. An explosion. People screaming. Jet engines. Wind howling nearby.

Nothing.

* * *

The child went limp in Anna's arms, eyes drifting closed as thick, black shadowstuff poured from her nose and mouth. "No, no, no," said Anna, rocking her, but it had no effect, and the smoke danced and writhed and tangled together until it formed a reptilian thing that lighted for a moment between them, its shadow-claws digging into the bright red fabric of a cocktail dress-turned-bedspread.

The creature opened its mouth exposing impossibly long crocodilian teeth, black and shiny like obsidian. Smoke dripped from its jaws as it roared. It looked warily at the child at their feet. It snorted, and then turned, rearing back on its haunches for a second before leaping into the air. Its shadowy form collapsed, thinned, and then streamed into a single point and was gone, leaving only the smell of ozone in its wake.

Celia's eyes were still closed and Anna couldn't tell if the child was breathing. Then, without warning, Celia gasped, opened her eyes, and screamed out a man's name: *Trent.*

Her eyes shut again, her head hit the floor, and she was gone.

13

Five and a half years ago…

THE CHAOS OF SOUND AND light and color and emotion, the tumultuous jumble of possibility and counter-possibility, the layers of reality all tore through each other, all assailing the creature bursting into existence near the back of the airplane cabin. Its clawed feet perched hesitantly upon the alien surface. Its mind (*a real mind!* it thinks) rebelled against the chosen reality, for it knew of many others, but this one had already been made. It could not undo this. It could not choose a different fate, not this time.

It looked down the aisle, saw an old mortal facing it. *No*, it thought, *not a mortal at all. A husk. A shell. One of the Fallen, occupying.* The demon wielded a red-hued blade and had waited for this moment, had waited to end the creature even before time had fully reasserted itself. The demon would undo what had been written, what was already known. *The demon knows what I am.*

And the creature wondered then exactly what it was. *A shade? Not a demon, nor an angel.* Remembrance danced in its gathering consciousness. A mortal woman, named Susan. A man. A child, its mother. A world and shade Prince, its father. *I am something different, something new, a Bringer of Nightmares, in some sense, but changed, born of two worlds, one part torn from immortal shadow and one from mortal womb.* It reveled at its uniqueness. It wanted a name. It so desperately wanted a name.

The creature roared, delighting in the feel of the air around its slavering jaws, rippling with vibration. It stepped forward, felt its shadow muscles become real, gathering energy and dove towards the knife-wielding demon.

Mortals all around erupted with shrieks and screams and lamentations at its arrival, and the creature tasted pride. It slammed full-force into the demon. They crashed together against seats and bloodied people. Beyond the demon, the creature spied another mortal, rising, acting differently than the rest. A mortal that was fated. Remembrance. It roared again, and this time attempted to bring its many-fanged jaws down upon the demon's wrist, that it might loose the red-hued dagger.

The demon, though, was strong, and wrestled the creature backwards, towards the gaping hole in the airplane's body. The sucking, screeching vortex called to them both. The creature planted its shadow-feet and dug black claws into the protesting metal floor. The demon leapt upon it again, grappling, thrusting the dagger, as the creature bit and tore with its claws to keep the red-hued blade away, knowing what a deep cut from the weapon would mean.

And then the mortal was upon them both. An explosion rocked the plane. They were thrown together, all three—mortal, demon, and shadow-made-flesh. The creature's claws punched through flesh and bone and it saw pain in the old demon's borrowed eyes. It felt arcane energies boiling out of the demon, disappearing through its own form into the place beyond, the Realms from which it was half-born. The demon was losing strength and power. It would kill nothing this day. The creature had won.

Until the man *did* something.

In a fit of madness (bravado?), the mortal gripped them both. The creature felt the human's warm touch, could sense the tenor of the man's thoughts. The man pulled, hard, and all three beings lost purchase and tumbled into the howling void.

The demon pulled away from the struggle, spread his arms, and smiled. The grey hat lifted from his head and took to the sky. *The demon falls*, the creature thinks, *like Raziel, the first time, when he fell through the black into shadow*. The mortal had no such grace. The man flipped and spun, buffeted by the wind, which tore open his shirt so it became like white wings fluttering behind him, rent and stained with ichor and blood.

The ground rushed up to meet them all.

The demon will survive this, the creature thought. *But the mortal man will not live. His soul is forfeit on impact.* Remembrance. A questioning grin. Blue eyes. Love.

The creature fell with the mortal, and when Trent Hawkins died, the creature filled that place within him that was ruined, returned like a child to the womb, and became a part of him, Bringer of Nightmares reborn into flesh, a shadow soul made from a child's sacrifice and a man's love.

No grave, it thought, as its last independent thought, *will take this mortal today. This name—Trent Hawkins—is now mine.*

14

THE FIRST THING TRENT THOUGHT of was Susan, standing there, white gown and blonde hair against the endless black landscape of the Realms of Shadow.

The second thing he thought was the fact that he had just thought about her, and the sudden realization of her memory sparked a flame in his gut. A tiny spark of hope burned. She had said he would forget when she was unmade, but he had not. Could it be possible? Could she still live?

The third thing he thought about was the red-hued dagger, still protruding from his chest, and the cold burning sensation that rippled across his skin and deep into his muscles and bone. He groaned in the small, dark room on the upper floor of Gadreel's church, and then forced himself to stifle the noise lest he be heard. He squeezed the blade's handle with his left hand and gripped one leg of the small bed with his right, fingers spasming with agony as he surveyed the room.

Empty.

The guards had left and with them, apparently so had Gadreel. The old man had not expected this. He had thought Trent banished to Abaddon for good. Trent wondered if the demon knew about Susan being a Shaper in the shadow realm, and how she opened a portal for Trent to that singular moment in his past, the moment that made him something else. He knew now that he was a shadow at heart, a man without a soul, with no connection to the old demon's powers. That bit had been a lie. Despite the pain, Trent grinned. He had an ace up his sleeve now.

With his free hand, he clawed harder at the floor and, with his left, he pulled. The metal slid through his insides, scraping bone, slipping between vein and artery. It caught once, sending agonizing cramps down into his stomach. His back arched and he gritted his teeth so hard he was sure they would shatter. To avoid screaming, he breathed in bursts. He sucked in through his nose, then out through his mouth in quick, pain-relieving huffs. In through the nose. Out through the mouth. Again and again. Fingers trembling, he *turned* the dagger, ever so slightly, so that its razor-thin blade might slip free. The pain lessened some, the blade moved more freely now, up, up, up, and out....

The tip of the red dagger brushed against the blood-caked skin of his chest and then, suddenly, he held the blade aloft. The wound was a clean, crisp line in his flesh; no ragged edges, no lacerations, just a razor-thin mark, slowly oozing blood. And was that a thin curl of black smoke boiling up from within?

He could hear nothing beyond the room and its open door. The glass window was shattered and blood stained its edges. He thought of Celia, and flitting remembrance danced just beyond recollection: something important, something he couldn't quite place.... But recent memory flooded back. The teenager scrabbling for the Book. The gunshot. Glass everywhere. Celia's body tumbling out the window. The terrible thump, and then nothing. But he knew now that she still lived.

You tried to kill her, he thought, teeth gritted. *You sonofabitch. And you lied to me.* For a moment, he wasn't sure if his thoughts were addressing Gadreel or himself.

He managed to stand, steadying himself against the wall, and took a few deep breaths. He looked at the red-hued dagger in his hand. From Hell itself, Charlie had explained in the note included with the "Educational Materials". Guilt ripped through him at the thought of Charlie.

"Dammit," he said aloud, startled by the loudness of his voice in the near-silent church.

He gripped the dagger's handle tight and headed into the hallway with a single purpose. He would find Gadreel. And he would end him.

*   *   *

Celia looked up into the pretty woman's face. "Get up," she was saying. "Wake up, Celia."

A crisp and heavy calm fell on Celia's mind. She wondered why she was lying here, in an abandoned, rearranged clothing store, half-naked in a dirty, soaked hospital gown, being shaken by a woman clearly gone mad. She sat up and could taste ice and shadow and ash on the air. It tasted good.

"Stop shaking me, Anna," she said, and turned away from the woman's face.

"Never turn away. Never look away."

Celia turned back to face her. "And why not? What is all your babbling about?"

Anna looked at her, astounded, mouth agape. "You— You— You *remembered* me."

"Yes, Anna, I remembered you." Celia reached out an arm. "Help me up," she said. "And find me some better clothes. Something clean. Jeans and a top. And a heavy coat. Grey, maybe, or silver. Long. And boots."

Anna helped her to her feet and then stood there staring.

Celia made a 'get going' gesture with her hand. She didn't know why, exactly, she did that, but she did, and she relished the power that she now commanded.

The woman twitched, then nodded, almost a slight bow, and scurried off towards a rack of clothes under a sign that read 'Petite'.

The teenager stretched and twisted her neck from side to side, feeling it pop. She breathed in the scents on the air. So many, so close in this place. She walked to the store's entrance.

In the abandoned mall, ice had formed haphazardly in places, patches adhered to the walls and floor, icicles hung from the decorative chandeliers, put there once to attract a *better* clientele. Celia grinned at the irony that it had now attracted something far, far different.

"Here, Celia." Anna handed her the requested clothes: black designer jeans; black boots; a grey long-sleeved top with a form-fitting cut; and a long, heavy silver coat with white trim and a high, flared collar. The sort of thing Celia would never wear. She held it in her hands. She loved it.

Unashamedly, she shucked off the ruined hospital gown and wrapped herself in the expensive clothes. She looked at herself in a nearby mirror and frowned at her stringy, sweat- and ice-laden blonde hair. She brushed it out a bit, letting it fall down over her face. She needed makeup, but didn't much care. Time for that later. She pulled the coat tight around her and stepped out of the shop into the mall. Ice crackled on the walls as she passed.

"Celia," said the madwoman. "Are you— Are you okay?"

"Yes," said Celia, without turning around. *Yes*, she thought, and noted that the thought had echoed, rebounded deep within her mind. *Yes*, she thought again. *I'm in control now. I'm not a child anymore. And I'm certainly not scared.*

And then the Shades burst from their hiding places.

Anna screamed, but Celia raised a hand to silence her.

"It's fine," she said. "It's all fine now. They're my friends. And as long as *you* are my friend," she said, turning to stop Anna in her tracks with a glare. She did not finish her sentence, but left it hanging there, a question floating in the icy air between them.

Anna caught on. "Yes, yes," she said, eyes wide, nodding. "Yes, I'm your friend, Celia. You saved me, remember? And then I saved you. And now you remember me."

Celia turned away, smiling. The woman sounded like an overly eager child. She made a dismissive wave with her hand. "Then the shadows are *your* friends, too. No need to fear them."

As they walked the mall concourse, the ghostly Shades poured from every interstitial space, every side passage, from behind old, dusty sales counters and empty metal shelves, from within shoe stores, clothing stores, and food stalls. They approached then and fell into a tumbling mass behind the two women, chittering, sibilant hisses, and the occasional roar or shriek.

They are, thought Celia, *my children*.

And yet a part of her yearned to see one shade that was missing from the ever-growing mass. A shade with a name. The only one so rewarded. A special shade whose memory flirted with her brain but danced away whenever she reached out to touch it. But the longing still remained....

"Where are we going?" said Anna, breaking Celia from her reverie.

Celia's eye twitched with irritation. "We're leaving this place, all of us," she said, her words clipped and dry. "We're going to destroy one of the Fallen."

"I— I don't understand..."

"A demon, Anna." Celia took a calming breath. "We're going to kill the demon, Gadreel."

"Why?"

Celia's irritation boiled over into anger. "Because of what he did to me! He sent me to die. Because of what he did to—" *Who? Who was I going to say?* "Because," she said, discouraged by the lost train of thought. "I'm the Prince's emissary now, his servant in this world. Gadreel is no longer required."

She spun on her heel, made a motion with her right hand to encourage the Shades to all gather closer, and proceeded toward the mall exit. Her boot heels crunched on the ice-covered floor.

The rain had picked back up again and fell in cold, withering sheets. But as Celia and her retinue stepped into the empty parking lot, the rain became sleet and snow. It was a strange sensation, she decided, to be walking amidst a rainstorm, surrounded personally by alternate, colder weather. With every step, the puddles of water on the ground near froze and crackled. The hiss of sleet hitting the pavement drowned out the sound of the pouring rain. Celia pulled her silver coat tighter and marched on.

With Anna by her side and a flickering, terrible mass of shadows streaming behind, none with physical counterparts from which they were cast, Celia walked north along the frozen mud of the Veterans Memorial Highway. The horizon ahead was nearly flat, and in the darkness, she could barely make out the distant apparition of Mount Charleston to the west. But she knew their destination: Gadreel's church.

The shadowy army passed planned communities of suburban homes and smaller, less-affluent collections of one-story ranch homes. Most of the homes were unoccupied, with mud-spattered For Sale signs gracing the lawns, but some still had residents. If any saw the strange cadre of things accompanying a teenage girl and a grown woman, none took any action. Nobody's business. Nobody's problem. *Not yet, at least.*

It was the simple, flat four-way intersection of Veterans Memorial and Kyle Canyon that changed all of that.

As the small army approached the intersection, they were suddenly cast in the alternating red and blue lights of a police cruiser. A traffic stop. An officer, stood on the side of the road, draped in a plastic poncho and plastic-covered cowboy hat, talking to someone in their car. At first, he didn't seem to notice Celia and her crew coming toward him, at least not until they were within a few hundred feet. And then he looked up, his eyes widened and dropped his pen and notebook into the mud. The car's driver craned his neck out the window to look behind.

The driver said, "My God, what the hell is that?"

The cop cursed and ran to his squad car to call for backup. Celia decided she didn't need the interference.

"No," said Anna. "No, don't, Celia. Please."

But Celia did not heed Anna's stuttering, sycophantic whining. A cold fog descended on her mind as a terrible, icy rush filled her veins and screamed its way to her fingertips. She walked towards the police cruiser.

"Stay back." The cop pointed an accusatory finger, hand trembling. "All of you, stay back." He had opened the cruiser's door and was reaching in for the radio. The dispatch operator's tinny voice called out inside the car. She ignored the cop's commands and kept moving, the Shades following eagerly behind her. Anna continued to plead.

The cop straightened up and drew his gun. He raised it, fired off three rounds at the advancing teenager, making a terrified, guttural "Aaaah!" sound as he pulled the trigger.

Celia raised her right hand, palm-forward. Ice burst out in every direction from her fingertips, like tendrils of glass, gleaming in the flashing lights, moving, swirling, racing to fill the space between her and the officer. And then the tendrils stopped. The mass of ice that filled the air held all three bullets aloft, frozen against strands like flies in a spider's web. Celia lowered her hand, and as she did, the ice fell out of the air and shattered on the asphalt at road's edge. The bullets clinked and clanked and rolled off into the mud.

"Oh God, no. What the hell—?"

The officer dove into car and pulled the passenger door shut behind him. The stopped driver, momentarily transfixed by the scene, regained his composure.

"Fuck this, man!" He stomped on the gas. The red compact revved up to a high-pitched whine. Its tires spun in the icy mud. "Fuck, fuck, fuck." He pounded a fist against the horn, over and over. "*Go!*"

Celia snorted, watching the spinning tires for a moment, and then raised her index finger. Stalagmites of ice burst from the ground beneath the car. The glistening spires crunched through the undercarriage and seat, and punched through the driver. Blood sprayed from the open window before he slumped forward onto the wheel, head settling on the horn, which droned against the noise of falling sleet.

Celia made a quick gesture, which catapulted the car off the icy mass. It crunched and shrieked and rolled off into the desert, flipping three times before coming to rest on its roof, horn dead and silent.

The cop, in his own car, was desperately fumbling to grab the radio mic, which had fallen onto the floor. He looked up at his assailants, eyes wide, filled with tears. Celia raised her hand and made a motion as though gripping some invisible object. Radiator fluid poured from the air vents inside the car, solidified around the radio mic in the cop's hand, and began to pull. The cop pulled back. Celia frowned, clawed her hand tighter around the metaphorical object, and *pulled*. The mic, cord, and the entire radio assembly from inside the dashboard blasted backwards into the engine compartment. The cop screamed. Celia made a tossing motion and the entire jumble of electronics punched its way out the side of the car, just above the wheel well, and crashed into a frozen heap on the side of the road.

The cop fumbled and crashed through the car's interior and got into the driver's seat. He was reaching for the parking brake when Celia turned and nodded toward the Shades.

Shadows of every shape and form, some tall and thin, almost humanoid, others indefinable wisps of dancing smoke, descended on the cruiser. They poured in through every crack and opening, disappearing beneath the car and pouring up like smoke into the interior. The red-and-blue lights went dark. The headlights dimmed, flickered, and died. The car bucked and rocked and Celia could see only the strange mass of shadow-things, grey-black, and the occasional flash of a white eye or indistinct, spiked tail or tentacle—

And then it was over.

Shadows poured from the vehicle in every direction, like cockroaches before the light. Celia moved closer to the car, Anna in tow, her movements nervous, cautious. Blood coated every surface. Wisps of smoke still drifted around the inside of the car. The cop's body was a ruined mass of flesh and bone and hair. A partial, disembodied hand still gripped one side of the steering wheel.

Celia felt nothing. She straightened, walked past the cop car, and continued along Kyle Canyon road, heading west.

Snow drifted in her wake, and the sound of sleet on the metal car rang out, uncontested in the pre-dawn black.

The walk to Gadreel's church would take a few hours. It would be dawn when they arrived. It would be the beginning of a new day, and Celia knew that she would have her revenge on the demon that had ruined her life. And then, she would be the Queen of Ice and Shadow. Raziel had promised it.

Deep in the recesses of her mind, she heard the voice of the mad angel, loud and jubilant. She reveled in its excitement. Behind her, an impossible army, chittering and hissing with enjoyment, marched toward the mountains.

15

THE BLADE'S METAL GRIP FELT warm in Trent's hand. It was not the warmth of a comfortable thing, but a sort of near-burning; a feeling that suggested, at any moment, the blade might choose to char his flesh straight through to the bone, but for now, it relented, this Hellforged blade with which he would kill the demon, Ramón—now Gadreel—his mentor, his confidant, consummate liar. The powermonger and architect of Trent's demise.

Failed demise, he corrected himself. *I'm back from the dead.* Though it hurt to think of it, he chuckled at the irony in that. He'd spent months looking for a way to bring Susan back from death, only to die and end up receiving the impossible gift himself.

Well, not exactly. I'm still dead, sort of.

He continued along the silent church corridor.

From ahead came the quiet chirp of a handheld radio and a man's voice. Trent flattened himself against the wall, crouched, and edged along the wall until he reached the corner. He peered around.

A lone guard stood there, radio in one hand, machine pistol in the other, hanging at his side. He shifted from foot to foot as he talked, bored.

Trent closed his eyes and searched the black for the layers of possibility that he had once been able to read. His breath caught, worry rising in him that his strange power over fate and chance had been ruined for good, that the resurrection and rebirth from the shadow realm had not restored it, as Michael had promised.

But the layers came. The visions, the fragments of reality danced off in every direction, more numerous now than ever before, more distinct. Sound, color, light, smell, movement, everything came rushing in, and he nearly fell to the floor as the sensations battered his mind. For a moment, he thought that he might not be able to control this, that the power had grown too strong for him, but he redoubled his focus, brought several possibilities into a tighter spiral, chose one and unleashed it upon the world.

"Come again?" said the guard, as Trent opened his eyes to watch. The guard shook the radio, smacked the back of it twice, and raised it back to his mouth. "Come again? Gettin' nothing here." The guard lowered the radio, looked at the screen, and cocked his head. "Dammit." He flipped the thing over and removed the battery cover.

With the guard distracted, Trent slipped out from behind the wall, walked up behind the man, and put the dagger to his throat covering the guard's mouth with his other hand. There was a momentary struggle, until the blade touched the guard's neck. A thin, pure line of blood dribbled from the cut. The guard went still.

"Where's Gadreel?" Trent kept his hand over the guard's mouth and his own voice low. "Nod. Is he on this floor, or downstairs?"

The guard nodded toward the floor twice. Sweat and fear oozed from the man's pores.

"More guards?"

The guard nodded.

"Thanks."

Trent pulled the dagger away, spun it in his hand, and then brought it pommel-first against the man's temple. It made a quiet, solid *clunk*. The guard let out a thin groan and crumpled to the floor, unconscious.

Trent headed down the nearest stairwell.

When he reached the ground floor, there were more voices, though none of them Ramón's. *Gadreel*, he corrected himself. *He's not my friend. He tried to kill Celia, tried to kill me.* He rounded the corner and saw two guards near a pair of large, ornate wooden double-doors. He flattened himself into the nearest shadow.

"Can't believe Gadreel keeps that weirdo around. Guy gives me the creeps."

"I saw him leaving with that kid, that girl. Made me sick to my stomach, just thinking about what he was going to do to her."

The first guard shook his head. "I know, man, I know." He winced. "I heard Gadreel tell him to kill her, though. Guess that's a mercy, right?"

"That was what? Like five hours ago?" He whistled. "Gadreel is pissed. Creep is taking *way* too long to get back."

Celia was alive; he knew that much from the scene played out on the wall of the canyon. She had survived the fall, the shot. *Of course*, he thought. *The rain. She fell outside into the rain.* He had seen water knit her wounds back together before. But now, if the guards were right, Palisade had taken the teenager off somewhere for sport and execution. He couldn't reconcile that with the image on the canyon wall of her, in pain, on the floor, with a woman nearby, not Palisade.

But she's alive, he thought. *That's all that matters.*

Rage and adrenaline washed though him like liquid flame. He could feel, smell, and hear the flesh of his palm sizzling as the Hell-dagger heated up.

He stepped out of the shadow and advanced on the guards. They looked up, surprised, and then moved to draw their guns. Trent whipped the dagger at the guard on the left, blinked once, and chose a reality where the blade pierced the man's throat. The machine pistol clattered to the floor as the guard reached for his neck with both hands, mouth agape, choking up blood in silence.

Before the other guard could pull the trigger, Trent was upon him. With his powers returned, it was trivial to jam his own hand against the guard's and grip his fingers so that he couldn't pull the trigger. With his other hand, Trent sent a roundhouse punch to the guard's head. The man dropped the gun, but remained standing, wavering. Trent gripped him by the jacket front and threw him against the double doors.

The wood splintered and the doors flew open, ejecting the unconscious guard onto the wood floor beyond. Trent pulled the Hellforged blade from the first guard's throat and looked up.

"Gadreel!"

Standing at the altar beneath a massive wooden Jesus, Gadreel turned to face the interloper, as did the guards on either side of him.

"Trent? You died— you—"

"Yeah, well I'm back now. Feel great."

The two guards raised machine pistols and pulled the triggers in unison. Trent blinked. The guns jammed. He never faltered as he strode down the aisle between the cherry wood pews.

The guards both looked at their guns, then up at Trent, then at Gadreel.

"Don't just stand there," he said. "Kill that bastard."

Trent spun the dagger in his left hand as the guards approached. The first one took the blade to the gut and stumbled backwards. Trent drew it out with a sharp, metallic song just as the other guard reached him. A quick swipe. Blood flew. The guard grasped his neck and fell into a nearby pew, gasping and shuddering, stomping his boots against the floor.

Trent continued toward Gadreel, blood dripping from the blade in his hand.

Gadreel raised his palms. "Now come on, Trent. All the talks we've had. All the things I've told you." He stepped backward, towards the naked legs of the massive Christ. His back bumped against the sculpture, which set the velvet red curtain at the back of the sanctuary rippling. "You knew this day would come. You had to."

Trent passed the first row of pews and ascended the shallow steps towards the altar. "You lied to me, Gadreel. Or is it Ramón? Or Ramiel? I keep getting confused."

"'Course I lied to you, son. I told you that's what we do, right? But you—" He leveled an accusatory finger at Trent. "You brought all this on yourself. This is all *your* fault."

Trent stopped a few feet away from the old Mexican, dagger hanging at his side. "My fault? You told me I'd die if you died. You told me you had my soul. Lies. Lies to keep me controlled."

"You've kept the Prince occupied for months. Delayed his ambitions. It was buying us time, Trent."

"Buying time for *who?* You?" Trent twirled the dagger. "So then why try to kill me?"

Gadreel sighed and ran a withered hand through his thinning hair. He shook his head. "Come on, kid. Just business. You quit on me to go after your stupid wife. You. The half-shade himself. Son of Raziel. I couldn't let you find Michael, couldn't let you end up there, where the Prince could have you. Needed to kill you here, regular-style, bury you in the desert for the rest of time." He snorted. "Then fuckin' Charlie goes and gives you a Hellforged blade." He gestured at the dagger in Trent's hand. "What did he think he was doing?"

Trent thought of Charlie, and Susan, and Celia. "You killed Charlie," he said, hands trembling, skin sizzling against the heated blade. "And you killed Susan and tried to kill Celia, too."

"No, *you* killed Susan. You. Your selfishness. You dragged her into this. And as for Celia...." He looked away, unable to meet Trent's withering gaze. "Well that's on Edward." He looked around, irritated. "Where *is* Edward? He'll walk in any minute now and strip that ridiculous power...."

"He works for *you*." Trent stepped up to the altar and swept a hand across it, knocking off several candlesticks and the Holy Bible, regaining Gadreel's attention. The heavy tome hit the floor with a thump. "And that girl, Fiamma, works for *you*. Does Vladimir work for you, too? Tricia? Snake?"

Gadreel shook his head. "You just don't get it, do you, kid?" His smile was sad, old, and tired. "All of this had to happen. Fiamma, Edward, Vretil, all of them just tools at my disposal, nothing personal. You screwed up the Prophecy when you started going after your wife, Trent. Things moved too fast. If you had been captured by the Prince while in the Realms, this world would have been doomed. If Celia had lived, this world would have been doomed. The Prophecy said she would bring Raziel's armies back into this world, and then it would be near impossible to sever the connection. Killing her first was the only way. Whatever that thing is inside of her—"

The radio on Gadreel's belt chirped, hissed, and then let out a high-pitched squelch that resolved to a man's panicked voice. "Oh, God— Boss— They're here—" The words came out clipped, hurried and breathless. "Shades everywhere— killing everyone—" Then the line went dead with a screech, static, and silence.

Gadreel's eyes widened. He ripped the radio from his belt and put it to his mouth, never taking his eyes off Trent. "What in God's name is going on out there? Hello? Come again? Report." But no reply came.

Trent stepped closer and chuckled. "Doomed, huh?" He shook his head. "Maybe so, but it sounds like you're going first. I don't think Cee's dead. Guessing your skinny little preacher ain't coming back either."

Gadreel frowned. His tired gaze locked with Trent's. "Sorry it's come to this," he said quietly. "At one point, I thought maybe you'd end up joining my cause, Trent." He shrugged and smiled, lifting both hands out in front of him.

Then, his right hand moved.

The Bible jumped from the floor and hurtled into the side of Trent's head, knocking him sideways. He stumbled a few steps, starbursts appearing and disappearing in his wavering vision.

Gadreel took off running, back behind the giant Christ, where he slipped through a hidden slit in the velvet curtains.

Trent cursed and leapt over the altar after the old man.

The opening in the curtains led into a low-ceilinged passage that Trent figured Gadreel used during church service when he wanted to make a grand entrance into the sanctuary. Along the walls were inset electric bulbs, which bathed the passage in rich, warm light. Ahead, he saw Gadreel round a corner.

The small bit of passage beyond the corner ended at a door, which slammed shut just as Trent reached it. From inside, he heard the heavy clunk of a bar dropping into place.

"Goddammit."

Trent put his boot to the door a few times, kicking with all of his strength, but it was solid and wouldn't budge. And without someone behind the door whose luck he could sour, he knew this door wasn't opening for him by chance either. Seething, he turned and went back the way he had come.

Once back in the nave, Trent headed down the aisle toward the big double-doors. Three guards stepped through as he reached the doors. Trent knifed one of them in the kidney, then planted a cowboy boot into the side of the second guy's knee, eliciting a sharp, crunching sound. In the worlds beyond the world, he saw a bone snapping, ligaments tearing loose. *Good enough*, he thought, and the guard went down screaming, clutching at his knee. The third guard pulled up short, shocked. Trent head-butted him in the nose. He went down in a cloud of blood.

Trent freed the dagger from first guard, who slumped away, and continued at a jog through the doors and into the church lobby. He reached the big doors that opened onto the front yard and parking lot, and threw them open—

His stomach turned at the sight.

A half-year prior, he had seen Zamagiel hang people from water pipes-turned-tentacles. He had seen a smokelike spider-creature tear men's shadows from their backs and leave them screaming, faces turned towards Heaven, minds ruined. He had seen Shades of every shape and size, and he had seen the grisly results of those times where he arrived a few minutes too late. But nothing he had seen had prepared him for what was happening in the parking lot of Gadreel's church. Nothing could have prepared him.

He stood on the front threshold of the church transfixed. Black-clad guards lay slumped over cars, sprawled in flowerbeds, crumpled on the rain-soaked pavement, their faces and bodies rent to shreds. Blood spatters coated the area, and the constant downpour had collected much of it into running streams of red. Snow and sleet was mixed into the sheets of rain, coming down so hard in some parts that he could barely see beyond the curtains of glittering white. Unnatural wind gusts whipped at the unmoving bodies, fluttering their blood-soaked jackets. He turned to his right to see a guard impaled against the façade of the church, a crystalline spear of ice jutting from his open mouth. The body hung limp, blood leaking from his pant legs, leaving a red smear down the church's exterior.

Squinting to see through the glare cast by the sodium lights upon the shining snow and ice, Trent looked for movement. And then he saw her, Celia, and another woman who was cowering nearby. At her feet, the teenager had trapped a guard, who was pleading for mercy, hands raised in defense.

Trent put his hands to his mouth in order to shout above the whipping, blizzard-like winds. "Celia! Stop!"

But if she could hear him, she made no indication. As if in defiant response to his plea, the teenager raised an arm and Trent watched as it transformed into an icy blade, swooped down, and separated the guard's head from his shoulders. Blood sprayed against the teen's silver coat. Then she turned and moved further away from Trent's position, walking, wintry forces dancing around her and a mass of black, swirling shadows following close behind.

The line of Shades extended far behind her, a line stretching well past the end of the parking lot. Her army numbered in the hundreds, he guessed. Maybe thousands. His heart broke as an immense feeling of failure swept over him.

He knew he had let the child down, left her to the burden of whatever she had done that night during the Blizzard, a thing that had set a transformation in motion that now couldn't be undone....

Wait, thought Trent. *Gadreel said that severing her connection to the Realms was "near impossible."*

He looked out into the swirling maelstrom of wintry violence and could now only barely see Celia moving further onto the church property. He had to get to Gadreel first, before Celia. *The old demon might be the only one who knows how to save her. If Celia kills him...*

He took off running, boots sliding awkwardly on the icy pavement as he rounded the nearest corner of the church, heading towards the gardens and the other buildings on the church campus. Gadreel had to be hiding in one of them.

Sure enough, as he rounded the back of the church, he saw faint footsteps embedded in the frost that had formed on the tops of the perfectly cut grass lawn. The trail led toward a one-story square building at the back edge of the campus. Somewhere in the distance, he heard a terrible, bloodcurdling man's scream. Not Gadreel's voice, though. He pushed the imagined scene from his thoughts. Celia would not stop if she found the old man.

He followed the trail through the snow, grimacing with every scream and cry that he heard in the distance behind him. He knew she was coming, a harbinger of ice and shadow and death. She had become something terrible. Guilt racked his insides as he ran toward the small building.

He reached the entrance, tried the door. Locked. He took a few steps back, ran, and launched his shoulder at the door.

There was a clang as the lock burst open. He slid to a stop inside.

The building was furnished like a small, but sparse apartment. The walls were barren. The old couch had seen better days. There was no television, only a card table with books and handwritten papers. A small kitchenette occupied one part of the open space. In the back, two doors, one open with a bathroom beyond, the other closed.

Trent threw himself against the closed door. It ripped from its hinges and deposited him on the floor of a small, unlit bedroom. He staggered to his feet.

Gadreel's voice cried out from the darkness. "Please, no. Help me. Get me out of here."

Trent fumbled with one hand until he found a light switch. The sudden glow illuminated a collage of monstrosities. The walls of the tiny room were papered exclusively with photographs, drawings, news clippings, some featuring naked men and women, or happy families, or murder scenes, hardcore pornography, pictures of corpses, children smiling for the camera in their Sunday best. Some of the images had black or red words scrawled across them in pen: whore, beggar, sloth, unbeliever. It was a nightmare amalgam of perversion and wholesomeness, a baffling display of two worlds, two lives competing for dominance. It was, Trent knew, Edward Palisade's room.

Gadreel cowered in the corner, more frightened and unimposing than Trent had ever witnessed. "Please," he said, "You have to let me leave." His voice wavered as he spoke.

Trent shook his head. "You can come with me, but you're gonna tell me how to save her. You're hiding something..."

"I can't come with you," he said. "You have to send me out of this world. He gestured at Trent's dagger. "Use the blade. Don't let Raziel come for me. The Prophecy has failed. He must know I've betrayed him. I'd rather take the Angels' Walk."

The mention of the Canyon set Trent's mind reeling with thoughts of Susan. That glimmer of hope, that spark again, as he realized that he still remembered her. She had said he would forget. He hadn't, not yet. He shook his head. "Not yet," he said. "Tell me. How can I save her from Raziel?" He looked behind him at the door to the small apartment. "Hurry."

Gadreel's eyes went wide. "It's impossible," he said, shaking his head. "It doesn't matter. The Prophecy, you, the girl, none of it really matters now. Raziel's here, through *her*, even if he doesn't have his black trinity. This is done. End me, please."

Trent stepped further into the room, grabbed Gadreel's collar, and half-led, half-dragged him back into the living area. He couldn't stand to be in that bedroom any longer than necessary.

"Fuck all that," he said. "Tell me now. Before she gets here. Then I'll end you."

"Sorry, Trent, but you've run out of luck on this one. You can try, but you'll just fail. No one has ever found it, no man, no angel, no one." Gadreel babbled, eyes darting all around the room, always returning back to the door beyond Trent. He wouldn't make eye contact. "It's here, somewhere, in the valley, but no one has ever found it. You're all gonna die."

"Dammit." Trent backhanded the old man to get his attention. "*What* is here, Gadreel? What has no one found—?"

"Trent." A voice he recognized. A girl's voice, but undercut with something more *ominous*, a second layer of tone and sibilance that sounded very, very familiar to him somehow.

Trent turned, still holding Gadreel's collar, to face Celia, now standing in the doorway of the tiny apartment. Her silver coat fluttered around her ankles, as did numerous black Shades, slipping in and out of her own shadows, connected to and separate from her at once. Behind her, beyond the doorway, an adult woman stood, fearful, in a blue gown. Part of him felt as though he'd seen her before, in the front parking lot, near Celia, but he knew that he never had. The sensation unnerved him.

"Celia, kiddo, you've gotta stop this."

"You're dead," she said, tone flat and emotionless.

Trent shrugged. "Yeah, kinda."

"Give me Gadreel."

"Just go, okay. Go home. Make those— those *things* go back wherever they came from. Go, Cee."

"No." That undercurrent boiled up louder in her voice this time. The familiar tones of the little girl that he had known were lost, somewhere in that voice. "He comes with me. Step aside."

Trent shook his head. "Sorry, but no, kiddo. This is for your own good."

Celia raised her hand then, and Trent realized that she meant to bring her powers to bear against him. Ice crackled as it formed along the walls and slithered its way across the floor extending from her feet. The walls of the small building groaned. The ceiling cracked and plaster rained in a faint dust down around them.

Trent locked eyes with her, uncompromising.

Gadreel made pitiful mewling noises.

Trent ignored him. The staring contest with Celia seemed crucial. In her eyes, he could see conflict dancing. Something held her back. Something was preventing her from ending him right where he stood. She lowered her hand. Ice receded. She broke her gaze.

He had won. Whatever held sway inside her had been fought off, for now. He'd seen it before, in the Shades that rode mortals, forcing them to do terrible things. The strong could resist, for a time. They'd resist it together, he and Celia, and Gadreel would tell them how to pry the teenager from Raziel's grip.

"Take him," said Celia then, and Trent's heart sank.

The Shades billowing about her legs leapt forward *en masse* and descended upon Trent and Gadreel. The old man screamed. Trent yelled in defiance as the black things curled around and over and beneath him, gripping him, tearing him away from his captive, throwing him backwards across the room with a mighty force. He smashed against the wall of the apartment and slumped to the floor. Through pain-dimmed, half-lidded eyes, he watched as one mass of Shades bore the struggling Gadreel aloft and floated him past Celia and out the door.

The other mass of Shades swept in at him. He raised his dagger in defiance and cut through several, banishing them into eternity, but there were more, so many more, and the shadows swirled about him and filled his mouth and ears and nostrils, poured down into his lungs and choked the breath out of him. He trembled as the light dimmed.

Before sight left him, he glimpsed Celia, the teenager he had loved like a daughter, standing tall, proud, bearer of powers unimaginable, unwavering. A line of tears streamed down her cheek.

NOWHERE

THERE IS A QUIET POPPING sound behind her. Susan doesn't turn around, doesn't turn back to see if he's still there. She knows he has gone. She's always known, from the day they first met at the theater, in line to see some terrible movie, both of them alone, pissed off at the world, looking for escape. She knew from that first moment that he would never leave her. And she also knew that he was already gone. He had the hero's look in his eyes, even then, a man searching for purpose.

She smiles at the thought. She loved his eyes. She loved what she saw in them. It hurt her to know that the last thing she had seen in his eyes was pain. *But then*, she thinks, *that's not really the last time I'll see him. Not exactly.*

Susan ponders that as she moves along the black-dust path, heading ever deeper into the canyon, taking the Angel's Walk. Michael, she notices, has already vanished from her sight, has already walked ahead and disappeared into the dark black distance of the canyon. She wonders where the angels go when they take the Walk. *Do they return to Heaven? Do they simply cease to be?* She fears the answer.

Raziel's Book feels heavy in her arms, unnaturally heavy, and its weight grows with every step she takes. Her fingers strain to hold it. She can feel it trying to escape, demanding to be set free, imploring her silently to drop it on the ground and continue on her damned way into nothingness, that it might be spared. She redoubles her grip on the leathery tome. She has no intention of doing what it wants.

As her footsteps grow heavier, she feels the weight of the black realm descend upon her. It is a crushing pressure on her skin, her bones, and her lungs. There is a deep, painful ache that boils up from her core and brings further tears to her eyes. She cries out, but refuses to falter, refuses to relinquish the Book to the ashen soil. Her bare feet become lead weights. Her nostrils fill with the acrid, ashen stench of the nothing-land. Every movement is torture. She realizes then that the Angel's Walk is as much punishment as it is execration. It is the last laugh of the Fallen, cast out into this land of nothing, but given rule over some part of it, to make Dis, the entrance to Hell, and to make this canyon, so that they might torture their unblemished brethren one final time before they are unmade.

Susan blanches at the thought of it. What God would allow its creatures to torture each other so? And then she thinks about the mortal world, and her tears burst forth anew. She falls to the ground. Despair settles over her like a leaden sheet, suffocating her will.

The Book stirs in her arms. She can sense its enjoyment of the moment, its ebullience at her failure.

No, she thinks, *I cannot stop.*

She stumbles to her feet, shoulders shuddering with tearful cries. The dust between her toes feels like shards of glass, but she continues on, one halting step after another. Her sight dims. Black rushes in to meet her—

The world around her explodes.

White-hot flame sears at the walls of the canyon. The edges of her white dress alight, flickering and singing and casting off smoke. She drops the Book. The onrushing blackness recedes, shooting backwards further and further until it disappears into a point of light and flame in the distance.

The canyon walls burn and crumble, throwing dense ash and smoke into the air, billowing clouds of unmaking as the canyon itself cracks and groans and collapses and turns to dust and is no more.

Around her, the Realms of Shadow are revealed again, spires arching toward the starless sky and vortices combing the landscape, mindless wanderers amidst the dust.

"About damn time."

Susan turns around then, confused. Behind her stands that same young woman, jet-black hair, tattered grey-black t-shirt, black pants. Her eyes glow orange, as do her fingers and arms and the tattoos that travel all the way up her arms to her neck and to the base of her jaw. Black ichor stains her clothes and skin. Flakes of ash drift around her fingers and arms.

"Fiamma?"

The younger woman is clearly injured. A gash on her left arm oozes thick black fluid. Another gash starts at her forehead and crosses diagonally across one eye and into the flesh of her opposite cheek. She shrugs. "What kind of fucking God would let its minions torture each other?"

Susan's laughter bursts out from amidst her sobs and she falls to her knees again, shaking, one hand upon the dropped book. She looks around, still baffled by the impossibility of what has just been done. "Where did it go? How can you do this?"

Fiamma kicks at the dust, watches it drift over the tops of her motorcycle boots. "They promoted me to King of Hell," she says, gesturing with one thumb back towards the iron city of Dis on the black horizon. She grins. "Well, after a little convincing." She makes a sweeping gesture with her arms. "A boss of Hell made the Canyon. Figured I could unmake it."

"You— you're—?"

"King of Hell. Or Queen. Lord. Whatever." Fiamma shrugs.

"And Zamagiel...? Lilith?"

"Lilith exited the Canyon and entered Dis. Both of them fled into the wastes during the fight. Cowards, though I doubt that's the last we'll see of them." She looks at the Book on the ground beneath Susan's hand. "Ah, you kept Raziel's Book."

Susan stands, holding the Book once more. She pulls it close against her chest, takes a step backward, away from the fiery young Queen of Hell. "I— I—," she stutters. "I don't think I should—"

Fiamma rolls her eyes and steps forward, offering a hand. "I don't want Raziel's stupid Book," she says. "You can keep it. I probably can't work it anyway. To be honest, I don't even think I have much control over this place." She turns a disdainful gaze on one of the vortices dancing across a nearby hill of ash and black rock. "Like those shitheads back there, I can't really do much once I leave the walls of Dis. I can unmake things that Hell made, like the Canyon, but when it comes to making things here, in the shadows...." She shrugs again.

Susan catches the implication. "You saved me from the Walk because—"

Fiamma nods vigorously. "Uh, yeah. I tortured a couple of those demons. They said some interesting things about you. I could use your help."

Susan frowns. "Use my help for what?"

"There's a big-ass war coming, lady. Even if the Prophecy is broken, the Prince isn't going to back down now. You just sent your husband back to fight him. But that's only one of the fronts. And I doubt he's going to pull off a win by himself, even if he does have a nightmare for a soul. I need you to help me fight the Prince. Keep him busy for a while. We've got armies to raise, fights to pick. We're gonna be rats in Raziel's basement."

Susan shakes her head. "But, where are we going to get an army?" She realizes then, with a sinking sense of dismay, that she has just used the word 'we.'

The younger woman's face cracks an impish grin. She winks and reaches out to grip the woman's hand as they both begin moving back towards the iron city, looming black and baleful on the horizon. "We're gonna rebuild Hell."

16

LOUIS BIRD'S FACE SWAM INTO view, one of the very last things Trent would have preferred to wake up to. Louis smiled. "Wakey wakey," he said.

Trent squinted. Bright beams of sunlight sneaked their way in around the edges of an old sheet hung up against his bedroom window. He sat up gingerly. The motion was stiff and painful. His back throbbed. At least one rib felt broken, maybe more. He groaned and grasped at his side as he tried to adjust to the light streaming in.

"How long?" he said, his voice hoarse and raw.

"You've been out four days, Sleeping Beauty. Welcome back to the land of the living."

Trent snorted and chuckled, eliciting another wave of groan-inducing pain from his midsection. He saw his clothes thrown over a chair, a pitcher of water and some straws on the nightstand, Louis still beaming at him. "Celia?"

Louis' face fell. He shook his head. "Sorry, man. Don't think she's coming home anytime soon."

"Where is she?" Trent coughed a few times to loosen the gravel from his voice. "Where the hell is she, Louis?"

"Whoa, calm down." Louis made a head gesture toward the window. "I suspect she's the so-called 'cult leader' they've got pinned down up at Gadreel's church, though I can't say I've been inside to see."

"A cult?"

"By the time I'd come up to the church to find you, there were already bums and weirdoes straggling up the hill, madness in their eyes. It was all I could do to sneak you out of that back building—"

"Wait, hold up." Trent fixed him with a squint. "How did you even know where I was? Hell, how did you know I was even *alive*?"

Louis shrugged. "Weird little guy showed up at my new place and told me. Pale, wispy hair, mouth like a sailor."

"Snake."

"What?"

"That's his name. Snake. I guess." Trent swung his feet out of the bed, stretched his arms, and tried to stand. His knees collapsed under his weight and he fell.

Louis caught him before he hit the floor. "Whoa," he said. "Easy there. Just sit for a minute."

Trent sat on the edge of the bed, head in his hands. His brain ached. "So Snake told you I was at the church? And you came and got me? And I was still there? Alive?"

Louis looked puzzled. "Yeah, why? I mean, you were beat up pretty bad, but still breathing and all."

Trent thought about that for a moment. Celia had let him live. She and the shadow creatures had taken Gadreel back inside, but they'd let him live. Just left him there, in the building out back, on the floor, until someone came and collected him. Why? He said as much to Louis.

Louis shrugged.

"So," Trent said, "they've got a cult in the church now?"

"Supposedly. National Guard has been called in. Police all around the place. For the first two days, I guess nobody even knew anything had happened, except for the crazies that started wandering up there. After enough of those folks, the police got interested. Rumor is they found carnage all over the front of the place."

"Yeah. I was there."

"Anyway, they're keeping everybody about a mile away."

Outside, Trent heard the sound of helicopters in the distance.

Louis nodded. "Yep. It's like goddamn Waco all over again. Without the oldies music."

"And the police have just stormed the place? Burned it down?"

"Apparently they tried something yesterday. They're not talking about it on the TV, though. Whatever happened, it wasn't good. They've backed off and are just holding the perimeter now, dealing with all the end-of-days idiots and religious wackos trying to get closer."

"Damn," Trent said, more of a pained sigh than a response.

"You really think your little girl is up there?"

Trent nodded. "I don't think she's my little girl anymore." He reached up and tore the sheet off the window. Bright, hot desert sunlight streamed in. On the horizon stood the gleaming black pyramid of the Luxor Hotel. He squinted at the bright light, but kept staring at that black triangle. "I guess she never really was."

Louis left the room for a moment and returned with a long, narrow cardboard box in his hands. He handed it to Trent. "Present for you. Showed up on the doorstep yesterday."

Trent turned the box over and looked at every side. It was heavy. No markings, no address labels, nothing. He pried it open and looked inside. There, nestled amidst linen wraps, lay a finely-wrought Hellforged dagger, the blade almost blood-red, even richer in color than any he had wielded before and wickedly shaped, with a subtle curve and a fishhook-like cut-in near the point. The handle was similarly ornate, and gleamed with artisan marks, curlicues, and slightly unsettling shapes and decorations. He lifted the dagger out, turned it in his hands. It was warm, as though it had just been taken from the forge. He turned it over, looked at the engraved pommel: TCH. His initials. Carved poorly, crudely even, not at all the mark of whoever had honed the razor-sharp blade or crafted the intricate handle. Someone had made him a Hellforged dagger, and someone else had carved his initials in it. He chuckled, put it back in the box, and closed the lid.

Louis busied himself gathering up dirty clothes and picking up empty food cartons and drinking glasses. Trent watched him until the small man left the room and left Trent to his own thoughts.

In the distance, he could hear the *chop-chop-chop* of the helicopters and the faint sounds of sirens. From the living room of the small townhouse, a woman's voice—a news reporter—droned on about the cult and the religious fanatics clamoring to go up to the church, and the street prophets that had gathered at the police barricade. They were calling it the End of Days. Armageddon. The Last Great War.

Trent looked out the window again at the Luxor. He thought about Celia, up there in the church, alone but for psychopaths and monsters. He knew she had Raziel riding shotgun with her now. He had seen what even the touch of his Book could do to her. He shuddered at the thought of what she had become now. He remembered the tear running down her cheek, even as she directed her minions to beat him down. He remembered Gadreel's mention of some impossible means of saving Celia.

He thought about that phrase: *End of Days*. It seemed, to him, that this was just the beginning. He was a man who'd died and been reborn. He was a man who'd lost his wife and his friends. He was an adoptive father who'd sworn to protect a little girl, growing up way too fast, and then lost her to evil. Each time, he'd had to start over. So be it. If this was a War, then it was one he would gladly fight, for them. He'd seen Prince Raziel's black realm. And he'd seen opposition there. Raziel could be defied. Maybe even beaten. Trent figured he'd just need a little luck.

About the Author

M. E. Patterson is an author of sci-fi, fantasy, horror, and thrillers, and an information technologist. He lives in the Texas Hill Country with his wife and their dog.

Burning Cards is his second novel, the sequel to Devil's Hand, available on Amazon, Barnes & Noble, and in bookstores.

Visit the Drawing Thin series website at:
http://drawing-thin.com

Catch up with Mr. Patterson on Twitter at:
http://twitter.com/mepatterson
or on his blog at:
http://mepatterson.net

And check out the official Facebook page at
http://facebook.com/devilshand.novel